Cord's instincts took charge of his body. Without con-
scious thought about what he was about to do, he launched
his body into the startled Charley, his shoulder into the
man's midsection, while grabbing the barrel of the rifle
with one hand. Ruby screamed and just managed to
jump out of the way of the hurling bodies before they
crashed against the wall. The rifle fired, sending a bullet into the ceiling and causing the women to scurry for
cover. It was the only shot Charley was able to get
off. There was a brief struggle over possession of the
weapon before Cord wrenched it out of his hands,
pulling Charley up from the floor with it before he was
slammed back down from a solid blow from Cord's left
fist.

MARK OF THE HUNTER

Charles G. West

A SIGNET BOOK

SIGNET
Published by the Penguin Group
Penguin Group (USA) LLC, 375 Hudson Street,
New York, New York 10014

USA | Canada | UK | Ireland | Australia | New Zealand | India | South Africa | China
penguin.com
A Penguin Random House Company

First published by Signet, an imprint of New American Library,
a division of Penguin Group (USA) LLC

First Printing, July 2013

ISBN 978-0-451-41990-3

Printed in the United States of America
10 9 8 7 6 5 4 3 2

For Ronda

Chapter I

The image of his mother's death had been etched upon his mind so clearly, a picture that would dwell in his subconscious forever, only to surface occasionally and remind him never to forget. He was only twelve years old when his father, outlaw Ned Malone, returned to the hardscrabble farm in southwestern Nebraska after an absence of nearly four months. Young Cord Malone was never glad to see his father return from one of his robbing or rustling sprees, for it usually meant a drunken session of abuse for his mother, Lottie. The only emotions the young boy had ever witnessed from his father were fits of contempt for his ill-treated wife and his undersized son. Cord had bitterly chastised himself for his failure to protect his mother from the terrible battering she suffered at the hands of a man who had held her in the same regard he had for his horse. When making even a feeble plea to his father to leave the poor woman alone, Cord was usually rewarded with a sharp

backhand for his efforts, along with a scornful remark
about the boy's lack of size or fight. A big and powerful
man, Ned Malone had never failed to tell the boy what
a disappointment he was.

On the night Cord's mother was killed, Ned Malone
had ridden in with one of his villainous partners, Levi
Creed, a man seemingly cut from the same evil stock
as Ned. When supper was finished and the drinking
started, Lottie told her son to leave the house and go to
the barn, for she knew what was going to follow. "Yeah,
you little shit," his father had roared, "get the hell outta
my sight. It makes me wanna throw up just lookin'
atcha." Cord did as he was told, knowing that his mother
did not want him to witness the wanton abuse of her
body that always accompanied Ned's drinking. As he
walked out the door, he felt a sickening chill when he
was met with the lascivious grin on the brutal face of
his father's friend, Levi Creed. The man reeked of evil,
especially to a twelve-year-old already fearful of what
misery the night might bring for his mother. He hurried out the door, anxious to be away from the scene.

What happened next remained vague in Cord's
mind because he could only construct a picture from
the loud sounds of cursing and an occasional cry of
pain from his mother that had carried across the yard
to the barn. The sounds told him that his mother was
suffering abuse from both men. Determined to stand
up to his father this time, he went to the feed room in
the barn to get the single-shot shotgun kept there for
the purpose of killing rats. The shells were only loaded
with bird shot, but they would do some damage at
close range. He had loaded one in the gun and dropped
a couple more in his pocket when he heard the pistol

shot and his mother's terrified scream. At once alarmed, he ran from the barn and up the steps to the front porch of the house.

The scene that confronted him when he ran into the room would linger to haunt his dreams for years to follow. His father's body lay facedown on the floor, shot through the head. The evil Levi Creed, with no shirt on and his trousers down around his boots, was lying atop his mother's limp body. Cord did not hesitate. He raised his shotgun and fired, sending a load of bird shot into Creed's back and buttocks. Roaring out in pain, Creed rolled off Lottie while Cord fumbled to reload his shotgun. Seeing it was the boy who had attacked him, Creed moved quickly to defend himself, and even with the hindrance of his trousers around his boots, he managed to reach the boy before he could remove the empty shell and replace it with another. There followed a brief struggle over possession of the weapon that quickly went in favor of the man. He wrenched the shotgun from Cord's hands and delivered a blow with the butt of it that landed on Cord's forehead, knocking the boy senseless. He stood over the unconscious boy for a few moments while he pulled up his trousers and strapped his gun belt on, deciding whether or not he should put a bullet in Cord's brain, leaving all three of them dead. Another shot might bring nosy neighbors to investigate. There were two small homesteads within two miles, so he thought it best to ride out while there was plenty of time. Hesitating briefly to ransack the little house for anything of value, he took another look at the fallen boy, lying motionless. "Hell, I believe I kilt him, anyway," he muttered. Then for good measure, he kicked the kitchen

stove over and piled the table and chairs over the
spilled coals. When satisfied that the fire was burning
steadily, he went to the barn and saddled his horse.
Leading his late partner's horse, he left the small farm
and headed north.

A little over a mile down a narrow, dusty wagon track,
Nettie Anderson stepped out on her back porch to
empty the supper dishwater from her dishpan. Uncertain about the gunshots she thought she might have
heard a few moments before, she listened, but there
were no more. Probably her young grandson shooting
at a rat, she thought, or a rabbit, although the two shots
didn't sound exactly the same—as if they came from
two different guns. She was about to go back inside
when she noticed a thick column of smoke wafting up
against the fading evening light. She paused to study it
for only a moment before calling her son. "Jesse!"

"Yes'um," Jesse answered, and walked out to the
porch to stand beside his mother.

Nettie pointed to the column of smoke. "Does that
look like it's coming from Lottie's house?"

Jesse squinted as he peered in the direction his
mother pointed. "It sure looks like it's comin' from
Lottie's," he said after a moment.

"You'd best jump on your horse and go see about it,"
Nettie said, genuinely concerned by then.

Equally concerned, since his sister lived alone, for
most of the time, save for her twelve-year-old son, Jesse
didn't hesitate. As far as he knew, Lottie's no-good husband was away on one of his lengthy absences, so he
ran to the corral and hastily put a bridle on one of the
horses. Not wishing to waste any more time, he didn't

bother with a saddle, jumping on the horse's bare back for the short ride up the road.

As he neared the house, he discovered a scene worse than he had anticipated, for it was not a brush fire. The small frame house was ablaze with flames licking the sides and sending up black smoke from the pine boards. At a gallop, he entered the barnyard, yelling, "Lottie! Cord!" There was no answer from his sister or his nephew, and there was no sign of anyone outside the house. Jesse didn't hesitate. Sliding off the horse even before it came to a complete stop, he ran, almost stumbling in his haste to reach the door, and plunged through it into the blazing building, still calling for Lottie and Cord.

Inside, the room was filled with heavy black smoke, causing his eyes to burn and making it difficult to see, and equally difficult to breathe. As he moved across the main room, on his way to the bedrooms, he almost fell when he stumbled over a body. Down on his hands and knees then, holding his shirttail over his nose and mouth, he identified the body as Ned Malone. He had not even known that Ned had returned. In a panic then, he looked to his side and discovered a second body and knew at once it was Lottie. He moved to her side, crying, "Lottie! Lottie!" But there was no response. She was dead, her skirt and undergarments torn away. "Oh, Lord, no!" he cried in anguish over the still body. "Please, Lord, no!" In the next instant, part of the roof over the kitchen came crashing down on the floor, and he knew it was only a matter of minutes before the rest of the roof collapsed, so he got his arms under his sister's body and struggled to his feet. With only a glance at Ned's body, he thought, *To hell with him*, and moved quickly back toward the door. It was only then that he remembered that Cord had not been accounted for, but there was no time to search the smoke-filled dwelling. So he staggered through the open doorway, his lungs screaming for fresh air. As he did, he almost tripped over the outstretched hand of his nephew. Startled, for he did not remember it there when he plunged through the opening in the flames on his way in. It could be no one but Cord, but he would have stepped on the extended hand, or tripped over it when he entered the smoke-filled house, as he had on Ned's body. *Maybe he moved*, he thought. *Maybe he's alive!* He couldn't stop then, however, so he carried Lottie out the front door, across the short porch, and laid her on the ground, away from the burning building.

Then he turned again to look at the inferno from which he had just escaped, wondering if he could risk another trip through the flames in hopes that Cord was alive. His common sense told him that the boy was dead, just as his mother—that somehow the heat from the fire had caused his arm to move. "But damn it, it moved." So he knew he had no choice but to make sure. Even if he was dead, his nephew's body should be removed from the fire, so Jesse took a couple of breaths of cool fresh air, then plunged back through the flames.

There was no time to be gentle. As soon as he found the outstretched arm again, he took it in both of his hands and dragged the body through the doorway. Once off the porch, and away from the flames, he picked up the undersized boy, whose face was covered in blood from a gaping gash across his forehead, and carried him to lie beside his mother. Totally exhausted then, Jesse sat down on the ground and coughed repeatedly

in an effort to clear his lungs of the smoke. When he
could breathe again, only then did he begin to sob over
the tragic loss of his sister and her son. It was especially painful for him, because he and his mother had
worried about Lottie ever since she had married the
no-good son of Hiram Malone. Jesse had tried to per-
suade Lottie on more than a few occasions to take Cord
and walk out on Ned, but she would not consider it.
She had married Ned for better or worse, she had said,
and she always hoped that the worse might someday
end. "Well, sweet Lottie," he said to her corpse, "I reckon
the worse is finally over now."

Seeing a quilt hanging on the clothesline near the
house, he went to get it to wrap around his sister's half-
naked body. It would be hard for his mother to see Lottie like this. The heat from the burning house was so
intense that he had to work quickly to take the clothes-
pins off the quilt and snatch it off the line. Even then it
was necessary to pat out a dozen sparks that had taken
root in the heavy quilt. Returning then to his sister, he
wrapped her body in the warm quilt.

He wondered then about Ned. The body still lying
in the cabin was surely that of Ned's, and he had been
shot in the head. Who shot him? Did he and Lottie kill
each other? From the marks on Lottie's neck, and the
location of the shot that killed Ned, it seemed impossible that they could have killed each other. Maybe he
would never know what had happened in that tragic
funeral pyre, but at the moment it didn't make sense.
Deep bruises around Lottie's throat indicated she had
been strangled. There must have been someone else
involved. He was startled in the next moment by a
weak moan from his nephew. Moving quickly to the

boy's side, he raised Cord's bloody head and called his name. "Cord! Can you hear me? It's Uncle Jesse!" But there was no response from the boy, whose eyes remained closed. Jesse pressed his ear against Cord's chest and listened. He was alive. There was a faint heartbeat, but no other signs of life.

Trying to determine what to do next, he decided first of all he should take Lottie and Cord back home, away from this evil place. Looking toward the barn, he spotted Ned's wagon, so he hurried down to hitch it up. It was then that he realized that the corral rails were down and the horse was gone, so he went back to get his horse. Finding a harness in the barn, he hitched his horse to the wagon, then gently loaded mother and son.

There was no doctor in the little settlement called Moore's Creek, so the care of Nettie Anderson's grandson was left entirely up to her. There was little for her to do, so much of her time was spent in grieving for her late daughter. It had been two days since his mother had been buried and Cord still lay unresponsive, seeming to be in a deep sleep. All Nettie could do was try to tend to the ugly wound on his forehead and pray for him until his heart finally ceased to beat. The spark of life within Cord Malone refused to die, however, and on the morning of the third day, he opened his eyes to startle Nettie, who was bending over him to change his bandage.

"Good Lord in heaven!" Nettie exclaimed, recoiling as if having been struck. "Cord, boy, can you hear me?" His only response was a nod, but it was enough. "Praise the Lord," Nettie blurted. "We thought you was dead!" She turned to yell through the doorway to alert the others, who were still at the breakfast table. "Jesse! He's awake!"

In a matter of moments, the rest of the family was gathered around the bed, with the exception of Nettie's other grandson, fourteen-year-old T.G., who deemed the biscuit he had just slathered with butter warranted first priority for his attention. "My stars!" Jesse's wife, Cindy, exclaimed. "He *is* awake." She reached over to pat Cord's hand in encouragement, although the boy still looked more dead than alive. There was movement in his eyes, however, shifting to gaze weakly at each person who spoke.

"I'll get him some water," Nettie said, then turned back to look at Cord. "Can you drink some water?" He nodded. "You ain't had nothing to drink for more'n two days," she went on. "I expect you're about dried up."

When he had recovered enough to talk about it, Cord told the anxious family what had happened on that fatal night as best he remembered. "We figured there had to be somebody else had a hand in it," Jesse remarked when Cord said the murderer was a friend of his father. "I went back down there yesterday and scouted around the barn till I picked up a trail where he had rode out—followed it for about eight or nine miles till I lost it at the river. I finally gave up. He'da been long gone by then, anyway."

In the months that followed, Cord became stronger, nurtured by the grieving family. Soon he recovered enough to work in the fields with his uncle Jesse, and his cousin T.G. The two cousins got along very well. T.G., whose name was Thomas Grant after his late grandfather, had always been a friend to his younger cousin. So the boys worked well together. Watching the two watering the horses one evening, Cindy was prompted to comment to her husband, "Those two don't ever argue. Do you suppose he talks more to T.G.?"

"I don't reckon," Jesse replied. "T.G. says Cord don't have much to say about anything. He didn't talk a helluva lot before gettin' knocked in the head, but he don't hardly say more'n two words at a time now, and that's only if you ask him somethin' he can't nod or shake his head to. You know, I ain't sure he'll ever be right in the head again. Hard to say—T.G. says he acts normal like he did before, except he just don't talk like he used to. I hope he ain't holdin' a grudge against me for givin' up on chasin' the man who killed Lottie. I swear, honey, there weren't no tracks to find on the other side of the river, or I'da sure as hell went after that son of a bitch."

"I know you woulda, Jesse," Cindy said. "I'm sure Cord knows that."

The dark clouds that lay behind the jagged scar across Cord's forehead were not enough to hide the deep wounds on the young boy's brain. Often in his sleep, the horrifying image of his mother's lifeless body came to haunt him. And the name he had come to despise flashed across his memory even when he was awake—*Levi Creed*. "This here's Levi Creed," he remembered his father telling his mother, as casually as if introducing a business associate. He tried to erase the picture of his mother's body, but he did not try to forget her murderer's name, for he was determined to avenge his mother's death someday. Smart enough to realize that he was too young to think of immediate revenge, he contented himself to wait until he was ready before going in search of Creed. He had time. Of that he was certain, for he felt confident that a man like Levi Creed would show up again in the thriving cow towns of Kansas or Nebraska. He would not be that hard to find. In the meantime Cord's every thought was directed at growing stronger.

The months turned into years. The changes in the undersized boy for the most part went unnoticed by those seeing him every day until Jesse took a good look at the two boys as they walked toward the house for supper. "You noticed Cord lately?" he asked his mother as she and Cindy set the table. "He's shootin' up like a weed. He's taller than T.G."

"I noticed," Nettie replied. She had been aware of the boy's growth spurt, but had not made mention of it, thinking it best not to, in case T.G. was concerned about it. She had suspected that Cord would eventually develop, even though he was still small at age twelve, for his father was a huge man and his mother was not a small woman. And now it was obvious to her that Cord was going to be a sizable man when he reached his full height—just like his father. The only trait he inherited from the evil man, she prayed.

The late Horace Anderson's small parcel of land was easily farmed by the three men of the family, so much so that as time went on, Cord spent a good portion of his time working on the parcel that became his with the death of his mother and father. It was a poor piece of land, evidence of his late father's lack of knowledge of farming and his reluctance to work for a living. Cord and his mother had done the best they could, which amounted to little more than a vegetable garden and a cornfield. He had no real interest in holding on to the land. It contained too many bad memories. Besides that, he was just biding his time until he felt ready to begin what was likely to be a long, long quest—to find Levi Creed.

Just after his nineteenth birthday, Cord decided it was time for him to leave his grandmother's house. T.G., having courted the preacher's daughter in Moore's Creek for over a year, finally popped the question, and the young lady said yes. While the family was pleased with the union, it did cause some problems. T.G. naturally planned to build his own house on his grandmother's farm, but initially, he and his bride would have to move into his grandmother's house, or his father-in-law's. And T.G. was not at all favorable toward moving in with the preacher. The problem was solved when Cord announced that he was leaving, making his room available for T.G. and his new wife.

Nettie was immediately concerned, for she feared the ever-somber, seldom-speaking young man would fare better close to the family that knew him and his tragic past. Jesse attempted to sway Cord's thinking, telling him that he was needed to work the farm with him and T.G. But Cord knew better than that. Jesse and T.G. could manage very well without him. "I know you're leavin' just so Mary Ann and I can have your room," T.G. told him. "You know I appreciate it, but I don't want you to leave on my account."

"You're givin' me too much credit," Cord said. "I was fixin' to go ever since my corn crop came in. I wouldn't have cared if you and your little wife had to sleep on the kitchen table."

"Liar," T.G. replied. "I know you better'n that."

Serious again, Cord said, "It's time I moved on. There's parts of the territory I ain't ever seen, and I reckon I'm ready now—matter of fact, I've been thinkin' that I've already stayed too long. I've got a little saved up to hold me for a little while till I find something else."

"It's that thing with your mother, ain't it?" He could tell by his cousin's expression that his guess was accurate. "Damn, Cord, that's been so long ago you'd do well to let it go for good. That feller's most likely dead by now, shot by one of the scum he rides with. You probably don't even remember his name."

"Levi Creed," Cord responded. "That's his name, and I got a feelin' he's still alive. He ain't gonna die till I kill him."

Frustrated with his cousin's stoic indifference to probability, T.G. continued to argue. "What are you gonna do, just ride from town to town askin' folks if they've seen Levi Creed? That don't make a bit of sense."

"I'll find him if he's still standin'," Cord said, with a patient smile for his cousin and friend. "Good luck on your weddin'. I'm proud of you. Mary Ann's a fine girl, and you might decide you wanna build a house on my mother's piece of land. That would be all right with me." There was a familiar sense of finality in his tone that T.G. had learned to recognize over the years. It meant the discussion was over.

The September morning that Cord left his home of seven years dawned cloudy and gray, which somehow seemed appropriate to Nettie Anderson, for it reminded her of the dark circumstances that had brought the doleful young man into her home. *Maybe it's best he leaves*, she thought, for his presence kept the grief for her daughter

always fresh in her mind. She stood by the porch with
Cindy, T.G., and Jesse as Cord led his old sorrel up to bid
them farewell. He had bought the horse with a little of
the money he had saved from his corn crop over the last
few years. She watched as Jesse and T.G. gave him a
strong handshake, and he turned to face her.

"I wanna thank you for everything you did for me,
Grandma," he said.

"Come here," she said, fighting back a tear, her arms
outstretched. She gave him a firm hug, holding him
close for a few moments before stepping back to arm's
length where she continued to hold him while she
gazed up into his face. It was hard to remember him as
the shy, undersized boy she had taken in. Tall and
powerfully built, he towered over her. She reached up
with one hand and touched the jagged scar running
across his forehead, and her tears started in earnest.
Wiping her eyes with her apron, she attempted to pull
herself together. "You take care of yourself," she said.
"And remember, you've always got a home here."

He nodded somberly. Then without another word,
he climbed in the saddle and turned the sorrel north-
ward, toward Ogallala, never looking back. The wild
little cow town across the Nebraska line was as good a
place as any to start his search for Levi Creed. The
odds were slim that he would find the murderous outlaw there, but it was a possibility. And he knew for certain that he was never going to find him if he remained
on his grandmother's farm.

Nettie stood on the porch and watched him until he
rode out of her sight, for she had a feeling that it was
the last time she would ever see her grandson. *Sorrow's
son,* she thought, because she sensed that Cord Malone

was destined to live a violent life. It seemed to her as if God had placed a mark on the young man, and pointed him down a troubled path. Maybe that was what the scar on Cord's forehead really was, a mark of violence. The troubled boy was now a troubled man. *God help him,* she silently prayed.

Chapter 2

Cord found the little town of Ogallala relatively peaceful on this day in early September, in sharp contrast to the noisy, brawling cattle center for which it had gained a reputation. The trail-hardened cowpunchers who drove the herds up from Texas were gone now until next summer when they would once again repeat the cycle and descend upon the saloons and hotel like an annual visit of locusts. With the cattle now grazing on the ranges of the cattle barons like the Bosler brothers, who filled huge contracts to supply beef to the Indian agencies, Ogallala had reverted to a nearly deserted little settlement in the valley between the forks of the Platte River. Cord knew very little about the cattle business, but he figured that with the great herds awaiting shipment on ranches around Ogallala, he should be able to find work at one of them. He worked well with horses, thanks to his uncle Jesse, so he was confident that he could learn to drive cattle.

Looking at the sleepy town now, however, he found it hard to imagine there could be any work for a willing hand. One hotel, one saloon, and one general merchandise store were the only businesses open, the others having evidently closed until summer. He was beginning to wonder if he should just move on to Cheyenne, or Omaha. He had been undecided where he was going when he left his grandmother's farm; he just knew that it was time to go. But now he was beginning to realize just how naive he was to set out to search for a man who might be anywhere from Texas to Canada. "What the hell?" he muttered, and turned the sorrel toward the saloon. "I reckon I can afford a glass of beer." He figured he could justify it as an official start of a quest that might take many years to fulfill.

Like every place else in town, the Crystal Palace was empty of patrons. The bartender got up from a table where he had been drinking a cup of coffee. "Howdy," he offered unenthusiastically. "Getcha somethin'?"

"I reckon I'd like to have a glass of beer," Cord answered.

The bartender set a glass on the bar, and watched with mild interest as Cord dug in his pocket for a coin. "I don't remember seein' you around here before," the bartender remarked, already deciding that the stranger wasn't likely to spend much more than the price of one beer.

"Ain't ever been here before," Cord said.

"On your way back to Texas?" the bartender asked, assuming that his customer was from one of the outfits that had driven cattle up from the south.

"Ain't ever been there, either," Cord replied.

His reply caused the bartender to chuckle. "Well, if

you rode in lookin' for a wild town, you got here at the wrong time of the year. Course, it'll pick up a little next month for a spell when the big outfits bring their cattle off the grass and ship 'em east to the markets. Then it'll be dead again till summer."

"What I'm lookin' for is work," Cord said.

"Is that a fact? What kinda work you lookin' for?"

"Anything that'll pay a decent wage," Cord answered.

Convinced then that Cord was not the typical aim-less drifter he was accustomed to seeing this time of year, the bartender offered his hand. "My name's Clyde Perkins. I run the Crystal when the owner ain't here."

Cord shook his hand and responded, "Cord Malone."

"Where you from, Cord?"

"Moore's Creek," Cord replied. When Clyde's expression registered no recognition of the name, Cord added, "About thirty miles south of here."

"Must not be a very big town," Clyde remarked.

"It ain't," Cord confirmed.

Clyde smiled. He was thinking the young stranger didn't waste a lot of words, and was probably serious about finding honest work. "If you're lookin' to work for one of the cattle outfits, you might be able to get on with the Bosler brothers. They're a big outfit, supply a lot of beef to the Red Cloud and Spotted Tail Indian agencies. I expect they're always lookin' for good hands. If they ain't hirin', you can try John Coad, or Joseph Carey. There's a few more outfits holdin' thousands of head of cattle on the grass that'll be drivin' 'em in to the shippin' pens in about a month."

"Much obliged," Cord said. "Reckon you could point me in the right direction to find one of those outfits?"

Clyde hesitated for a moment when a thought struck

him. "You know, your best bet might be Willard Murphy. He ain't as big as Bosler Brothers, and I know for a fact that he had a couple of men leave his outfit to go with the Boslers. Murphy might need some help."

"Sounds like what I'm lookin' for," Cord said. Clyde gave him general directions to Willard Murphy's range on the North Platte near the mouth of Blue Creek and wished him good luck. Standing in the doorway, watching the somber stranger step up in the saddle, he couldn't help thinking that the young man would need to get himself a stouter horse. The sorrel he was riding didn't look to be much of a working horse.

Clyde Perkins was not the only one who held a critical opinion of Cord's tired old sorrel. "You're gonna have to get a better horse under you," Willard Murphy, owner of the Triple-T, informed his new hire. "That damn nag is kinda gray around the muzzle, ain't she? She's gotta be close to twenty years old."

"She's eighteen, accordin' to the man who sold her to me," Cord replied. "She's better'n walkin', and she don't complain."

Murphy shook his head and laughed. "Go on down to the south pasture and find Mike Duffy. Tell him I said for you to pick out a good horse. You can let that old mare retire and take it easy for a while. Tell Mike I sent you down there to work with his crew. He'll fix you up with a bed in the bunkhouse."

"Yes, sir," Cord said. "I 'preciate it." He climbed back into the saddle and urged the sorrel into a comfortable lope to show Murphy the old girl wasn't quite ready to fall over and die. "I hope he didn't hurt your feelin's," he told the mare as he rode away.

* * *

Mike Duffy, a short, wiry man with a shock of red hair
and a full beard, seemed not at all surprised when Cord
showed up. It was not the first time Will Murphy had
hired a man to work with his crew without getting
Mike's prior approval. Mike could usually use an extra
man, and more times than not, the new hire didn't stay
with the job for very long, anyway. A couple of the bigger spreads paid more money than the wage that Willard Murphy paid. He had just lost two men over the
summer. After talking to Cord for a few minutes, he figured that he would have offered him a job as well. This
new hire looked as if he had worked hard before. His
hands were callused and tough, his eyes were clear and
alert, and he was certainly big enough. Mike helped
him pick out a good horse from the herd grazing near
the creek. Cord's pick, a bay gelding, would serve as
replacement for his tired old sorrel. When it was time to
move the cattle down to the holding pens in Ogallala,
he would pick out a string of horses to work. For the
time being, however, he would simply be riding herd,
watching for strays, keeping an eye out for wolves, and
ensuring that Murphy didn't lose any cattle. With a
good horse under him, Cord felt a real sense of confidence, and he was sure he was going to get along well
with Mike Duffy.

Mike rode back to the barn with him and waited
while Cord turned the bay out in the corral. Then they
walked to the bunkhouse where a tall, gaunt man
Mike introduced as Slop was busy cooking supper in
the kitchen at one end of the long building. Cord would
find out later that Slop's real name was Sloope; it had
been shortened by the men he cooked for. Slop paused

briefly to give Cord a nod of his head before returning his attention to his oven and the biscuits that were browning inside. "They come and they go," he muttered to himself when Mike and Cord proceeded to the far end of the room, where Cord threw his modest possessions on one of four empty cots.

"Mind if I take a look at that?" Mike asked, nodding toward Cord's Henry rifle. Cord handed the rifle to him. Mike sat down on one of the bunks and looked the weapon over with interest, hefting it up to his shoulder, aiming at a rack of deer antlers on the wall at the end of the building. "That's one of the old ones," he commented. "Looks like one of the sixty models." When Cord nodded in confirmation, Mike said, "Everything you've got is old, that mare, your rifle. Was this a hand-me-down from your pa?"

Cord almost grunted aloud in response when a picture of Ned Malone flashed across his mind, and he tried to recall anything his father had given him other than a hard time. His answer was calm, however. "No, it's just the best I could buy with the money I had. I'll get a better one when I've got the money."

Duffy handed the rifle back, studying Cord's expressionless face. "You ain't ever worked cattle before, have you?"

"No, I ain't," Cord replied. "I never told Mr. Murphy I had. I just told him I needed work."

"That's what I figured. I just had a feelin'," Mike said with a smile. "Well, it don't make no difference. I think you'll be just fine." He got up to leave. "You just take it easy. The rest of the crew will be gettin' back before long and we'll be eatin' some supper." He left Cord to pass the time until supper while he attended to a few chores.

The smell of baking biscuits reminded Cord of how little he had eaten that day, but he figured he'd best not ask for anything before supper was announced by the sour-looking man in the kitchen. He turned his attention to the cot he had selected, unrolled the straw tick mattress, and spread the blanket over it. There was no pillow. Looking at the other beds, he saw a variety of makeshift pillows, most of which consisted of rolled-up shirts and trousers, although one of the beds sported a fancy, fringed silk pillow with the words *Chicago Stock Fair 1869* embroidered across it. Cord had never seen a pillow like that before, and he moved closer to admire it.

"That there's Slick's pillow." The voice came from behind him, startling him. He turned to see Slop standing between him and the kitchen. Before Cord could respond, the doleful cook tossed an object at him. Reacting quickly, Cord caught it. It turned out to be a hot biscuit, fresh from the oven. "You look like you ain't et in a while," Slop said. "You might as well try the cookin' before you start complainin' about it." He turned abruptly and returned to his kitchen.

Somewhat astonished, Cord called out after him, "Much obliged," and hurriedly consumed the biscuit. There was nothing to complain about, he immediately decided. It was as good as his grandmother's. When he finished it, he walked back to the kitchen and said as much to Slop. There was no way to tell by the slothful cook's expression, but Cord had made a friend from that point on.

In twos and threes, the rest of Mike Duffy's crew arrived back at the ranch until all twelve were assembled to gather around the table. Thinking it best not to seat himself in someone's customary position on the long benches on either side of the table, Cord waited until it appeared all were present. He was met with open-eyed curiosity by the hungry cowhands as they filed by him, with a few nods from some. Mike walked in the next moment, saving Cord the task of introducing himself. "Say howdy to Cord Malone," Mike announced. "He's just hired on. Set yourself down anywhere you can find a space," he told Cord.

Cord chose a spot at the end of the bench next to a thin, sallow man with a dark, drooping mustache that gave him a constant expression of sadness. Looking to be one of the elder drovers, he offered Cord his hand. "Lem Jenkins," he said. "You come up with one of the herds?"

"Nope," Cord replied, "I'm from Kansas."

"Well, we ain't gonna hold that against you," a broad-shouldered, solidly built young man, sitting across the table from him, said. With a friendly smile, he offered his hand as well. "My name's Stony Watts. I'm glad to see Mike's finally hired somebody to help shape up this sorry crew." He laughed at his attempt at humor.

"I might have to hire a dozen to shape this crew up," Mike replied, also chuckling.

Cord was immediately at ease. Having never worked with a crew of cowhands before, he wasn't sure what to expect, halfway anticipating the necessity to prove himself before being accepted—and possibly being tested by a resident bully. But that seemed not to be the case with Mike Duffy's crew. It was a practice not tolerated by Duffy. By the time supper was over, and the three men riding night herd that night departed, everyone made it a point to say howdy. With his positive introduction to Mike's crew, Cord felt he had taken a step in the right direction. He looked forward to learning the ropes in his new job, and even for a short time forgot the primary reason he had come to Ogallala, to begin a search for Levi Creed.

When Lem Jenkins got up from the table, he remarked that he was one of the men whose turn it was to ride night herd. "You probably got your own way of doin' things," he told Cord. "But if you wanna ride night herd, I'd be glad to show you how we do it here."

Cord glanced at Mike Duffy before responding. Mike shrugged indifferently, so Cord replied, "I ain't got no set ways. Sounds like a good idea to me."

"Sounds like a good idea to me, too," Mike said. "Lem's a good one to show you the ropes." So far, Mike was satisfied with the new man's attitude, especially considering that he volunteered to ride night herd his first night on the job. He had a good feeling about the somber young man, but he sensed there was something deeper driving him than a simple need for a job. He was not discounting the fact that he had briefly considered the possibility of an ulterior motive behind Cord's request for employment. It would not have been the first time a band of cattle rustlers sent one of their gang seeking a job with a big ranch, only to cut out a large portion of the herd to drive away in the middle of the night. He wasn't sure why the thought had occurred to him. Maybe it was the cheerless countenance of the young man, or possibly the jagged scar across his forehead. He soon discarded the notion after a few minutes' conversation with him, however. *He might have fooled me,* he thought, *but if he did, he fooled Will Murphy, too.* His boss was a pretty good judge of men.

"Come on," Lem said, nodding to Cord to follow him to the kitchen, where Stony Watts and a short, dark-haired man with a bushy beard stood by the stove. "Slop will fix you up with a little somethin' to keep your belly from curlin' up before breakfast."

Stony turned to grin at Cord when he and Lem walked up. "You get the privilege of ridin' night herd with me and Lem on your first night. Course, you have to ride with Blackie here, too, so it ain't all good."

Blackie shook his head in mock disgust. "You're about as funny as a saddle sore on the crack of my ass, Stony. Come to think of it, there's a right smart resemblance there, too." They all laughed. "You're lucky you're ridin' with Lem," he told Cord. "Before the night's over, the cows will be comin' to Mike to complain about Stony's jokes."

"Here," Slop said, handing Cord a biscuit with a slab of bacon in it. "Find you somethin' to wrap this up in. And don't pay no attention to them two." Indicating Blackie and Stony.

"Much obliged," Cord said.

The night passed peacefully enough, with Lem showing Cord the boundaries of the range the cattle were grazing. They met Stony and Blackie several times before dawn as they circled the herd. It was only necessary to drive a small number of strays back to the herd on two occasions before darkness set in for the night. On the first occasion, Lem suggested that Cord should cut the strays off and push them back to the main herd. Cord managed to get the job done, but with a lot of extra trouble to Lem's way of thinking. "That horse you're ridin' is a cow pony," Lem told Cord after it was done. "He knows what to do, if you'll just let him know where you want 'em to go." On the second bunch, Lem led off so Cord could watch him turn them back. "Ain't much to it," Lem said. "Horse does all the work." As far as Cord ever knew, Lem made no mention of his inexperience working cattle to any of the other men.

In the weeks that followed that first night with Lem, Stony, and Blackie, Cord developed into a first-rate cowhand. It seemed to come naturally to him, and it suited his lonesome disposition. By the time the crew drove the cattle into the holding pens in Ogallala, Duffy knew he had himself a top hand. Cord soon gained a reputation with the other men as a hard worker, uncomplaining, even when called upon to ride night herd in the brutal winter that followed his first fall in Ogallala. Mike Duffy's daughter, Eileen, had taken notice of the quiet young man. "He never goes into town with the other men on payday," she commented. "Is he a religious man?"

Mike had to think about that. "Well, I never thought about it," he said, "but I don't think so. At least he ain't never talked about his religion." He paused again, this time to chuckle over his remark. "Course, he don't say much about anythin'. I don't think religion's got anythin' to do with why he don't go to town with the other men, though. I think he's just savin' up his money." Mike happened to glance at his wife, who had paused in the midst of drying the dishes Eileen was washing. He immediately picked up on the look of concern in her eyes, causing him to question his daughter. "How come you're so interested in Cord, anyway?"

Eileen shrugged indifferently. "I'm not *interested* in

him," she asserted, emphasizing the word. "He just seems like a nice man—quieter than the others."

Mike was quick to warn his daughter. "Well, quiet don't always mean nice. A rattlesnake's pretty quiet till he's fixin' to strike. Don't you go gettin' interested in that man. We don't know a thing about him before the day he set foot on this ranch. One thing for sure, though, that boy's got somethin' locked up inside him that he don't wanna talk about."

"I thought you liked him," Eileen protested.

"I do," Mike said, "but somethin's eatin' inside him, and I'd just as soon not know what it is." For all practical purposes, that pretty much ended all discussion concerning Cord Malone, but it was not enough to curb Eileen's curiosity—a fact that her mother continued to notice, even if her father did not.

After a winter that Mike Duffy claimed to be one of the hardest since sixty-eight finally gave way to spring, work on the ranch turned to repairs and preparations for the arrival of the herds coming up the Western Trail from Texas. The cabin that housed Mike and his wife and daughter was one of the buildings in need of repair. The job had been given to Stony and Blackie, but Stony recruited Cord to help them, knowing that his quiet friend never shied away from hard work. He justified it by pointing out that Cord was a good bit taller than Blackie and would, consequently, make it easier to hand up shingles from the wagon. So when Cord came in after helping move some twenty-five hundred head of stock cattle to a new range, Stony gave him barely enough time to grab a biscuit before riding down to the boss's house to work on the roof. Blackie had just returned from Ogallala, where he had picked up the new shingles at the railroad, and Stony was hoping to finish the repair job before dark. As he expected, Cord made no complaint, although he was going without supper. "Don't worry," he told Cord. "Mrs. Duffy will most likely offer us some coffee or somethin', and we might even get a peek at Eileen."

Cord had paid very little attention to Duffy's young daughter on the few occasions he had seen her—those times usually at a distance, even though there had been one morning he had been in the barn when she came in searching for some chicken nests. She had wished him a good morning, and he had returned the same. There was no conversation beyond that and he had led his horse outside and ridden off to his assigned work.

On this afternoon, knowing that Mike was not around, Stony made it a point to knock on the door, telling Cord and Blackie that it was the proper thing to do to let the ladies know they were going to work on the roof. His real purpose was the chance for an opportunity to get a look at Eileen. When he returned to tell his two partners what success he had, he was grinning from ear to ear. "Mrs. Duffy said she'd put some coffee on after a while, when we was ready to take a rest." He looked at Cord then and winked. "I saw her," he said. "She was standin' in the kitchen door, lookin' at me while I was talkin' to her mama. I swear, she's lookin' fine. She's got herself a fair-sized pair of chest warts since last summer, 'cause somethin' was makin' that apron poke out in the front." His mischievous chuckle brought a like reaction from Blackie, but an unintentional scowl from Cord.

"Whaddaya doin' eyein' the boss's daughter?" Blackie said, enjoying the mischief. "I thought your true love was big ol' Flo down at the Crystal Palace. Now, there's a real pair of chest warts, and Flo will let you see 'em for two dollars."

His remark brought forth a chuckle from Stony. "Well, now, that's a fact. The trouble is, Flo will let *you* see 'em, too, if you've got two dollars, but I'd pay a heap more'n that to take a little peek at Eileen's."

"Ha," Blackie huffed. "You ain't gonna get a look inside that bodice for a year's pay."

"Let's get it done," Cord finally interrupted, and climbed up on the roof. Stony's harmless remarks were not meant to vilify the young lady. He knew Stony well enough by then to know he would never do anything to disrespect the boss's daughter. It was just typical male bluster, but Cord was suddenly chilled by the reference to her body, and his thoughts were drawn back to the little regard his father had shown for his mother's feelings. The peaceful months he had spent working for Mike had dulled the intensity he had left home with, and the vow he had made to avenge his mother. It now surfaced once more to remind him never to forget. "Hand up that hammer," he ordered Blackie.

"Damn," Stony swore softly, surprised by Cord's sudden irritation, "what did you say to him?"

"Nothin'," Blackie replied. "I reckon he just wants to get this roof fixed."

Working at a pace set by the determined quiet man, ripping up rotted shingles and replacing them with new ones, they repaired the weakened places in the roof in about half the time calculated. When they started throwing their tools down into the bed of the wagon, Muriel Duffy came out to take a look. "Knocking off already?" she asked while she stared up at the roof, shielding her eyes from the sun still high above the horizon.

"Done finished," Stony replied as he hopped down from the roof.

"Well, my goodness," she said. "I expected it would take you till dark. I just made some fresh coffee I was fixing to offer you, and some sugar cookies to go with it." She interrupted herself to call back inside to her daughter. "Eileen, see if those cookies are ready to come out of the oven." Turning back to the three workers, she said, "I guess, if you're not in a hurry to get back, you can take a little time for a cookie."

"Yes, ma'am," Stony answered for the three. "We've got time for a cookie, all right." He favored her with a warm smile.

Eileen came out the door then, carrying three coffee cups in one hand, and the large coffeepot in the other. "We don't have a big tray," she explained as she set the cups and the pot down in the wagon bed. She grabbed Cord by the elbow. "Come on, you can help me bring out the cookies and some dishes."

"I doubt we'll need any dishes," her mother quickly remarked.

"Well, he can carry out the plate of cookies," Eileen countered, and continued on toward the door with Cord still in tow. She was still curious about the quiet young stranger with the cruel scar across his forehead, and she didn't expect many opportunities to observe him up close. She smiled at Cord and asked, "You can do that, can't you?"

"Yes, ma'am," he replied dutifully, unaware of the game of wits being played between mother and daughter.

Taking no chances with her daughter's immaturity, Muriel followed them into the cabin. In her mind, there was no reasonable explanation for Eileen's interest in the strangely serious young man, so she had to credit it as just that, immaturity. She had shown not the slightest awareness of any of the young men hired by her father before this seemingly aimless stray showed up at the ranch. Muriel's concern was to make sure no foolish mistakes were made before Eileen got over her fascination, so she planted herself between Cord and Eileen when they got to the kitchen. "Go ahead and pull them out of the oven if you think they're done," she instructed her daughter. When Eileen pulled the pan out, Muriel quickly slid the cookies off onto a plate and handed it to Cord. "There you go," she said, and nodded toward the door. "I hope you and the boys enjoy them."

"Yes, ma'am," Cord said, still without a clue, "I'm sure we will. Thank you, ma'am."

Fully aware of her mother's concern, and finding it amusing, Eileen caused him to pause at the door when she asked a question. "Papa said you were from Kansas. Is that right?"

"Yes, ma'am."

"Where in Kansas?" Eileen persisted.

"Moore's Creek."

"I guess you still have family there. What brought you up here to Ogallala?" She could see right away that it was going to be difficult to pry conversation out of the stoic young man.

"I needed a job," was all he offered.

She gave up for the time being, but his reluctance to talk only increased her curiosity. Her mother and father's suspicions that an unwillingness to talk probably meant he had something to hide was not shared by Eileen. To the contrary, she saw honesty in the somber face, despite the granitelike features and the scarred forehead. She gave her mother a smile and held the door open for Cord, stood in the open doorway for a moment to watch Stony and Blackie assault the plate of cookies, then returned to the kitchen to clean the pan and mixing bowl.

"Honey," Muriel said, "you need to leave that boy alone. He's got trouble written all over him."

Eileen only smiled in response and went on with her cleanup.

Chapter 3

The summer came with the first herds driven up from Texas arriving in Ogallala during the second week of June. There were few opportunities for even chance encounters between Eileen and Cord since the men were busy moving the Texas longhorns to graze on Willard Murphy's range to fatten up before shipping them to the markets. Long days, with many nights camping out on the prairie, gave Cord little time to think of much beyond watching the cattle. Stony, Blackie, and usually Slick never hesitated to ride into Ogallala whenever the opportunity presented itself, but Cord never accompanied them, causing Stony some concern. He had grown to like the private young man, and he feared that, if Cord didn't blow off some steam from time to time, he was going to explode one day like a cartridge in a campfire. Cord would give him one of his infrequent smiles and assure him that he just wanted to save his money. "I swear," Stony predicted, "you're gonna swell up like a tick if you don't take a drink of likker once in a while. Ain't that right, Blackie?"

"I swear, Cord," Blackie confirmed.

The campaign to get Cord to the saloon amused Lem Jenkins. "You oughta leave him be," he told Stony. "He's got more sense than the rest of us—helluva lot more than you and Blackie."

Cord held to his resolve throughout the summer, but when it finally wound down and Mike Duffy's crew drove the last shipment into the pens at the railroad, he allowed that he could celebrate the season with a round of drinks with Stony and Blackie. Overjoyed that his friend was finally going to let off some steam, Stony proposed a visit to the Crystal Palace to start with, and a follow-up at the Cowboy's Rest if the Crystal was unsuccessful in providing the added pleasures that accompanied drinking. "You know, it wouldn't hurt you, and probably do you some good, if you was to visit with ol' Flo or Betty Lou upstairs. You know, to make sure everythin' is workin' like it's supposed to."

Stony's serious advice almost made Cord smile. "I ain't figurin' on spendin' my money on any of the fine ladies in the saloon," he replied, and maintained that he was limiting his drinking to a couple of shots of whiskey. Stony hoped he would change his mind once the fun started. Leaving the cattle loading chutes, the three friends walked their horses down the short main thoroughfare, known as Railroad Street, to the Crystal Palace.

Although most of the Texas drovers had departed the town on their way back home, there were still four cowhands lagging behind to enjoy the pleasures offered by the bartender and the prostitutes at the Crystal. Without the usual summer crowd of cowboys to compete for the services of the ladies, the four drovers commanded the attention of all three remaining prostitutes—their sisters in sin having already gone to Omaha for the winter. Judging by the loud conversation and the raucous laughter, the Texas crew was well along with their last celebration before leaving town. Clyde Perkins, tending bar, offered a "Howdy" when he saw the three local men walk in.

"Howdy, Clyde," Stony returned, and headed for a table across the room from the Texans. "Bring us a bottle of that rye whiskey you had last time I was in here."

In half a minute, Clyde came over to the table with a full bottle and three glasses. "Stony, Blackie," he acknowledged, then nodded toward Cord. "I remember your face, mister, but I don't recollect if you was in here before."

"I've been here before," Cord said.

The way he said it, short and factual, triggered Clyde's memory. "'Bout this time last year," he recalled with a grin. "Looks like you found a job. I swear, though, I didn't see you no more after that, so I figured you musta not had no luck." He was about to say more but was interrupted by a call from one of the soiled doves attending the Texans.

"Hey, Stony," she bellowed, "it's about time you showed up. Me and Betty Lou are fixing to pull outta here in a couple of days." She was a large woman, tall with still some feminine shape in a body that had seen many miles of hard road. She was not really overly heavy. Big-boned was her description of herself, with

enough padding to give a man a handhold. Her name
was Flo, Stony's favorite whenever he had occasion to
visit town.

"I figured you and Betty Lou might be gettin' ready
to head out to Omaha or Cheyenne for the winter,"
Stony yelled back to her. "That's the main reason we
came to town today."

"Liar," she responded. "I don't reckon all them cows
over there in the holdin' pens had anything to do
with it."

"You know I couldn't ride through town without
comin' to see you," Stony insisted, holding one hand
over his heart for emphasis. Flo threw her head back and
laughed. "Come on over and say hello," Stony invited.

Not particularly amused by the playful conversation between Flo and the three cowhands across the
room, the Texans attempted to regain the attention
they had enjoyed before Stony came in. Three of them
looked little more than boys. The other one, however,
was a heavyset, square-jawed brute with coal black
hair pulled back and tied like a pig's tail, and he took
personal offense when Flo started to get out of her
chair. "Where the hell do you think you're goin'?" he
said, and grabbed her wrist.

She favored him with a patient smile, and replied,
"I'm just goin' over to say hello to a friend."

"The hell you are," he informed her, "not after I spent
my money fillin' your gut with whiskey."

Flo maintained her patience, having dealt with countless bully types over the years. "I'll just be gone a few
minutes," she said. "Betty Lou and Frances will take
care of you boys."

"Set your ass back down in that chair," Pig Tail

ordered, tightening his grip on her wrist until she winced.

"You're hurtin' my wrist," she told him, still standing. "Let me go." He responded by clamping down on her wrist until she cried out in pain.

Her sudden cry interrupted all conversation at the table as everyone became aware of a situation suddenly turned threatening. Hoping to head off an ugly scene, Betty Lou and Frances both tried to calm the Texans down, insisting that they would make sure none of them would be slighted. The incident had caught the attention of everyone in the saloon now, including the three men at the table across the room, as well as Clyde behind the bar. As Pig Tail continued to crush her wrist, now forcing her back toward the chair, she struggled against him and said, "I'm gonna ask you one more time to let me go."

"Or you'll do what?" Pig Tail slurred. Her answer was swift. Using her free hand, she reached up and pulled a long hat pin from her hair. And in one quick move, she plunged it deep into the back of his hand. With a great roar of pain, he freed her wrist immediately to yank the pin out of his hand, releasing a spurt of blood when he did. The sight of it, and the pain throbbing from the wound, sent him into an insane rage. He sprang to his feet, knocking his chair over in the process. "Now you're gonna pay for that, you damn slut," he promised.

Alerted by the sudden commotion at the table across from them, Stony, Blackie, and Cord realized that a serious confrontation had developed. Stony rose from his chair, preparing to intervene, unaware of the quiet rage flaring up in Cord's mind. His young friend's

attention was captured with the first sign of an argu-
ment between the woman and the rude cowboy when
their voices rose in heated exchange. Thoughts of his
mother's abuse came back to fill Cord's mind with
images of her blatant mistreatment at the hands of his
father. Vivid pictures of his mother's suffering caused
the muscles in his arms and shoulders to tense with
each threat that issued from Pig Tail's mouth, and for a
brief moment, he saw Pig Tail as the incarnate of his
father. Ever frustrated by his inability to protect his
mother then, he now sought to punish the brute lung-
ing after the woman.

As Flo instinctively backed away toward Stony, he
stood ready to defend the prostitute while Blackie kept
his eye on the Texan's companions. In the midst of this
tense situation when the opposing cowhands eyed one
another, and Flo's girlfriends tried to calm the men
down, striving to head off a brawl, no one was prepared for what happened next. Like a wolf on the
attack, Cord struck quickly and savagely. Launching
his body like a human battering ram, he drove his
shoulder into Pig Tail's chest, and the force of his strike
carried the two of them hurtling backward to land in
the middle of the Texans' table. The impact of the two
sizable bodies caused the table to collapse under them,
landing them on the floor with whiskey glasses and
bottles scattered in all directions as the women screamed
and the drovers jumped back out of the way. His rage
fed now by the fury of his attack, Cord hammered his
victim with a series of left and right punches, each one
with every ounce of strength he could muster. So lost
in the determination to punish all men who victim-
ized women, he failed to notice when Pig Tail no longer

tried to defend himself and lay unconscious, his head rocking back and forth with each blow delivered.

"Cord!" a shocked Stony yelled. "He's had enough!" When Cord continued his brutal assault, both Blackie and Stony tried to penetrate the blind fury that consumed him. "Cord! He's done! You'll kill him!" When words failed, Stony grabbed him by his belt and pulled him off the beaten man. Cord spun around to defend himself. "Whoa!" Stony yelled. "It's me, Stony!" His words finally registered and Cord relaxed and looked around him at the shocked witnesses. Staring in disbelief, as if having witnessed the strike of a cougar, everyone was stunned to the point of paralysis, never thinking to join the fight. Aware now that he had lost control of his emotions, Cord stood numb, his hands bloody and swollen.

"He ain't dead, is he?" The question came from behind them, and everyone turned to find Clyde standing there, holding a double-barreled shotgun.

"If he ain't, it's a miracle," one of the Texans said. At that moment, Pig Tail moaned and rolled his head back and forth as if recreating the beating just administered.

"Looks like he's alive," Clyde decided. "I expect it's best if you boys get him outta here before the sheriff finds out and throws the lot of you in jail. That goes for you, too, Stony. It's best you and your friends leave."

"Right, Clyde," Stony replied, but made no effort to move, still unable to believe what he had just witnessed.

Clyde lowered his voice and spoke softly to Blackie. "Get him outta here," he said, nodding toward Cord.

"Right," Blackie said, and took Cord by the elbow.

"Come on, Cord, we gotta get goin'." He kept one eye on the cowhands helping the beaten bully to his feet, but there was no indication they entertained thoughts of making any further trouble. "Let's go, Stony."

Finally back to his senses after the shocking exhibition he had just seen, Stony looked at Cord and muttered, "Damn, Cord!" That was all he could think to say at the moment.

Blackie was intent upon taking Clyde's advice, however, and started herding Stony and Cord toward the door. While her two friends stood back from the broken table, still shaken by the brutal beating of the belligerent bully, Flo stepped in front of Cord. "Honey, I wanna say thanks for what you did. That bastard was fixin' to give me a real beatin'. Thank you." He nodded, but made no reply, and Blackie pressed him toward the door again.

Outside, the three younger men were lifting Pig Tail up into the saddle. The opposing parties paused only momentarily to stare at one another before getting about the business of leaving town. There was nothing said between the two groups. They got on their horses and rode out on opposite ends of Railroad Street.

It was a somber ride back to the ranch for the three friends. For Cord's part, he was slowly coming down from the violent rage that had overcome him when he had seen the bully's mistreatment of Flo. Prostitute or preacher's wife, it made no difference—no woman should be treated like that by any man. As for Stony and Blackie, they were still somewhat stunned to have been introduced to a side of their quiet friend that they never suspected. The attack on Pig Tail had been as violent as any they had ever seen, and was only a few minutes short of a killing. "It don't pay to rile him none." Blackie summed it up when he and Stony told the rest of the crew about it out of Cord's presence.

In the days that followed the near-fatal beating, Cord could not help noticing a difference in the attitude of the other men with whom he worked. They seemed to be more guarded and less inclined to jape him as much as they were inclined to do with everyone else. Stony was the one exception. He seemed to know that there might have been something deeper inside that caused the quiet man to react so violently. Cord regretted the change in their treatment of him, and he wished that he had not totally lost control of his rage that night. But he did not regret stopping Pig Tail from harming Flo.

As was bound to happen, word reached Eileen of the savage beating of the Texas trail drover a few days past the incident when she overheard her father relating the story to her mother. "Hard to tell about that boy," Mike had said. "Looks like he's got a little rattlesnake in him." The comment was enough to worry Muriel, for she was already concerned about Eileen's apparent curiosity about the quiet man. She talked to her husband about the peril that might lie ahead for their daughter if her odd fascination for the man was not nipped in the bud, and suggested that it might be in Eileen's best interest if Cord was let go. The decision was a tough one for Mike, since Cord had proven to be hardworking and dependable. "Problem is, honey," he complained, "there ain't a man on the place that works harder than Cord. And he ain't ever showed no violent streak before, least not against the men he works with." He promised her he'd think about it, however. Before he was moved to take action on the matter, an opportunity arrived to delay any permanent settlement of the problem.

Word arrived in Ogallala early one morning in late September that the Union Pacific train had been held up twenty miles west of town at Big Springs Station. It was the first time that a Union Pacific train had been robbed, and the bandits had reportedly escaped with some sixty thousand dollars, all in twenty-dollar gold pieces. There was great speculation as to who the guilty parties were. Some suspected Jesse James or the Youngers, but a witness aboard the train recognized one of the robbers as Joel Collins, one of Sam Bass's gang, and the call went out to the ranches to form a posse to hopefully pick up the robbers' trail. Mike Duffy was willing to let a couple of his men ride with the posse. His first choice was Cord, hoping this would give Muriel some temporary peace of mind, having him away from the ranch for a while, and maybe out of Eileen's mind. When he approached Cord with the proposition, the quiet young man agreed to go without hesitation. Mike asked Lem Jenkins to volunteer as well. He, too, was agreeable to participate, not being averse to an opportunity to get away from the daily chores of the ranch. "No tellin' how long you'll be gone," Mike told them. "So get what supplies you think you'll need for a week or two at the general store and tell Homer to put it on Murphy's bill. I expect you'd better head for town right away, 'cause they'll be ridin' out as soon as they get a posse together."

It was already late in the afternoon by the time Cord and Lem rode into Ogallala, and judging by the number of horses tied up in front of the Crystal Palace, they figured that was the place to find the posse. When they walked into the noisy saloon, they saw a group of men standing around one who appeared to be in charge. "That's J. G. Hughes," Lem told Cord. "He was given the job of sheriff after the last one left last spring."

"Lem," Hughes acknowledged when he noticed the two latest arrivals, "'Preciate you and your partner there joinin' up with us." He paused only a few seconds to consider the man with Lem, since he had never met Cord. "We was just talkin' about it bein' too late to start out this evenin', so I think it best if we bed down here in town tonight and start out for Big Springs in the mornin'." He raised his voice then, so that all could hear. "And I'm talkin' about first thing in the mornin', first light, so don't spend half the night in here drinkin' whiskey."

From behind the bar, Clyde Perkins, always concerned about business, called out, "He don't mean you ought not have yourself a little bedtime toddy to help you sleep good."

"I'm ridin' with whoever shows up at first light," Hughes repeated. "Might be a good idea to make camp by the river so we'll all be ready to go, come mornin'."

"Me and Cord need to pick up some supplies before we head out," Lem said.

"Homer's still open," Hughes told him. "He said he'd stay open later, in case anybody needed supplies." When Cord and Lem started for the door, Hughes walked over to the bar for another glass of beer. He took a drink from the glass, then asked Clyde, "Who's the young feller with Lem Jenkins? He ain't the feller who damn near beat one of them boys from Texas to death, is he?"

"He is," Clyde said, and chuckled. "And from what I saw that day, you just need to turn him loose on that

Bass gang. You might not need the rest of the posse, if you get him riled enough."

Hughes thought about that for a moment. "Maybe he might be more trouble than I need to deal with," he remarked.

"Nah, I wouldn't think so," Clyde said. "He didn't seem the kind to give you any trouble—quiet, don't hardly say a word. It just don't pay to make him mad. Anyway, I doubt Mike Duffy woulda kept him on this long if he was a troublemaker."

"I reckon you're right," Hughes said. "Funny I ain't ever run into him in town. What's his name?"

"He don't ever come to town. That time a couple weeks ago, when he gave that feller a lickin', was the first time I'd seen him all summer. His name's Cord Malone, says he's from some little place in Kansas."

Early the next morning, the posse set out for Big Springs Station on the South Platte. Sixteen strong, they arrived well before noon to find there was very little trace of the train robbers except for tracks leaving the station and heading south across the prairie. There was some disagreement over the number of men that made up the gang. It was hard to tell from the tracks alone. Some might have been left by packhorses, but at the least, there were six bandits, according to J. G. Hughes, and maybe as many as eight. Stationmaster and telegraph operator Quincy Johnson listened until Hughes's speculation was finished before stating, "There were six."

"How do you know that for sure?" Hughes asked.

"I counted 'em when they held up the train," Quincy said. "Then they rode off across the tracks that way." He pointed toward the south.

"Why in hell didn't you say so to begin with?" Hughes asked.

"You never asked me how many," Quincy replied. "The word has been wired out to every marshal's office in the territory and Union Pacific has already got their detectives on the job."

Perturbed to be wasting time, Hughes asked, "Any other information you can offer to help us track down the robbers?"

"Well, Sam Bass and Tom Nixon was two of 'em."

"How do you know that?" one of the posse asked.

"I've seen 'em around here before. I ain't ever seen the others."

"I reckon ol' Bass got tired of holdin' up stage-coaches," Lem remarked. He turned to Hughes then. "Whaddaya aim to do now, J.G.?"

"Hell, whaddaya think? Go after 'em, follow that trail south, and we'd best get started right now. We've wasted enough time." When no one moved immediately, he raised his voice. "Let's go! Everybody in the saddle."

"Hold on a minute, Sheriff," one of the ranch hands from H. V. Redington's spread interrupted. "Those fellers have got a pretty good head start on us. It could take a helluva long time to track 'em down—if we ever do. And my boss only figured on me bein' gone for a couple of days. Maybe we just oughta let the law and the Union Pacific take care of this." His words were echoed by a few others in the posse.

"Well, I'm aimin' to track those bastards down if I can. Anybody else wantin' to quit with Ed here?" To his disappointment, several others were of a like opinion. Disgusted, he looked at Lem and Cord. "What about you boys? You gotta run home to Daddy?"

Lem looked at Cord for his reaction, which was nothing more than an indifferent shrug. "No," Lem told Hughes, "I reckon me and Cord will ride along with you." So the posse set out following the train robbers' tracks with eight of their number heading back to Ogallala.

They were fortunate to have no rain for the two and a half days it took them to follow the gang's tracks from Big Springs. The robbers seemed to take no real efforts to hide their trail. On the morning of the third day, the posse struck the Republican River, and from the signs they found, it appeared Bass and his gang had camped there for a couple of days. That meant the posse had gained a day on them, which would have been encouraging news except for one thing. After they'd studied the tracks around the camp, it was obvious that the gang had split up in three pairs when they left the river, heading out in three separate directions. The decision had to be made as to how to split the posse. Hughes suggested that he should follow the trail leading southeast, and invited Lem and Cord to ride with him. The other posse men seemed reluctant to continue deeper into Kansas, their numbers reduced by the three-way split. A couple of them grumbled that they should have turned back with the others at Big Springs. When it became clear that any enthusiasm they might have had for capturing the train robbers was now waning, Lem asked Cord if he was still willing to stay in the hunt. "Ol' Hughes seems to have his mind set on catchin' some of these outlaws, so I figured somebody oughta go along to keep him outta trouble." He cast a broad grin in Hughes's direction, knowing the sheriff could hear his remark.

"It's all right by me," Cord said. "We told Mike we'd most likely be gone a week."

"'Preciate it, Cord," Hughes said, looking at him while aiming his next comment at Lem. "I might need your help to keep Lem from fallin' off his horse."

Lem chuckled. "Hell, you're lucky to have me along on this little picnic."

While the others turned back north, the three lone posse men followed the trail left by the two outlaws heading southeast. "I hope to hell one of these riders is Sam Bass," Hughes remarked.

Chapter 4

After almost four days following a trail left by two horses, losing it half a dozen times before finding it again, the three-man posse pushed their horses close to a hundred miles over flat Kansas prairie. Finally Lem asked Hughes just how far he was planning to follow the outlaws. "Hell, them boys is long gone. If we ain't caught up with 'em after this long, we ain't likely to catch 'em before they get clean to Texas."

"We'll call it quits if we don't overtake 'em before they get to Buffalo Station," Hughes said. He was reluctant to end the chase, since a reward of ten thousand dollars had been offered by Union Pacific for the capture of the robbers and recovery of the money, a small detail he had neglected to tell any of his volunteer posse.

Late in the afternoon of the fourth day, they spotted a strange object on the distant horizon looming up from the flat landscape. "Look yonder," Lem exclaimed. "What the hell is that?"

"Buffalo Station," Hughes said, "couldn't be nothin' else. That's gotta be the water tank at Buffalo Station— train stops there. I heard that water tank is a hundred and twenty feet high, so we're still a long way from the station."

"I just hope they've got a saloon there," Lem said. "My throat's a little dusty."

"They got a general store with a saloon built on the back," Hughes told him. "Least they did the last time I was there. They may have more'n that by now. That was over four years ago, but there was folks comin' from miles around to trade there at that time."

"Well, good," Lem remarked, "maybe these two jaspers we're trailin' decided to stop there awhile and wait for us."

"Maybe so," Hughes said. Then he glanced over at Cord, riding silently beside him, his gaze focused on the water tower that now seemed to be rising higher as the three riders steadily closed the distance. "Damned if you ain't the gabbiest feller I've ever rode with," he joked. Shifting his gaze back to Lem then, he asked, "Does he ever say anythin'?"

Lem chuckled. "Once in a while he'll say somethin' if he's got a good enough reason. Ain't that right, Cord?"

"If you say so," Cord answered, unperturbed by Hughes's attempt to jape him.

A little closer to the water tower now, the rooftops of a handful of buildings pushed up out of the prairie. "I believe they *have* added some folks since I was here," Hughes remarked. "Maybe those outlaws mighta stopped here awhile to spend some of them gold coins they stole." Thinking then of the possible confrontation that might occur as a result, he asked Cord, "You any good with that old Henry rifle?"

"Fair, I reckon," Cord replied. "Least I most times hit what I'm aimin' at if I'm huntin' deer or antelope. Course a deer ain't ever been shootin' back at me," he answered honestly. "Once in a while it misfires. I think I need a new firin' pin."

"Well, you might get a chance to find out if we catch up with these two," Hughes said, shaking his head in astonishment.

"I wouldn't worry about Cord," Lem felt compelled to comment, having seen how he responded to danger before.

As it turned out, there would be no occasion to test Cord's proficiency with the old Henry rifle, for the little settlement that had risen around Buffalo Station appeared as peaceful as a town could be. There was no activity on the short, dusty street when the three riders pulled up before a newly constructed building that proclaimed itself to be the Water Hole. "What'll it be, boys?" Wally Simon, the short, rotund bartender asked when the three strangers walked into his establishment.

"Somethin' strong enough to cut the dust in my throat," Lem replied.

Wally laughed and set three shot glasses on the bar. "Come a long way?" he asked as he poured.

"A piece," Hughes answered. "We're lookin' for somebody we think rode through here a couple of days ago."

Aware immediately what the strangers' business was in his sleepy town, Wally informed them, "You're a day late on the excitement, if you're chasin' them train robbers."

"Whaddaya mean?" Hughes asked.

"Two of 'em, Joel Collins and Bill Heffridge, was here, all right, right here in my saloon, but the sheriff from over in Ellis County and ten soldiers from Fort Hays came and arrested 'em. They was peaceful enough at first, went along with the sheriff with no trouble a'tall. I reckon they figured they was done for, though. And one of 'em, I think it was Collins, pulled his pistol. He didn't get off a shot. Them soldiers cut down on the both of 'em, killed 'em deader'n hell."

"Well, I'll be . . . ," Lem started, never finishing. Hughes, obviously disappointed, said nothing, as did Cord. "Looks like we just rode a long way to get a drink," Lem said then. "Might as well have another'n. We got a long ride back to Ogallala."

"How'd the sheriff and the soldiers know it was them two?" Hughes asked. "Somebody know 'em?"

"Yeah," Wally replied, "feller named Levi Creed—been hangin' around here for about a week—I think he was a friend of Collins. They sat down at that table in the back corner and bragged about the train holdup. I reckon they didn't think anybody could hear 'em, but Danny Green—young feller who works for me—was sweepin' out the storeroom and he overheard 'em talkin' about holdin' up the Union Pacific. When he told me what he'd heard, I sent him to Fort Hays to get the law."

Far too engrossed in Wally's account of the apprehension of the two outlaws they had trailed, neither Lem nor Hughes noticed the immediate tensing of their young companion when the name Levi Creed dropped from the bartender's lips. Shocked, as if struck by lightning, every muscle in Cord's body was clenched, his heart pounding. He forced himself to calm down enough to control his emotions while Wally went on with the story. When finally able to speak calmly, he asked, "Levi Creed, is he still here?"

"Levi? No. He took off as soon as the soldiers showed up. He didn't have nothin' to do with the train robbery, but he was wanted for a bunch of other things, so I reckon he figured it weren't too healthy to hang around. Collins and Heffridge musta figured those soldiers hadn't come for them."

"Do you know which way he ran?" Cord asked, his face expressionless, giving no indication of the fire burning inside him.

"Why, no, I ain't got no idea," Wally answered, "but I'm damn glad he did. He's a right mean son of a bitch when he's drunk, and he stayed drunk most of the time." He paused for a moment to study the young man with the jagged scar across his forehead. "You thinkin' 'bout goin' after Levi?" Cord didn't answer, so Wally continued. "'Cause if you are, you'd best be awful damn careful. That man's got a mean streak a mile wide. There's some men that's best just to step around, like you would a rattlesnake."

Lem was alerted now to the sudden pall over Cord, and was prompted to ask a question. "You know this feller Creed?"

"Yeah," Cord replied, his voice low, almost in a whisper, "I know him." He turned his attention back to Wally then. "You have any idea where he might have been headin'?"

"Well, come to think of it, the first day Collins and Heffridge came in and saw Levi, he told 'em he was fixin' to head out to Cheyenne," Wally said. "But, hell, I don't know nothin' about the man, and like I said, I sure as hell wasn't sorry to see him go."

"Cheyenne, huh?" Cord echoed, his mind already working on how far and in what direction Cheyenne was from where he now sat. Like an old wound, the memory of his mother's tragic death was throbbing in his brain, and the demand for justice flamed anew in his soul. There was no decision for him to weigh. He had no choice. There was only one way to free his mind of the burden of guilt he carried for not protecting his mother. He turned to Lem and said, "Then I reckon we can head for home right away."

"I reckon," Lem replied, still waiting for an explanation for Cord's sudden sense of urgency. When there was still none forthcoming, he asked, "What's workin' on your mind so heavy?"

"Nothing," Cord answered. "Just no sense wastin' time around here when there's plenty to do back home."

"It'll get done without us," Lem insisted. "We can take a little time to rest up our horses before we start back."

"Suit yourself," Cord told him. "I'm headin' back right now. It's a good four days' ride back and we've got about two more hours of daylight today. I'll rest my horse when I make camp."

"All right," Lem conceded. "We'll start back tonight. Just give me time to finish my drink. No sense in you ridin' back alone." His real concern was that Mike Duffy might want an explanation for his late arrival if Cord showed up alone. "What about you, Sheriff?" he asked Hughes. "You ready to go back now?"

"I don't think so," Hughes said. "I don't see no reason for me to start back before tomorrow mornin'. But
I 'preciate you boys ridin' with me, even if we didn't
get the credit for capturin' any of that gang of train
robbers."

It was not easy to break through the wall of silence
Cord had built when it came to talking about his quest
to find the man who killed his parents. Lem, being
older and almost like an uncle to the younger man,
knew there was something eating away inside Cord's
brain, and he was determined to find out what it was.
The story came out gradually over the four full days of
hard riding, and in the last camp before reaching the
ranch, he finally found out what was driving his young
friend. It was a terrible burden for any man to carry,
and in his opinion, the odds of Cord finding the killer
were slim at best. "How do you know you'll recognize
this Levi feller?" Lem asked. "It's been a lotta years since
you saw him. He most likely changed a lot since then.
Hell, he's a lot older. Men in his line of work sometimes
have to change their whole appearance when the law
gets on their tails, anyway."

"I'll know him," Cord replied confidently. "I don't
care how much he's changed."

"Maybe so," Lem allowed, stroking his chin thoughtfully. He was not comfortable with the idea of Cord
going after a hardened criminal like Levi Creed. He
decided to make one more attempt to dissuade him
from the task he had set upon. "Look here, Cord, you're
about as tough a young feller as I've ever seen, but
you're talkin' 'bout goin' after somebody who kills for

a livin'. Might be best to just let it go. I expect your mama would tell you the same thing if she could."

"If I was to listen to you, I might as well shoot myself in the head right now, 'cause I sure as hell wouldn't be worth the price of a horse turd," Cord told him. "I've already told you more than I ever intended to, so I'd appreciate it if you just keep what I've told you to yourself. All right?"

That was the reaction Lem pretty much expected from his determined young friend, but he figured it was worth the attempt to change his mind. "All right," he said. "I reckon it's your business and none of nobody else's." He didn't bring the matter up again.

"Why?" Eileen Duffy asked when she overheard her father telling her mother that Cord was leaving.

"I don't know for sure," Mike said. "You know how Cord is. He don't say much, anyhow, and all he would tell me is that he had somethin' he had to do, somethin' important by the way he sounded, and he didn't seem to wanna talk about it."

"But I thought he was satisfied here, working for you," Eileen insisted.

"I thought so, too," Mike replied, "and he said so himself—said he hated to give up his job, but he didn't have any choice—said he'd like to have it back when he got done with whatever it is he's got to take care of."

"You said he was a hard worker," Eileen reminded him.

"He is at that," Mike allowed. "I told him to come talk to me after he's done with it."

Muriel Duffy stood listening to the conversation

between her husband and her daughter, the plate she had been drying still in her hand. She had felt a sense of relief when Mike told her Cord was leaving. Now she wondered if there was any cause for her to be concerned over Eileen's apparent distress over the young man's leaving. "Just like most of the drifters," she finally commented. "Nothing ties them to any place for very long before they're itching to try a new spot. He must be up to some mischief if he won't tell why he's going. I'm surprised he stayed this long." As she spoke, she watched Eileen closely for her reaction, not sure how deeply infatuated with the young man her daughter had become.

Eileen, however, seemed not to notice her mother's pointed comments, addressing her comments to her father instead. "I bet if you asked Lem Jenkins he could tell you where Cord was going. Lem's the only one that Cord says much to, anyway."

"Maybe so," Mike replied, "but I reckon if Cord wanted me to know, he'da told me. It's his business if he wants to quit." He glanced at Muriel and her stern expression told him to end the speculation. "Anyway, he's leavin' in the mornin', and that's that. At least he ain't quittin' to go to work for one of the bigger outfits." He grabbed his hat from the back of his chair and went out the kitchen door.

"Well," Muriel said cheerfully when the door closed, "we'd best finish up the dishes. I was thinking that tomorrow would be a good day for you and me to get out that material I bought at Homer's store and cut out a new dress for you."

Eileen, her mind somewhere else, stood staring at the kitchen door. Aware then of her mother's comment, she turned to her and said, "Oh, Mother, don't worry yourself so much over things that don't matter. I'm not going to run off to follow Cord Malone." With that, she turned and went to her room, leaving her mother to finish the dishes.

"I wasn't worried about any such thing. . . ." Muriel's voice trailed off as she called after her, even though her face flushed slightly in embarrassment over her obvious ploy to get her daughter's mind off of the quiet young man.

"Mike said you ain't gonna be ridin' night herd tonight," Stony said when he walked into the bunkhouse, where Cord was packing up his few belongings in his saddlebags. He watched Cord for a few moments, then commented, "Looks like you're fixin' to pack up and go somewhere."

"That's a fact," Cord said. "That's the reason I ain't gonna ride night herd."

"Where you goin'?"

"Got somethin' I need to tend to," Cord replied.

"What?" Stony persisted. "You ain't said two words ever since you and Lem came back." When Cord merely shrugged in reply, Stony asked sarcastically, "You on some secret business for the government, or somethin'?"

"Personal business," Cord replied, stuffed his clean shirt into the saddlebag, and headed toward the door. "If I get it done, I'll most likely be back."

"Damn, Cord," was all Stony could think to say. His quiet friend sometimes confounded him.

On his way to the barn, Cord saw Lem Jenkins coming to meet him. He was carrying his rifle. "I was just comin' to find you," Lem said. "You all set to leave in the mornin'?"

"I reckon," Cord replied. "Figured I'd best take a look at my saddle and see if it'll hold up for a while yet. What are you fixin' to do with that rifle?"

"Like I said, lookin' for you," Lem said. "See if I can talk you into a trade for that old Henry you're carryin'."

Cord was confused. "My rifle? What are you talkin' about? Why do you wanna trade for this old rifle? That's a Winchester '73 you're totin'."

"I ain't talkin' about tradin' for good," Lem was quick to explain. "I'm just talkin' about loanin' it to you till you get back. If you wind up findin' the feller you're goin' after, you're gonna need a weapon you can count on, and that still might not be enough to keep you from gettin' yourself shot. But it'll sure as hell give you a rifle you can depend on, better'n that old rifle that don't shoot half the time."

Cord was dumbfounded. "I can't take your rifle. I don't know how long I'm gonna be gone. Hell, I might not come back at all."

"Don't argue," Lem insisted. "It'll make me feel better, knowin' I could help you out a little bit." He shoved the Winchester in Cord's hand and took Cord's Henry before his confused young friend could resist. "Now, good huntin' and be careful you don't get yourself killed." Not waiting to hear Cord's protests, he turned and continued on toward the bunkhouse, leaving his friend to stand amazed.

Standing in the kitchen door, Eileen saw Cord come from the bunkhouse and head toward the barn. She threw her shawl over her shoulders, grabbed the egg basket, and got as far as the kitchen door again before hesitating when she saw Lem approach him. Impatient, she waited for the two men to finish their conversation, and when they parted, she stepped out the back door and headed to the barn. She found him in the tack room, checking the girth strap on his saddle. "Looks like you're gonna have to repair that pretty soon," she said, startling him.

"Sorry," he apologized for jumping. "I didn't hear you come in the barn." He looked at the strap again. "I reckon I'd better before I find myself sittin' on the ground one day."

"Papa says you're thinking about leaving us." She made an effort to be cheerful in her tone.

"Did he?"

"Are you?" she pressed when he failed to answer her question.

"Leavin'? Yes, ma'am," he replied, "after breakfast in the mornin'." He glanced around him in the tack room, wondering if there was something he wasn't noticing. "Was there somethin' you needed help with?"

"No. I was just checking to see if the chickens had laid any more eggs in the barn. A couple of them made some new nests here." Without pausing, she returned to her questioning. "Papa said you aren't telling anyone where you're off to and why. Is that so?"

He hesitated to answer, not wanting to appear to be rude. "It's somethin' that needs to be done, that's all. And I reckon I'm the only one who can do it."

"My goodness," she remarked, "it sounds important, and you're the only one who can do it?" There was a hint of sarcasm in her tone.

He wasn't sure if she was being sarcastic or not, and he wished at this point that he had simply left without telling anyone he was going. But he knew that wasn't the proper way to quit his job. "Look, miss, I don't want—" That's as far as he got before she interrupted him.

"When are you going to stop calling me miss or ma'am? My name is Eileen. You must think I'm about forty years old."

"No, ma'am, I don't think you're hardly that old."

"Then call me Eileen."

"Yes, ma'am."

Exasperated, she demanded, "What's my name?"

"Eileen," he answered, perplexed by her seemingly disturbed attitude.

"Well, there, you said it. I was beginning to think you couldn't form the word *Eileen*. But you can, so from now on that's what you must call me." She took a step back and looked at him as one would gaze at a problem child. "You are planning to come back, aren't you? I mean, whenever you finish with this important job you have to do."

He took a minute to answer, unable to understand why she was interrogating him in such fashion. Stony and Slick were always talking about what a fine-looking woman Eileen was, but no one ever suggested that she was a little bit loco. It would be a shame if she was touched in the head, because Stony and Slick were right. She was a fine-looking woman. He was not at all blind to that, but he never fantasized anything about her for the simple reason that he figured she was far above men like him—that and the fact that, for some reason he could not explain, he always felt uncomfortable when she came around. There was no room in his life for a woman, anyway, as long as he had his vow to complete. "I reckon I'll be comin' back," he finally said. "I ain't got nowhere else to go."

"And that's the only reason you'd come back here—because you don't have anywhere else to go?" She was pressing him hard, hoping he might realize there was a better reason to return to the Triple-T.

"I guess so," he answered, puzzled by her question.

"Well, when you're deciding whether you are or not, here's something to think about." She stepped quickly to him, rose on her tiptoes, and kissed him hard. She stepped away then, spun on her heel, and was gone, leaving him standing, confused and dazed, trying to figure out what had just happened. Whatever possessed her to kiss him, and why? Of all the issues he had encountered in his young life, women were the subject he knew the least. He suddenly had a strong desire to change his mind and forget about leaving. After a few moments of indecision, however, he reminded himself of his sworn obligation to find Levi Creed and punish him for the death of his mother. He knew there would never be peace in his mind until that promise to her was fulfilled. He hesitated a moment more when another thought occurred. There was a good possibility that Mike's daughter, Eileen, might be *tetched in the head*. He decided on that explanation for her impulsive kiss, although it would be difficult to dismiss the strange tingling he imagined he still felt on his lips.

Equally uncertain about what had just happened in the tack room, Eileen questioned her sanity as she walked back to the kitchen. *What on earth was I thinking?* she asked herself. The trouble was, and she knew it, that she was not thinking rationally. The sudden impulse to kiss him was the only way she could think to shock him out of his constant emotionless detachment. She smiled to herself when a picture of her horrified mother formed in her mind. *She would have had a cow,* she thought. She shook her head then, wondering if she had just opened a door that would have best remained closed. After all, her mother was right—they had known absolutely nothing about Cord Malone before he set foot on their ranch. But she had to admit that the strange young man had stirred feelings in her, at least enough so that she wanted to know more about him. Maybe she was wrong, but she thought that she sensed a decent soul behind the scarred forehead— *and malleable enough so that I could shape him any way I wanted,* she thought. "Hell," she swore aloud, "he's leaving and we'll probably never see him again. It was just a kiss, anyway."

"What did you say, dear?" Muriel Duffy asked when Eileen walked into the kitchen.

"Oh, nothing," Eileen said. "I was just thinking that it's getting colder outside."

The morning broke chilly and clear, and Cord was saddled up soon after taking advantage of a hearty breakfast provided by Slop, who was one of the few, along with Stony and Blackie, who made it a point to offer Cord a casual "so long." Settled in the saddle, Cord nodded to Lem, who was standing near the corner of the house, as he rode out toward the road. Lem returned the nod and stood watching him for a few moments as he led the tired old sorrel he had first ridden in on behind him. He chuckled to himself when he thought about it. Mike had told Cord he needed a pack-horse, and he might as well take his old sorrel since the horse wasn't of much use as a cow horse. A few more moments passed before he realized that Eileen had come out on the porch and stood watching Cord's departure. It occurred to him then that it was not typical of the young lady, and it got him to thinking. After a few more moments, he walked over to stand at the corner of the porch. "He'll be back," he said.

Startled by his comment, for she had not seen him at the corner, her mind having been occupied with other thoughts. "How do you know that?" she asked.

"He's got my rifle, and he's too doggoned honest not to bring it back."

Chapter 5

Following the directions Lem had suggested, Cord
rode west along the South Platte for about thirty-five
miles looking for the point where Lodgepole Creek
branched off. With one stop to rest his horse, he arrived
at the confluence of the creek and the river a little before
sundown, so he made his first night's camp there. He
started out early the next morning, leaving the South
Platte and following Lodgepole Creek. Lem had told
him that the creek would take him all the way to Cheyenne and to figure it to be a little over a hundred miles
from that point. Cord planned to bite off the major portion of that distance in one day's time, hoping to make
Fort Sidney late that afternoon. With a good horse
under him, and a dependable rifle now in his possession, he felt confident that he would somehow find the
man he hunted. He was not flush with cash, but he had
a little, thanks to his scrimping and saving, which had
provoked predictions of eventual despair from Stony

and Blackie. Slop had stuffed a sack of coffee beans in his war bag to be boiled in the small tin coffeepot he had been given by his grandmother. That, coupled with a supply of antelope jerky and a slab of sowbelly, he figured he had all he needed to survive, with the exception of maybe some dried beans. Lem had told him that there was a settlement near the fort, so he figured he could buy some beans there, and maybe a little bit of salt.

Created primarily to protect track-laying crews for the Union Pacific from Indian attacks, Fort Sidney had progressed from an original blockhouse with tents pitched nearby to a modern-day fort with quarters for three companies of soldiers. It appeared sizable to Cord at the end of a long fall day over a frosty prairie that seemed endless in all directions. With no business to conduct with the army, however, he guided his horses toward the town of Sidney and a stable, thinking they could use a night inside and a portion of grain.

He was greeted by the stable owner, Dewey Gillespie, when he pulled the bay to a halt and dismounted stiffly in front of the door. "How do?" Gillespie asked. "Looks like you've been ridin' for a spell."

"That's a fact," Cord responded.

"It's startin' to get a little chilly, ain't it? We're gonna turn around one of these mornin's and find old man winter lookin' right down our backs. I swear, this mornin' there was a thin little layer of ice on that water trough out yonder."

"Is that a fact?" Cord replied.

"Yes, sir," Gillespie went on. "I can feel it comin' in my bones. We're in for a rough winter this year." He paused to allow room for Cord's comments. When there were none, he asked, "You lookin' to stable your horses?"

"Yes, sir," Cord answered, "if the rate ain't too high."

"Fifty cents with a ration of oats throwed in," Gillespie said.

"Fair enough. How much for me *and* the horses?"

"Another fifty cents," Gillespie said. "Same as the horse, only you don't get no oats." He laughed good-naturedly at his remark, then studied the somber young man as Cord fished in his coat pocket for the money. "First time in Sidney?" he asked. Cord nodded, and Gillespie went on. "You gonna stay awhile, or just passin' through?"

"Just passin' through," Cord answered, "on my way to Cheyenne."

"If you're lookin' for a place to get a hot supper, Maggie's Diner is right up the street. That's about the best place for the money, and the cookin's better'n that over at the hotel—and a helluva lot better'n what you'd get at the saloon."

Cord nodded again while he considered the suggestion. He had not planned to spend any more of his money than was absolutely necessary, and already he had decided to put his horse in the stable for the night. The prospect of a good hot meal was tempting. He had not been away from Slop's cooking long enough to become fully adapted to camp meals of sowbelly and coffee again. "I might do that," he finally said.

"Just tell 'em Dewey sent you," Gillespie said, "and maybe they'll shave a little more offa the price."

"I'll do that," Cord said, and led the bay into the

stable to the stall Gillespie pointed out, where he pulled the saddle off and dropped it in the back corner.

Gillespie picked up a pitchfork and tossed some more hay in the stall. "Make your bed a little softer," he volunteered.

"Much obliged," Cord said, pulled the Winchester from his saddle scabbard, and headed toward the door. "Dewey sent me, right?"

"Dewey sent you," Gillespie confirmed. "She'll take care of you." He nodded toward the rifle in Cord's hand. "I doubt you'll need that in the diner."

"This rifle don't get outta my sight," Cord replied. He had every intention of returning the Winchester to its owner.

There were two women cleaning up the small diner when Cord walked in. The only customers were four soldiers seated at a table near the front door. From the number of tables yet to be cleared of dirty dishes, it appeared that business had been brisk. "Looks like I might be a touch late to get somethin' to eat," Cord said, still holding the door open. "Dewey sent me," he remembered to say then.

One of the women looked to be older than the other, so he assumed that she was Maggie, for whom the diner was named. She set the tray of dishes she was holding on one of the tables, wiped her hands on her apron, and looked beyond him to see if he was alone. When it appeared that he was, she took another moment or two to look him over. "No, we can still feed you." She paused before commenting, "Dewey sent you, huh? Well, I reckon we can scrape you up a plate of food. Set yourself down right here and we'll see what ain't been throwed out yet." She called out to her helper, who was just walking through the kitchen door carrying a tray of dirty dishes. "Bessie, you might as well put another pot of coffee on."

In just a couple of minutes, the woman came back with a plate piled high with potatoes, beans, and two thick slices of ham. "This ain't hardly had time to cool down yet. We just emptied it outta the pots."

Bessie walked up beside her and filled his cup with the dregs of the old pot. "You're new in town, ain'tcha?"

"Yes, ma'am," Cord said, "just passin' through."

As Maggie placed the plate before him, she introduced herself. "I'm Maggie Gillespie," she said. "Did Dewey say he was comin' to get his supper anytime soon?"

"Ah, no, ma'am, he didn't say." It was obvious to him now why Gillespie had recommended this diner so highly. Cord looked at the plate piled high with food, and imagined the woman in the kitchen scraping every scrap out of the pots and pans. "I hope there was a little bit left for his supper."

Maggie chuckled. "Did he look like he was missin' many meals?" Cord pictured the round little man he had just left in the stable, but Maggie didn't wait for a response. "Dewey's supper's warmin' in the oven. He oughta be here directly."

Cord propped his rifle against the wall behind his chair and sat down to eat. After a few mouthfuls, he decided that Dewey wasn't far off when he had praised the cooking at the diner. He wondered if that was the reason the four soldiers were eating there, instead of the mess hall at the fort, but it occurred to him then that at this hour the mess hall was probably closed. All four had turned to look him over when he had walked in, pausing in their conversation until he propped the rifle against the wall. Cord took a sip of the scalding-hot coffee, unable to prevent a grimace as he set the cup back on the table. Noticing his reaction, Bessie paused in her clearing of a table and grinned at him. "I expect that's a little strong. It was the bottom of the pot I made about two hours ago."

"It has got plenty of bite," Cord replied. "That's a fact."

She laughed then. "I've got a fresh pot on the stove—oughta be ready in a minute or two."

"Don't even bring mine till it's done."

Cord turned to see Dewey coming in the door.

"Tell Maggie I'm about to starve to death, so hurry up with my supper."

"Hmph," Bessie grunted, "I believe we already throwed your supper out." It was obvious that the women were accustomed to joking with the rotund stable owner.

Dewey sat down at the table with Cord. "Mind if I join you?"

"Reckon not," Cord replied.

"How are the vittles?" Dewey asked. "Did I lie?" With his mouth full, Cord could only shake his head in response. "The little woman can cook," he said, and leaned back to give his wife a wide grin as she approached with a plate piled equally high to the one she had served Cord. "I see you're still feedin' soldiers," he said to Maggie.

"Yes," she replied. "That's the third bunch we've had tonight. If any more of 'em show up, they're gonna be out of luck, 'cause we're closin' up as soon as those four are finished." She returned to the kitchen to get the coffeepot.

"They've been lookin' for an escaped prisoner," Dewey explained. "They had ol' Bill Dooley locked up in the guardhouse over at the fort for stealin' a couple of horses, and I reckon they musta sent troopers out in all directions tryin' to find him. They musta split 'em up in details of four men. I reckon they didn't figure Dooley would be too tough to handle. From what I hear, some years back he was a real hell-raiser, though. Used to ride with that Sam Bass bunch. But I reckon a few years in the territorial prison softened him up a little. He musta had some fire left in him, though, 'cause he managed to steal a cavalry horse and take off. From what I hear, it was when they was escortin' him to the hospital after he come down sick." He gestured toward the soldiers at the other table. "I reckon they could tell you the straight of it, if you was interested." Cord wasn't. He continued eating, pausing only when Maggie came from the kitchen with the coffeepot and two clean cups.

They ate in silence for a while until both men began to get full, and then Gillespie rekindled the conversation. "Did you say you was on your way to Cheyenne?" Cord nodded, but continued eating. Dewey studied the face of the seemingly serious young man, especially the jagged scar across his forehead. It appeared to be an old scar and not from a recent injury. "You don't talk very much, do ya?"

"Every time I got somethin' I need to say, I reckon."

Since Cord didn't appear to be irritated by the questioning, Dewey asked another. "How'd you come by that scar on your forehead? That looks like it mighta hurt somethin' fierce."

Cord glanced up to meet Dewey's gaze, the feeling finally striking him that the round little man was getting mighty inquisitive. "Got hit in the head when I was a kid," he answered him.

Dewey waited a few moments for more, but when it appeared there were no details to follow, he shrugged and said, "I reckon I'm askin' a lot of questions that ain't none of my business. I better shut up and let you eat."

Not wishing to seem unfriendly, Cord said, "Nothin' to tell, just some tomfoolery kids get into." He finished up his supper and had another cup of coffee before paying Maggie for the meal. Satisfied that he had gotten his money's worth, he headed back to the stable to sleep. Dewey came by later to tell him to put the bar on the inside of the door, and to close the padlock on the outside if he should happen to leave before he came back in the morning.

Cord was saddled up and leading the bay out of the stable when Gillespie showed up the next morning. "Mornin'," Dewey greeted him. "If you're thinkin' 'bout gettin' some breakfast, Maggie will be open in about thirty minutes."

"Thanks just the same," Cord replied, "but I reckon I'll be on my way. I'll stop to eat somethin' when I rest my horses."

"Well, good luck to ya," Dewey said. "Maybe you'll get back this way again sometime."

"Maybe so," Cord said as he stepped up in the saddle, turned the bay back toward the wagon track by the creek, and started out again for Cheyenne.

Like on the morning before, there was a heavy frost on the rough road along Lodgepole Creek and a chilly

wind sweeping across the prairie, unimpeded by the
occasional bluffs of limestone. He pulled the collar of
his heavy jacket up close around his neck, even as the
sun reflected from the silvery whiteness of the frost-
covered prairie caused him to squint. The big bay horse
maintained a steady pace, seemingly unconcerned
with the cold while his breath formed miniature clouds
of white vapor around his muzzle. Thinking primarily
about his packhorse, he decided not to push on too far
before stopping to let it rest. After a ride of about three
hours, the sun climbed high enough to take a little of
the chill from the air, so Cord began to look for the best
place to stop. He finally settled on a long grove of trees
that formed a belt along the creek, thinking there would
be wood there for a fire.

The sorrel was not carrying much of a load, because
Cord had few possessions and not a great lot of supplies, but he took the packs off anyway. After pulling
his saddle off the bay, he let the horses drink before
building his fire and charging up his coffeepot. In a
short amount of time, he was warming his insides
with the fresh, hot coffee and chewing on a stick of
antelope jerky.

By nature a man very much aware of his surround-
ings when away from other people, Cord felt the soft
current of the creek and the slight rustle of cottonwood
leaves overhead. He sat real still, absorbing the quiet
that suddenly shrouded the creek bank when the breeze
stopped for a few moments. There was something else
he sensed, something that was not part of the creek or
the trees, and he slowly pulled his rifle up to lie across
his legs when he heard the bay whinny. Without mov-

ing, he spoke. "You gonna hang back there in the trees, or you gonna come on in by the fire?"

"I'm comin' in," a voice called from behind him. "Don't shoot. I ain't got no gun."

"Come on, then," Cord said, and turned to face the direction from which the voice had emanated. Although there was no outward sign, he was somewhat startled by the response because he had been going on nothing more than the sense of a presence. In a moment, a man came from behind a large cottonwood. On foot, and true to his word, without weapons of any kind, his visitor came eagerly toward the fire. Haggard and limping, he moved up beside the flame and reached for its warmth. "You look like you could use some coffee," Cord said. He dumped the last little bit from his cup, refilled it with fresh, and handed it to the eagerly awaiting man.

"Lord bless you, friend," the man croaked as he took the cup. After taking a few gulps of the hot liquid as fast as his lips would permit, he paused to look at his Samaritan. "How'd you know I was back there watchin' you? You must have eyes in the back of your head."

Instead of answering the question, one he had no explanation for, anyway, he made a statement. "You'd be Bill Dooley, I reckon."

Dooley immediately tensed, certain that he had picked a lawman from which to seek help. "I reckon there ain't no use to run for it now," he said, discouraged, and eyeing the Winchester still lying across Cord's thighs. "I'm 'bout run out, anyway." He reached out eagerly to accept the piece of jerky Cord offered. "I'da got

away from them damn soldiers if they hadn't shot my
horse—and hell, it was the army's horse at that. I rode
the poor ol' horse with a bullet wound in his rump till he
give out and left me on foot. I doubled back on them soldiers and headed the other way. I saw 'em when they
rode past me. I coulda throwed a rock and hit one of 'em,
but they just kept on chargin' up the road, just like ol'
Custer at Little Big Horn." He threw up his arm in a
"what the hell?" gesture. "I shoulda knowed a marshal
would be smart enough to know I'd double back. How'd
you know I'd strike the creek about here?"

Cord was amazed by the man's tendency to ramble
on. The words fell out of his mouth like spent cartridges from a Gatling gun. When he paused to take a
gulp of coffee, Cord answered his question. "I didn't,"
he said. "I ain't a lawman."

"You ain't?" Dooley blurted, barely able to believe it.
Relieved for a second, he frowned when it occurred to
him. "You a bounty hunter? They already got a reward
posted for me?"

"I ain't a bounty hunter," Cord replied calmly.

Confused, Dooley couldn't talk for a moment. "Well,
what the hell . . . ? You ain't?" Unsure now what Cord
intended to do with him, he asked, "What are you
fixin' to do?"

"I'm fixin' to saddle my horse and get on my way to
Cheyenne," he stated matter-of-factly.

"You ain't got no idea about takin' me back to Fort
Sidney?" Dooley could not believe the stoic stranger's
indifference.

"I could do that, if that's what you want me to do,"
Cord answered.

"No, hell no!" Dooley was quick to respond. "Why

do you think I'm runnin' around on this prairie on foot? That's the last place I wanna go."

"What did they arrest you for?"

"They said horse stealin'," Dooley replied. "But I tried to tell 'em I wasn't fixin' to steal a horse. I just wanted to swap a couple of tired horses for some fresh ones, you know, even swap." He couldn't help grinning. "I just didn't have the tired horses with me at the time they caught me, but I was goin' to get 'em. I told 'em so."

"Is that a fact?" Cord responded with an undisguised tone of skepticism. Dooley detected it, but made no attempt to protest. Instead, he shrugged and favored Cord with a sheepish grin, still waiting to see what his fate was to be at the hands of his benefactor. "Now that you've gotten away from the soldiers, what are you plannin' to do? Where are you goin'?"

"I need to get someplace where I know I'll be safe to lay low for a while," Dooley said. "I know the place, if I can just get there before another patrol runs up on me."

"Well, I don't like to leave a man on foot," Cord said, "even a damn horse thief. I'm headin' toward Cheyenne, and you can ride my packhorse if you're headin' that way, too. She ain't much of a horse, but she'll beat walkin'."

"Why, that's mighty neighborly of you, young feller. I'll sure as hell take you up on that and give you my thanks to boot." His smile spread all the way across his whiskered face. "What is your name, if you don't mind me askin'?"

"Cord Malone," he replied as he slipped the Winchester back in the saddle sling.

"Malone," Dooley repeated. "I used to ride with a

feller named Malone. That was a few years back, when I wasn't so down on my luck. Ned Malone was his name, and he was a hell-raiser. There ain't no joke about that—don't s'pose you're any kin?"

"He's my pa," Cord replied.

"Well, I'll be kiss a pig! You don't mean it! You're ol' Ned Malone's boy? I ain't heard nothin' about Ned for years. Some of the others from the old bunch are showin' up ever' once in a while. We figured Ned decided it was time to retire and just found him a hole some-where to hide—maybe that little farm he had near that little town in Kansas."

"Moore's Creek," Cord supplied, content to let Dooley ramble on.

"Yeah, Moore's Creek," Dooley continued. "Fact is, I recollect Levi Creed said your pa had gone back to that farm. I expect Levi's the last one of the old gang to see Ned. Him and Ned was pretty good friends, but I reckon you'd know that. How is your pa? Is he still at that farm in Moore's Creek?"

Cord did not flinch when Levi's name was men-tioned. He decided to play along with Dooley's apparent assumption that the son of an outlaw was an outlaw, too. He hoped there was a chance to gain some clue as to Levi's whereabouts. "He's still there," he said, answer-ing Dooley's question.

"I swear," Dooley exclaimed in wonder for the coin-cidence. "If this ain't somethin'—me hightailin' it for my life, and runnin' into Ned Malone's son. And Ned Malone gone to farmin'." He shook his head, chuckling at the picture. "But not you, huh, boy? Looks like you ain't no more for farmin' than I am. You're more suited to the high life like me and your daddy was before we got too damn old." Then an idea struck him. "You said you was headin' to Cheyenne. You got some particular reason for goin' to Cheyenne?"

"Nope, just thought I'd see what was what," Cord replied.

"Well, if you're lookin' to get in with some boys that are still livin' the easy life, where there ain't no mules or plows, then you need to go where I'm headin'."

"Where's that?" Cord asked, thinking that he might have stumbled onto a road that would lead him to Levi Creed.

"Rat's Nest on the Cache la Poudre," Dooley announced grandly. He waited for Cord's reaction, but when there was nothing more than a blank stare on the face of the young man, he asked, "Didn't your pa ever tell you about Rat's Nest?" Cord shook his head, so Dooley went on. "Rat's Nest is a couple of log cabins back up in the mountains where more'n a few outlaws has hid out when the law got too hot on their heels. Your pa's been there many a time. Levi Creed, Sam Bass, Joel Collins, Jim Murphy, Jim Berry, and a lot of the old gang that me and your pa rode with—they all used Rat's Nest. It ain't easy to find, and the Cache la Poudre is a pretty rough river to go up." Seeing a definite spark of interest in Cord's eyes, he continued. "Whaddaya say? Wanna go there with me?"

"Might as well," Cord answered in as indifferent a tone as he could manage. Inside, he could feel an increase in his heartbeat for what might result in a face-to-face meeting with Levi Creed.

"Hot damn!" Dooley exclaimed. "Now you're talkin'. We'll lay up in the mountains for a spell and maybe you can catch on with some of the younger fellers that are workin' the stage road from Cheyenne to the Black Hills."

"Fine," Cord said. "Where is this place?"

"From where we are here, I'd say it's about three and a half days south and west." He laughed. "It was gonna be a helluva lot farther on foot. It was a lucky day when I ran into you."

Yes, sir, Cord thought, it was a lucky day, all right.

Chapter 6

Thinking it best to leave the well-traveled trail along Lodgepole Creek, because of the high probability of encountering an army patrol, they set out to the south into Colorado Territory. This route would take them south of Cheyenne and any Wyoming lawmen on the lookout for the escaped prisoner. With Dooley as guide, since he assured Cord that he knew the country like the back of his hand, they continued on that course until striking Two Mile Creek. "We'll head straight west from here in the mornin'," Dooley said as they set up camp by the creek.

After a supper made from the meager supplies Cord was carrying, the two new partners sat by the fire to finish the last of the coffee. "About that sorrel I'm ridin'," Dooley said. "Is that mare somethin' special to you? I mean, is that the first horse your pa gave you, or somethin', so you wanna keep her for sentimental reasons?"

Cord snorted a laugh. "Not hardly. She was about the only thing I could afford at the time I bought her. When I got the bay, I decided to keep the mare for a packhorse, since I didn't have one."

"So you wouldn't mind tradin' her for a little younger one. Is that so?"

"I reckon."

"Good," Dooley said. "'Cause I was worryin' that I might end up totin' her before we get to Rat's Nest. It just so happens there's a place between here and Crow Creek where you can get a fair trade for that horse." He grinned and gave Cord a wink of his eye. "You know what I mean? I've done business there before."

Cord nodded. He knew what Dooley meant. *Helluva note*, he thought. *I'm fixing to become a horse thief.* He wasn't crazy about the idea, but he couldn't very well refuse to do it, if he expected Dooley to lead him to Levi Creed. He turned his coffee cup sideways and stared at it as he dumped the dregs from it, as if looking up a stream running dry. Two people on his scant supplies were going to use them up pretty quickly. "We might need to hunt somethin' to eat before long," he commented. "I've seen plenty of sign of deer or antelope."

"Antelope," Dooley said. "There's plenty of 'em in these parts. We'll take us a day to go huntin', but it'd be best after we leave Crow Creek, if that's all right with you."

"Crow Creek," Cord asked, "how far is that?"

"Well, we could make it in a day," Dooley answered. "But we need to hold up for a little bit before we get to Crow Creek so I can trade horses."

"We'll be gettin' pretty low on somethin' to eat by

then," Cord speculated, "but I guess we won't starve if we go easy on the little bit of sowbelly I've got left."

Dooley cocked his head to the side and affected a sly grin. "Course, if you're partial to beef, we could get some of that, too, before we get to Crow Creek."

Cattle rustling, too, Cord immediately thought. He quickly replied, "To tell you the truth, I'm partial to some fresh venison, but I like beef as well as the next man. The trouble is, I don't think it's a good idea to leave a trail across the prairie, from a slaughtered steer to a stolen horse. We might find ourselves with a sheriff's posse on our tail. Besides, if you're gonna steal a horse, I don't think we wanna stick around long enough to butcher a steer."

"You may be right," Dooley conceded. "I hadn't thought of that."

It was decided then. They would get an early start in the morning and continue on toward the west.

Late in the afternoon, they found a herd of cattle southeast of Cheyenne where it appeared a crew of cowhands had moved them to new grazing near a small stream, and were in the process of settling them down for the night. Cord and Dooley gave them plenty of room as they circled, looking for the horses. They found them on the western side of the cattle herd. It was a small herd of maybe forty horses, under the care of a single wrangler. "Don't look like no trouble a'tall," Dooley said. "We'll just wait till dark, then walk right in and pick us out a new horse." With little cover for concealment close up, they withdrew to wait it out by the side of the small stream, far enough away to prevent Cord's horses from greeting the ranch horses with an inquisitive whinny.

"I expect I'll just stick with the one I'm ridin'," Cord said. "I doubt I'd find one I like any better."

"All right," Dooley said, apparently with no reason to suspect Cord's choice was due to a sense of honesty when it came to another man's property. "It'll be dark enough in a little while to ride old Grandma here right into the middle of that herd and slip her bridle on another'n—if that wrangler ever goes to get him some coffee or somethin'. He won't even know what happened till mornin'—if he figures it out then." He chuckled, amused by the picture forming in his mind. "By the time they figure out they got a new mare, me and you'll be huntin' antelope on the other side of Crow Creek." He sat back down on the creek bank beside Cord. "I swear, it's times like these that I wish I hadn't got so damn old. Back when me and your pa and the other boys was ridin' together, we'da rode in there and run off with the whole herd, and woe be the poor cowhand that tried to stop us." He paused before adding, "Damn, those were good days." He said no more then, left alone with memories made sweeter with the passage of time, blaming age for the moisture in his eyes, his emotion unseen by the young man sitting next to him.

Chilled by the evening air, for they could not take a chance on building a fire, the two horse thieves waited for the night to darken. "We'd best get at it," Dooley finally announced. "It looks to me like there's gonna be a moon tonight, and we'd best get our business done before she comes up." So, walking and leading the horses, they made their way back up the wide draw where the remuda was gathered. When Dooley deemed it close enough, they stopped to watch the herd for a few minutes. "Yonder he goes!" he whispered. "Just like I

told you, he's gone to get hisself some coffee or somethin' to eat." Cord nodded. The man charged with
watching the horses did, in fact, get on his horse and
ride off toward the main cattle herd. Dooley turned
quickly to Cord and whispered, "You change your
mind about another horse?" When Cord said no,
Dooley jumped on the mare's back and headed toward
the horses.

"I believe I picked a good'un," Dooley boasted, "even if
I do say so, myself. The only thing better woulda been
if he had a saddle on him. I ain't all that partial to ridin'
bareback. Got too comfortable settin' in a saddle over
the years, I reckon."

Cord agreed. Dooley had selected a good, stout
horse with little time to look him over. A sturdy buckskin. Cord was confident that the horse was a gelding,
but there had been no time, and not very good light, to
confirm it at the moment of trade. Daylight confirmed
his opinion when a brief inspection revealed the absence
of reproductive equipment. "Looks like they gelded
him pretty young," Dooley remarked, "'cause he rides
nice and gentle." Cord tried to pacify his conscience by
telling himself that it was Dooley who had stolen the
rancher's horse, but he couldn't escape the knowledge
that he was certainly an accomplice. He didn't hold
himself to be especially innocent in all his thoughts
and actions, and surely his intention to kill a man was
less than Christian. But in his mind, there were few
men lower than a damn horse thief. Bill Dooley's cheerful, guilt-free attitude, however, made it seem like
nothing more than schoolboy high jinks and it was difficult to dislike the man.

Because of their delay to acquire Dooley's buckskin, they did not reach Crow Creek until late morning the next day. The hardy creek, bordered by trees already shed of leaves, snaked its way across the prairie before them and confirmed Dooley's prediction of available game—for there was ample evidence of recent deer activity at the very spot the two riders picked to cross the creek. They had obviously found a favorite watering hole. Thinking it a good time, and a perfect place to rest the horses while they tried their luck at possibly getting a shot at a deer, they led their mounts downstream and tied them in the bushes next to the water. Back at the water hole, they found some concealment in the midst of some berry bushes and sat down to wait.

It turned out to be a long wait. Sitting cold and still for over an hour, they were about ready to admit their poor luck when Cord sighted a small herd of deer approaching the creek from the west. At first, it appeared the animals were going to cross the creek a hundred or more yards north of the place where the two men sat huddled against the chill. "Damn," Dooley whispered, "they ain't comin' this way." It appeared that he might be correct; then the deer turned and came toward them, but stopped after closing the distance to within seventy-five yards. "Are you a good shot with that Winchester?" Dooley whispered.

"I don't know," Cord replied, also in a whisper. "I ain't ever shot it before."

Astonished, Dooley was about to express it, but Cord signaled for him to be quiet. The leader of the herd, a large buck, seemed reluctant to come closer, seeming to sense danger. At that unfortunate moment, Dooley's new buckskin decided to call out with an inquiring whinny. Already sensing something amiss, the buck bolted, springing the rest of his herd in flight. Cord didn't wait. Plunging out of the screen of bushes, he ran up the bank to get a clear shot at the fleeing animals, knowing he would have time for only one before they were out of range. He would have preferred a doe, but the best target he had was a young buck right behind the older leader. Cocking the rifle as he dropped to one knee, he took aim quickly and squeezed the trigger. The buck stumbled momentarily, wobbled drunkenly for a few more yards, before collapsing to the ground.

"Hot damn!" Dooley exclaimed. "That was a helluva shot! I swear, I'd already give up on havin' venison for dinner." He was satisfied that he would never have to ask again if Cord could handle a rifle. As for Cord, he held no illusions. He chalked it up for a lucky shot under the circumstances, but he saw no reason to volunteer that to his traveling companion. Like Dooley's, his belly was grumbling for lack of attention and he was relieved that he would not have to hear it for much longer.

"Was you japin' me when you said you ain't ever shot that rifle before?" Dooley asked while they were skinning the deer.

"Nope," Cord replied. "That was the first time. I just traded an old Henry rifle for it, and I ain't had a chance to see how it shoots till now."

"Kinda like I just traded for that buckskin," Dooley said with a mischievous grin.

"Yeah," Cord replied, "kinda like that." He thought it wouldn't be a bad idea to let Dooley think he stole the rifle. It might further satisfy the old outlaw that

Cord was of the same stock as his father and the apple had not fallen far from the tree.

They delayed their trip a day to butcher the deer and smoke the greater portion of it over a fire to be tied up in packs. Dooley feasted on the liver and heart, while Cord contented himself with the animal's flesh. The liver and heart were considered delicacies by most, especially Indians, but Cord would only eat the insides of an animal if starvation was the alternative. By the end of the day, both men were sufficiently sated. With bellies full, they turned in by the fire to give their over-worked stomachs time to digest.

Ready to begin anew with morning's first light, they continued their westward journey, crossing a sizable creek that Dooley called Owl Creek, then another about five miles past that he couldn't call by name. Lofty mountains loomed in the distance, their snowcapped peaks testament to the fact that winter was already in the higher elevations. In spite of the weighty issues on his mind, Cord could not help a natural feeling of awe and an awakening of a latent desire to know their peaks and valleys. His mind, set adrift by the majesty of the distant horizon, was drawn back to his reality by a comment from Dooley.

"I expect we ain't more'n a couple of miles from the road into Fort Collins," he said. "Last chance to get some more coffee beans before we go up the river into the mountains."

"I reckon we could," Cord said. "But it might be the last coffee we'll buy, 'cause I'm runnin' short of money."

"I need to do a little shoppin' myself," Dooley said. His comment brought an immediate reaction in the form of a questioning face on his partner. "I didn't say

I had any money to buy anythin'," Dooley quickly explained. "I'm just curious about what's for sale." He flashed a wide grin to reassure Cord. "If I had a cent on me, I'da sure kicked in to buy some of the supplies." Cord's response was no more than a grunt. He was becoming accustomed to Dooley's nonsensical remarks. Dooley went on. "It ain't a good idea to ride on into Fort Collins—too big a risk of somebody wantin' to ask a lot of questions. But there's a saloon and a general store on the north end of town where we can make a quick stop and head right back outta town."

"If you're afraid somebody might recognize you, I can ride in alone and get coffee beans. You can wait for me on the edge of town."

"Well, like I said," Dooley replied, "I need to do a little shoppin' myself. If we stay outta the middle of town, I ain't too worried."

They followed the road toward town until coming to a small store fifty yards from a saloon that appeared to be doing a fair business late in the afternoon. They pulled up in front of the store, but Dooley didn't dismount. "I'm gonna look around a little while you're in the store," he said. "I'll meet you back the way we rode in, if I ain't back here when you're finished."

"Suit yourself," Cord said. He could see that Dooley was eyeing the saloon, but he wasn't about to spend any of the money he had left to buy any whiskey. He thought he knew what the scruffy old outlaw had in mind, but doubted his odds of having one of the saloon patrons spring for a drink. He looped his reins over the rail and went into the store.

"Afternoon," a thin man with a shock of black hair and a mustache to match called out to him when he entered. "What can I do for you?" He laid a feather duster on the counter to give his full attention to his customer.

"Need some coffee beans," Cord answered, then scanned the shelves while the store clerk went about the business of weighing out the beans. He decided he could also afford some dried beans to go with the smoked venison he was packing, so he told the clerk to weigh him out a couple of pounds.

His purchases completed, he stepped out on the front stoop and glanced at the saloon. He was startled by what he saw. There at the hitching rail where half a dozen horses were tied, he saw Dooley's buckskin pulled up to the rail in the middle. Hardly able to believe his eyes, he watched while Dooley unhurriedly pulled the saddle off a dun horse and nonchalantly threw it on the buckskin's back. While he was tightening the cinch strap, a man walked out of the saloon and stood talking to Dooley. After a few short moments, Dooley stepped up in the saddle, turned the buckskin's head toward the road, and rode away at a slow lope. Looking quickly back at the door of the saloon, Cord expected to see someone charging out to give chase, but there was no one. Dooley touched his finger to his hat as a salute as he rode by the store. After another look back toward the saloon, Cord wasted no time in jumping into the saddle and riding after him.

When out of sight of the store, Dooley kicked his horse into a full gallop. Cord urged his horse to catch him. After about a mile, racing north on the road, Dooley reined the buckskin back to a walk, allowing Cord to catch up to him. "We'd best leave the road now and head for the Cache la Poudre," Dooley told him.

"There's gonna be some feller lookin' for his saddle pretty soon."

"I thought you'd gone loco," Cord said, "in broad daylight, right out in front of that saloon."

Dooley chuckled heartily. "Hell, nobody thinks you're stealin' somethin' when you ain't tryin' to hide it and actin' sneakylike."

"I saw one fellow stop and ask you somethin'. What the hell did you tell him? He just walked away and let you steal that saddle."

The question brought on an amused response and another chuckle. "He asked me what I was doin'," Dooley said. "I told him that dun belonged to a feller in the saloon, and I was just leaving him there so he could pick him up. 'So you're leavin' a horse,' he says. I said I sure am—gonna tie him right here to the rail just as soon as I get my saddle off."

"And he believed you?"

"I reckon so, 'cause he didn't go runnin' back in the saloon to tell nobody. I guess he was concerned about somebody stealin' a horse, so when I didn't take one, he figured everythin' was all right."

"Damn," Cord swore, amazed by the blatant theft, performed with the same carefree attitude as his earlier horse trade. "Damn," he repeated, shaking his head in disbelief.

"How you like my saddle?" Dooley asked then, still laughing at Cord's amazement. "It came with a Winchester like the one you carry." He pulled the rifle halfway out of the scabbard so Cord could see it.

"We'd better get the hell outta here," Cord said, and nudged the bay with his heels.

* * *

They struck the river a little before sundown with enough daylight to set up their camp for the night. Peaceful and wide at this point after it flowed down from the mountains that spawned it, the river was bordered with a thick grove of trees that offered them protection from the chilly night. Once a good fire was going, and the coffeepot chuckling, they settled down in their blankets with time to talk about the events of the day. Dooley related the story of his acquisition of a saddle once again, enjoying it more than the first telling. "A man can get away with a helluva lot more in broad daylight than he would at night. Folks just get naturally suspicious when it's dark." He laughed good-naturedly when Cord told him he was crazy. "Me and your pa used to do a lot of things crazier'n that when we was a helluva lot younger." He took a long swallow of coffee and lay back on his new saddle. "I'm gonna ride a lot better with my feet in the stirrups again. Tomorrow we'll follow this ol'-lady river up Cache la Poudre Canyon where she'll start showin' her feisty side. When we get higher up to where we're goin', she'll turn into a fickle bitch that had just as soon dump your ass as look at you."

"How far is Rat's Nest?" Cord asked.

"It'll take us a day," Dooley said. "It ain't that it's that far. It's just that there's a roundabout trail to find it. You ain't likely to stumble on it accidental-like, and even if you did, there ain't but one way into the clearin'. So any strangers comin' in better have an invitation, or they'll play hell tryin' to get back out. You'll see when we get there."

"What makes you think there'll be somebody up there now?" Cord wanted to know.

"'Cause there's almost always *somebody* there," Dooley replied. "There *is* a chance nobody's there now, with winter comin' on as close as it is. Most of the time the only fellers holin' up there in the winter is fellers who've got the law hot on their trail."

Cord found Dooley to be accurate in his speculation regarding the amount of time it would take to climb up to the outlaws' hideout. The little man led him up a series of game trails, often coming back to the river, which became more and more defiant as the incline steepened, forming long areas of white-water rapids. Most of the day was spent climbing the mountain before they reached a stone ledge beside a waterfall, where Dooley announced, "Well, we made it. This is it."

His announcement confused Cord, for he could not see that they had reached anything beyond yet another stretch of rough water, with a lot of mountain still to climb. There were no cabins, no clearing even. With a question on his face, he turned to see a grinning Bill Dooley. "There's nothin' here," Cord commented.

"Ya see," Dooley said with a chuckle, "I told you nobody ain't found the Rat's Nest that ain't supposed to." When he was satisfied that his new friend was properly baffled, he turned in his saddle and pointed toward what appeared to be the stone face of a cliff. "See that cliff yonder? We're gonna ride right through it." He laughed when Cord looked skeptical, then nudged his horse and rode straight for it. Cord followed, not seeing the narrow passageway hidden behind a large pine until Dooley guided the buckskin around to enter it.

"Well, I'll be damned," Cord murmured to himself when he entered a crevice wide enough for a man on horseback to pass through, and about twenty yards long. When approaching the other end of the stone passage, Dooley reined his horse to a stop, pulled his rifle from the scabbard, and fired three times in the air in quick succession. "Hold on a minute," he called back to Cord. They waited for what seemed a long time, standing in the dark passage, and then they heard one lone shot from the other side of the passage. "Somebody's home, all right," Dooley said to Cord. Then he called out loudly, "Bill Dooley and Cord Malone." He was answered by a voice that Cord could barely hear, muffled by the thickness of the rock wall. "Come on," Dooley said to Cord, and rode out of the passage.

Leaving the crevice, Dooley and Cord rode into a wide clearing surrounded by thick pine forests. There were two log cabins with a corral between them. The clearing itself was a field of stumps from which the logs to build the cabins came. Waiting on either side of the passage, each kneeling behind a stump, two men watched them carefully. "I swear," Nate Taylor exclaimed, "it *is* Bill Dooley." He got up and walked toward them. His partner on the other side of the opening got up as well. "Dooley, you ol' buzzard, I heard you was in jail," Nate said.

"Who'd you say this feller is?" his partner, John Skully, asked.

"This here is Ned Malone's boy, Cord," Dooley said. Turning to Cord then, he introduced his friends. "Cord, this is John Skully and Nate Taylor." They both nodded to Cord and he returned the gesture. Dooley continued. "Cord here came along just in time to keep me from havin' to run all the way up this mountain on foot. How 'bout you two? How come you're holed up here?"

"'Cause Nate thought it'd be a good idea to hold up the stagecoach at Horse Creek," Skully volunteered.

"There you go again," Nate came back. "We both thought the two of us could take that stage, and we coulda if our luck had been a little better."

"We was lucky to get outta there without gettin' kilt," Skully said. "Bob Allen was ridin' shotgun, and a deputy sheriff from Cheyenne was inside the coach. We had to run for it, but the bad part was Bob recognized Nate, so we had to make ourselves scarce, holed up here on this mountain."

"It mighta been different if more of the old gang was still together," Nate said. "We'da most likely shot Bob and the deputy and been done with it. Hell, Levi Creed passed through this way last week. If he'd been here when we held up the stage, it mighta been a whole different story." A thought occurred to him then, and he said to Cord, "Levi and your daddy used to be big friends back when we had the old bunch together."

"Most of the boys is dead, in prison, or hidin' out like us now," Skully commented. Neither he nor the other two outlaws noticed the slight twitch in Cord's eye and the clenching of his fists when the name Levi Creed was dropped.

Feeling the increase of his heartbeat and the tightening of the muscles in his arms, Cord cautioned himself to calm down enough to play his part. "It's been a long time since I've seen Levi Creed," he said. "Did he say where he was headin'?"

"Well, not exactly," Skully replied. "He was talkin' about maybe headin' back up in the Black Hills—said he'd had pretty good luck before up there, and he didn't see nothin' around Cheyenne any better. I think ol' Levi don't realize he's gettin' old, just like the rest of us. He asked me and Nate if we wanted to go with him. I know you and your daddy mighta been friends with Levi, but to tell you the truth, I never felt easy ridin' with that man. He's liable to take a notion to shoot you, just 'cause he ain't got nothin' else to do."

With his emotions more under control now, Cord asked, "Was he ridin' a chestnut sorrel? He was ridin' one the last time he came home with my pa. I think he always rode a chestnut."

Skully looked at Nate and shrugged. "I never knew Levi to be partial to chestnuts or any other color horse. Did you, Nate?"

"Nope," Nate replied. "He was ridin' a dapple gray when he was here last week."

"Well, like I said, it was a long time ago when I saw him," Cord said. "I reckon I just don't remember that well."

"How is your pa?" Nate asked. "Ain't nobody heard much about him. Levi said he went to farmin' over in Kansas."

"He's still there," Cord said. "He ain't likely to leave. I'll bet ol' Levi is gettin' kinda gray around the muzzle, just like my pa."

"Yeah, a little," Nate said, "mostly in his beard, though." Ready to talk about more important things, he abruptly left the subject of Levi Creed. "You fellers bring any coffee or sugar with you? We're about outta what we brung with us."

"No sugar," Cord said, his mind already occupied with thoughts of taking leave of Rat's Nest, now that he knew where Levi was heading, the horse he rode, and a general notion that his mother's murderer hadn't changed a great deal. "We've got a little coffee and some sowbelly, and a good bit of smoked deer meat."

"We've got plenty of venison," Skully remarked. "Nate shot a doe and butchered it yesterday. I'd sure love to have some coffee to go with it. We figured one of us was gonna have to go down the mountain to that tradin' post this side of Fort Collins, but if you've got some to spare, we can wait a day or two longer."

"I reckon I can spare enough to last you a couple of days," Cord said.

"Much obliged," Nate said. "You know, you and Bill mighta come along at just the right time. Me and Skully have been talkin' about that little bank over in Fort Collins. We could handle it, just the two of us, but if you boys want a piece of it, it might make the job a whole lot easier." It was obvious that his offer was directed at Cord. "Big ol' strong buck like you oughta come in handy." He grinned at Dooley, teasing, "Might even find some use for an old cuss like you."

"Huh," Dooley snorted. "I ain't that much older'n you or Skully, but I reckon I could handle my end of it, if I was wantin' to. But I'm old enough to know I ain't as fast as I used to be, so my days of robbin' banks in the middle of town and gettin' shot at by everybody on the street are over." He nodded toward Cord. "Cord here is his own man. He might wanna join in the fun."

"Reckon not," Cord said. "I'm leavin' in the mornin'."

His remark surprised Dooley and caused him to cast a questioning gaze in Cord's direction. When Cord offered nothing more, Dooley asked, "Where you in such a hurry to get to?"

"I'm thinkin' about headin' out to Cheyenne, maybe follow the stagecoach road up to Fort Laramie and the Black Hills." Dooley continued to favor him with the look of surprise, so Cord reminded him that he had been on his way to Cheyenne when the two of them first met.

"Matter of fact, you were," Dooley replied. "I recollect now." He was disappointed to hear that the quiet young man had no plans to linger in the Rat's Nest. "Well, hell," he finally said after a pause in the conversation, "let's take care of the horses and help Nate and Skully eat up some of their deer meat." He had known the young man for only a few days, but he sensed that something had occurred to make him suddenly in a hurry to move on. He had given no indication of that hurry before they arrived at the hideout.

After the horses were taken care of, Cord and Dooley took their gear inside the cabin that Skully and Nate were using since there was already a fire built in that one. Cord would have left his supply of meat out in the lean-to at the back of the small corral, but Nate advised him to store it inside the other cabin, because of the likely visit of a nighttime critter. "There's plenty of coons and wildcats about these woods, and once in a while a bear," he warned.

This captured Cord's attention. "What about the horses?" he asked.

"Our horses ain't ever been bothered," Skully replied. "'Specially with four horses in there, a bear most likely wouldn't bother 'em." Cord took his word for it, but he almost decided to sleep near his horse anyway. He was not that far from the memory of the time when he didn't have a good horse.

There was plenty of room inside the cabin, even though it was small, for the only furniture was a table and four chairs. There were no beds, none of the cabins' many guests over the years having had the inclination to build any. It was just as easy to spread one's blankets on the dirt floor near the fireplace.

After a supper of fresh venison, roasted on a spit in the fireplace, the four men sat close by the fire, finishing the coffee Cord had provided. "You must not have anybody lookin' for you right now," Skully commented to Cord.

Dooley answered for him. "No, I'm the one had an army patrol on my tail. Cord just came along for the ride."

"I don't know as how I'd be headin' up in the Black Hills this time of year," Nate remarked. "Too damn cold. I told Levi the same thing."

"It ain't gonna be no colder than where you're settin' right now," Dooley reminded him.

"That's true," Nate responded. "But I'm holed up in a warm cabin with plenty of firewood and plenty of game."

"We'd better get on down in the valley and pick up some more supplies before winter really decides to set in," Skully remarked, also thinking about the approaching winter. "I don't wanna get caught up here snowed in because we didn't get down in time."

The conversation went on into the evening as the three outlaws reminisced about the glory days gone by when they rode with Sam Bass and the others, and complained about the restrictions put upon them by advancing years. Dooley participated equally in recalling holdups that were successful and some that were not, all the while noticing a hint of impatience on his young friend's part. He decided for sure that Cord might have been sired by Ned Malone, but he was not carved out of the same block of wood. So when Cord got to his feet and announced that he had to empty some of the coffee he had been drinking, Dooley said he had a call, too, and walked out the door behind him. "You two been ridin' together too long," Nate chided as they closed the door behind them.

Walking to the corner of the cabin, Cord turned to look out toward the valley below as he tended to the business of emptying his bladder. It was a dark, moonless night with millions of stars filling the sky above him. A few yards away, Dooley assumed the same posture, and after a few moments, commented, "There ain't no better feelin' of freedom than to stand at the top of the world and piss like a natural man." When Cord only grunted in response, he continued. "I already know you good enough to tell when there's somethin' eatin' away at you, and I've been thinkin' about it. And seems to me it's got somethin' to do with Levi Creed. Now before you tell me to go to hell and mind my own business, I just wanna warn you that, if you're goin' after Levi, you need to know that there ain't ever been born a meaner snake than that man. Your pa was the only man I know who would ride with him when it was just the two of 'em, and the rest of the gang wasn't with 'em. Hell, I never would."

"What makes you think I'm goin' after Levi?" Cord asked.

"Well, then, tell me you ain't," Dooley challenged at once. "I see you get all drawed up anytime somebody mentions Levi. Listen, what I'm sayin' is you're gonna need some help if you've got anything on your mind about settling anything with that man, whatever it is. And I reckon I can help."

"What are you sayin'—you wanna go with me?" Nature's call completed, Cord turned to question him. "Why in hell would you wanna go with me?"

"'Cause I know a lot more about the man than you do—where he's likely to show up for one thing. There are some places up there between Custer City and Deadwood where a man on the run can hole up. I know where they are, 'cause we used 'em when I was ridin' with Sam and some of the other boys a few years back. If Levi's holin' up in one of those hideouts, you might be too old to do anythin' by the time you found him."

"I ain't said anything about lookin' for Levi Creed," Cord insisted. "You're puttin' two and two together and comin' up with five."

"I'll admit you ain't knowed me long enough to tell the difference," Dooley said, "but I ain't as dumb as I look. One thing I know for sure, you don't add up to be no outlaw. I've been a thief and a robber long enough to recognize an honest man when I see one, and I'll bet you ain't ever stole nothin' in your life. I'm not even sure you're Ned Malone's son." He paused to observe the young man's reaction to his comments. "I ain't gonna say nothin' to them fellers inside, so you might as well tell me why you're dead set on trackin' Levi Creed."

Cord was at a loss as to how to respond to Dooley's accurate assessment of his character. He was not of the opinion that he needed any help to accomplish what he had set out to do. But if the odd little man was truthful about what he knew in regards to Levi's likely haunts, he might help him find him quicker. He decided it was useless to try to maintain the image that he was one of them, at least with Dooley. "Well, the part about bein' Ned Malone's son is true. He was my pa, and he was a no-good son of a bitch at that."

"I couldn't agree more," Dooley commented quickly, encouraging Cord to continue.

"Levi Creed murdered my mother and father seven years ago, and that's why I wanna find him."

"Seven years ago," Dooley echoed. "So Ned didn't go to farmin' like Levi said, and you waited this long to go after him." He took a look at the formidable young man standing before him, gaining a new sense of respect for Cord's patience and wisdom. Instead of flying off the handle at age twelve, when he had little chance against a hardened killer like Levi, the boy was smart enough to wait until he was more likely to gain his vengeance. "That scar across your forehead, Levi give it to ya?"

"He did," Cord replied, "set the house on fire and left us all for dead. His mistake was he didn't hit me as hard as he thought."

Dooley shook his head slowly as he recalled the man he once rode with. "I ain't surprised none. That sounds like ol' Levi, all right." He thought about it for a few moments longer until Cord started to turn back toward the cabin. "Lemme help you, son. It'd be better'n you goin' after him alone."

"It ain't your concern," Cord insisted, baffled as to why Dooley wanted to get involved in something that might cost him his life.

"I ain't got nothin' better to do right now," Dooley said with a shrug. "Besides, you need somebody like me to help you—unless you've got a whole lot of money—which you said you ain't. What are you figurin' on doin' when your supplies run out, or you use up your ammunition for that Winchester—you bein' an honest citizen and all? You're gonna need a scavenger to come up with that stuff, and you're lookin' at one of the best."

It suddenly struck Dooley why he wanted to ride with the young man. It would give him a reason to feel alive again. He had been reluctant to admit to himself that his best days were over. Men like Skully and Nate might offer a chance to provide an extra gun on one bank robbery attempt, but they were really more interested in Cord. As soon as Cord had turned down the offer, there was no more effort on their part to enlist Dooley. Before that, he had almost decided he was at the end of the line while trying to escape the cavalry patrol. And he would not have offered much resistance had Cord decided to turn him in to the army. On foot, with no weapon or ammunition, no supplies, not even a sack of tobacco to roll a smoke, a return to a prison cell had not looked so bad. Now the thought of riding off to the Black Hills with a new partner gave him hope that there might be some good years left in him. Aside from that, he really liked the young man. Able and strong, Cord seemed to possess the one quality lacking in partners he had ridden with in the past: honesty. "Whaddaya say, partner?" Dooley asked, his hand extended.

Not really sure how he felt about the proposition, Cord hesitated for a moment. Bill Dooley was a horse thief and a stagecoach road agent, albeit a semiretired one, and certainly not the kind of partner he would have considered. In fact, he had never considered taking on a partner of any kind. But Dooley was easy to get along with, and as he insisted, he might be of help with his *special* qualifications. He had ridden with Sam Bass when Bass's gang of road agents was making a living holding up stagecoaches and freight wagons on the Cheyenne to Deadwood road. He was probably right when he claimed to know every hideout the outlaws used. "What the hell . . . ?" he finally decided, and shook Dooley's hand.

It was done then, the partnership formed between the tall young man and the stumpy little man with a bald spot on the back of his head, and a shaggy gray beard—an alliance formed to deliver cruel justice to one Levi Creed.

Chapter 7

The new partnership rode out of the Rat's Nest after breakfast the next morning. Nate and Skully followed them down the series of game trails to the valley below, where they bade them farewell and headed toward Fort Collins to get supplies for the coming winter. Cord and Dooley turned their horses north, toward Cheyenne with Dooley acting as guide, since he was well familiar with the territory. They could have made it to Cheyenne in one long day's ride, had they not waited until after breakfast to leave the mountain. Since they had, Dooley figured they would make camp eight or ten miles south of the town. It made little difference, since their scant financial holdings prohibited them from patronizing any of Cheyenne's hotels. Wearing heavy jackets and bandannas tied over their ears, they left the banks of the Cache la Poudre, prepared for a long, cold day in the saddle. "I'm damn shore gonna look for me some more clothes when we hit Cheyenne,"

Dooley declared, "an extra shirt and pair of socks, any-way. When I left those soldier boys back at Fort Sidney, I didn't have time to pack my bags." He chuckled at his comment. "I reckon I was lucky I had my coat on when I ran." Cord didn't bother to ask him what he intended to use for money.

After camping for the night by a small stream south of Cheyenne, they were in the saddle again early the next morning. At Dooley's request, they entered the town on the east side. The army's Fort D. A. Russell was located three miles west of Cheyenne, and Dooley wasn't comfortable in passing close by. There was always the possibility, he said, that word of his escape from the Nebraska fort had been telegraphed to other forts nearby. "I'd be surprised," Cord told him, "since you were runnin' on foot the last time they saw you."

"I hope you're right," Dooley said. "But I reckon they'd really love to get their hands on me again 'cause I rode with the Bass gang."

"Maybe so," Cord allowed, even though he seri-ously doubted that the army held Dooley to be impor-tant enough to spend much manpower on. He imag-ined they would be content just knowing Dooley had fled the territory. Nevertheless, they rode a few miles out of their way to circle in from the east side, arriving before noon.

Cheyenne was much bigger than Cord had expected, with many stores and shops, one saloon after another, and a few buildings two stories high, among them the Union Pacific Hotel next to the depot, and Dyer's Hotel on Eddy Street. Riding farther into town, they approached a three-story building that Dooley identi-fied as the Inter-Ocean Hotel. The size of the town

caused Cord to experience a feeling of discourage-
ment, for it seemed unlikely they could pick up a trace
of one man passing through.

"The thing is," Dooley assured him, "there ain't but
a couple of places where Levi was liable to go—
Frenchy's Saloon was where he always went when we
was in town. They didn't ask no questions at Frenchy's,
and they didn't give no information to the sheriff.
Besides, that street's where most of the red lanterns are
hangin' by the door." Cord responded with a questioning look, so Dooley explained. "Whores. That's where
the whores live. When you see a door with a red lantern hangin' beside it, that means there's a friendly
lady there that's ready to offer you some comfort."

"Oh," Cord replied, looking astonished.

Dooley studied his young partner's face intently.
"You ain't never been off the farm before, have you?"
He marveled that a man nineteen years of age had not
known what a red-light district was. "I might have a
bigger job on my hands than just bein' a guide," he
commented with a chuckle.

"You just help me find Levi Creed," Cord said. "I
don't need you to teach me anything else." He had no
time, and little money, to waste on Cheyenne's places
of physical gratification. He was hoping that Levi might
have decided to linger in town to partake of them,
however.

The statement brought another chuckle from Dooley.
"All right, partner. Best place to start is Frenchy's. If
they ain't seen him, I know a couple more places to
look."

It was still a little before noon when they tied up at
the saloon's hitching post and walked in. As a matter

of habit, Dooley paused at the door to get a look at the room before proceeding toward the bar. The only patrons in the saloon were two men sitting at a table in the back corner of the room, so Dooley continued. "Mickey, you old cuss, you ain't got no prettier since I was last in this place," he called out to a thin little man with a dark drooping mustache working the bar.

Mickey did a double take, then replied, "Well, I'll be damned. . . . Bill Dooley, I thought you'd gone down to Texas with the rest of that wild bunch you rode with."

"I ain't lost nothin' in Texas," Dooley replied.

"Well, times has changed a little around here since you were in town," Mickey said. "Cheyenne's gettin' downright respectable, so I'd recommend you better keep your head down and cast a small shadow." He paused then to ask, "Whiskey?"

"You offerin' one on the house for old times' sake?" Dooley asked.

"No, I ain't," Mickey replied, causing Dooley to look inquiringly at Cord.

"I'll have a glass of beer," Cord said, "and whatever he wants." His comment brought an instant smile of appreciation from his thirsty partner.

"Who's your friend?" Mickey asked as he drew a glass of beer and poured a shot for Dooley.

"Cord Malone," Dooley answered, then tossed his whiskey down. Banging the glass down on the bar, he smacked his lips loudly and sighed as if lamenting a long-lost friend. "Whaddaya mean, the town's gettin' respectable?"

"There's a lot of honest businesses movin' into town," Mickey said. "There's more law than we used to have when you boys were runnin' so free. Hell, half the whores and gamblers have left and gone up to Deadwood. That's the hot spot now, and a better place for fellers in your line of business. Friend of yours passed through here a few days ago. I told him the same thing."

"Levi Creed?" Dooley asked.

"Yeah, Creed," Mickey replied, surprised. "You fellows tryin' to catch up with him?"

"Yep," Dooley said. "We were hopin' to catch up with ol' Levi right here in Cheyenne."

"Well, you're about three days too late. He's already gone. At least, he ain't come back in here. It might be just a coincidence, but a masked man stuck a gun in Jack Thompson's face and made him open the hotel safe. He cleaned out a pile of money and some valuables, then pistol-whipped poor Jack and left him lying in front of the safe with a cracked skull. Sheriff didn't have no idea who to go after, but it happened the night Levi left here, and like I said, he ain't been back in."

"Did you tell the sheriff that Levi had been in town?" Dooley asked.

"He didn't ask me," Mickey said. Dooley nodded his approval.

"Where did Levi say he was headin'?" Cord spoke up for the first time.

Mickey glanced at Dooley to get a nod from him before answering, "He didn't come right out and say where he was goin', but he talked a lot about Deadwood and all the folks headin' up that way. Does he know you're tryin' to catch up with him?"

"No," Dooley drawled, "we just thought we'd surprise him, since we're headin' up that way, too."

Suspecting that there was an underlying reason

they were trying to overtake Levi, Mickey remarked, "If I remember right, you and Levi were never real close friends—I mean, like him and Ned Malone were." As soon as he said the name, he remembered then, and looked quickly back at Cord. "Did you say your name was Malone?" Cord did not speak, but nodded slowly. Concerned then that he might be asking too many questions, the bartender said, "Ain't none of it any of my business, but I hope you catch up with Levi. He didn't have no cause to crack Jack Thompson's head like that." Seeming to have a sudden change of heart, he volunteered, "Why don't you fellows have another drink? This one's on the house."

"Well, now, that's bein' right neighborly," Dooley said. "We'll take time for one more, won't we, partner?"

"I reckon," Cord replied. None of the three noticed one of the men at the table in back when he quietly got up and slipped out the back door of the saloon.

Outside the saloon afterward, Dooley said, "Levi's headin' for the Black Hills, all right, and it sounds like he picked up a little money while he was here. Ain't no use hangin' around any longer. The horses are in good shape. We can get halfway to Horse Creek before sundown before we need to rest 'em again."

That suited Cord. He was anxious to close the distance between Levi and himself. He shoved his rifle back in the saddle scabbard and had one foot in the stirrup when he heard the voice behind him in the street. "Let's just hold it right there, fellows." He turned to see Sheriff George A. Draper and one of his deputies come from behind his horse. Although they both had guns drawn and leveled at them, the sheriff addressed them in a civil tone, almost approaching apology.

"You'll be Bill Dooley," he said. "I've got paper on you, for stealing horses and escaping U.S. Army custody, and stealing a horse belonging to the army in the process. If I ain't mistaken, I believe I've got some old papers that link you to the Sam Bass gang of stage-coach robbers." He looked at Cord then. "As for you, young fellow, I don't know if you're wanted or not. I'll have to look into it."

There was no use to think about resisting. The two lawmen had them at a distinct disadvantage. Dooley looked at Cord with an expression that could almost be described as pride in the knowledge that he had a name that was recognized. He turned to address the sheriff. "You're right, Sheriff. I rode with Sam and some of the old bunch, but that was a while back. I've reformed since then, and I ain't never killed nobody. Now, this boy here, he ain't no outlaw. He just hired me to take him up to Fort Laramie. That's the kinda work I do now. I've give up my sinful ways, and that's a fact. Ask anybody. Ask Mickey in the saloon. He'll tell you that I ride on the right side of the law now. I was just foolish in my younger days."

A smile slowly formed on Draper's face. "Is that a fact? Well, I'm mighty pleased to know that you've mended your ways, but I think it'd be a good idea for you to spend a little time in my jail till we find out a little bit more about what you've been up to lately." He nodded toward his deputy. "Put them irons on him, Fred, and put him in the storeroom while I find out a little bit more about his partner. After you lock him up, take his horse down to the stable."

Cord watched helplessly as the deputy led Dooley away. "Now, young fellow, let's start with your name."

When Cord told him, Draper paused as if trying to remember. "Cord Malone, huh? I don't recall any recent notices on you." He stroked his chin thoughtfully. "And you're too young to have run with Sam Bass when they were workin' this part of the territory. "Where'd you hook up with Bill Dooley?"

"Fort Collins," Cord said. "Like he said, I paid him to guide me to Fort Laramie."

"You didn't know you were dealin' with an outlaw?"

"No, sir," Cord answered respectfully.

"Where you from?"

"Moore's Creek, Kansas Territory," Cord said.

"Hell, Sheriff," Dooley said, "he didn't have no idea who I was. He sure as hell ain't done nothin' to go to jail for. He don't even know how to get to Fort Laramie without a guide." He looked over at Cord then and said, "I'm sorry, Cord. I shoulda told you I was wanted by the law, but if I had, you might notta hired me to take you to Fort Laramie."

His soulful apology was convincing enough to sway Sheriff Draper's opinion toward giving the young man the benefit of the doubt. Draper took another long look at Cord while he made up his mind. Finally he released him. "All right, young fellow, I reckon I ain't got nothin' to hold you for, so I'm gonna let you go on about your business. It'd be a good idea to mind who you're dealin' with from now on." He started to follow his deputy, who was herding Dooley toward the jail, but stopped to make one more comment. "If you're still goin' to Fort Laramie, you don't need a guide. Just follow the stagecoach road. It's about ninety miles from here, give or take a few miles."

"Yes, sir," Cord replied politely. "Thank you, sir."

He stood there, holding the bay's reins, and watched the two lawmen march Dooley off to jail. *Now what the hell am I going to do?* The sheriff was right, he didn't need a guide to find Fort Laramie, or to ride all the way to Deadwood, for that matter. What he needed, however, was his guide to take him to the outlaws' favorite haunts and hideouts. He had a decision to make and he didn't have to think about it for very long. He needed Bill Dooley more than the law needed to hold him. He felt that he knew Dooley well enough by now to know that the aging outlaw was no threat to anyone as long as that person wasn't careless about keeping an eye on his possessions. So the real problem was how to free him without causing serious harm to anyone. *I'll have to think about this,* he told himself as he stepped up in the saddle, and started out in the opposite direction when the sheriff glanced back at him.

He didn't know where the jail was, so when he got almost to the end of the street, he turned between two stores and rode back up the alley until he caught sight of the three men and the horse between the buildings. Holding the bay back by the corner of a dry goods store, he watched when the sheriff led his party down a side street toward a one-story building boasting a sign that said SHERIFF'S OFFICE. Instead of taking Dooley inside the jail, however, the deputy took him around behind the building to a small log building. *That must be the storeroom,* Cord thought, remembering the instructions the sheriff had given his deputy. *Why didn't he put him in the jail?*

Farther up the street was a livery stable, and this was where the deputy took Dooley's buckskin. In a few minutes, the deputy came out of the stable and walked back to the sheriff's office, leaving Cord to think about the best way to solve his problem. Giving the bay a gentle nudge, he slow-walked the horse down to the corner of the street and stopped again to think about the situation. He noticed a small diner a little way up the street that proclaimed itself to be the Supper Table, and thought, *If you lock him up, you gotta feed him.* And maybe that little café was the place that took care of that.

He tied the bay at the rail and stepped inside the door. A pleasant aroma of food cooking teased his nostrils as he stood for a moment deciding which of the empty tables he would choose. The choice was his because he was the only customer in the place. A pleasant-looking lady, appropriately plump, with her gray hair pulled back in a bun, came from the kitchen, having heard him come in the door. "Good afternoon," she said cheerfully. "You're either late for dinner or early for supper."

"Yes'um, I guess I am at that. I was just hopin' I could maybe get a cup of coffee if it wouldn't be too much trouble."

She smiled cordially. "No, of course not. I'd be glad to get you a cup of coffee. Would you like a slice of apple pie to go with it?"

"Uh, no, ma'am. Like you say, it's a little early for supper."

She disappeared into the kitchen to reappear a few minutes later with a steaming cup of coffee and a saucer with a slice of pie on it. "You take sugar and cream with your coffee?" she asked.

"No, ma'am, just black, but I didn't order the pie," he replied.

"I know," she said, "but you looked to me like you needed a slice of my apple pie, so I'm giving it to you. There's no charge."

"That's mighty kind of you, ma'am. That pie sure looks good, all right, but I can pay you for it." The pie did look good to him, and it had been a long time since he had had anything to eat other than deer jerky and beans. But he had already spent more of his money than he had intended on some beer and a shot of whiskey for Dooley.

"Nonsense," she told him. "I want you to have it— no charge, but you have to tell me that it's the best apple pie you've ever eaten." Something about the solemn young stranger aroused the motherly instincts in her soul, for she certainly knew nothing about the character of the man. With his broad shoulders and square jaw—and the ominous scar across his forehead, he could have been the most vile of outlaws. But somehow she didn't think he was—just a young cowboy down on his luck.

Her comment brought a grin to his face. "Yes, ma'am," he said. "I can tell that just by lookin' at it."

"I think I'll have a cup of that coffee with you," she said, and went back into the kitchen to get a cup. "If you don't object, I'll sit down with you," she said when she returned. Without waiting for his reply, she pulled a chair out and sat down. "This way I can make sure you eat every crumb of that pie."

He grinned at her again. "You don't have to worry about that."

She smiled and took a tiny sip of the hot coffee. "Mighta let this boil a little too long, Fanny," she said as a girl passed by with an armload of dishes for the long table in the center of the room. "It's a bit strong." Turning her attention back to Cord, she asked, "You're new in town, aren't you?"

"Yes, ma'am, I'm just passing through."

"Going to the Black Hills?"

"Yes, ma'am. How'd you know that?"

She laughed. "That's where everybody's going." She took another sip of her coffee, glanced over her shoulder to see if Fanny needed any help, then turned back to her guest again. "My name's Ocilla Bussey. If you end up staying in town longer, this is the best place to eat." She favored him with a warm smile and asked, "What's your name, son?"

"Cord Malone," he said, "and you're right—this is the best apple pie I ever ate."

Pleased by his comment, she sat there a few minutes more before picking up her cup and getting to her feet. "Well, Cord Malone, it's been real nice talking to you, but I'd best get back to my kitchen. Fred Beasley will be in here soon to let me know how many prisoners I have to fix for. I hope I'll see you again sometime. Fanny will get you more coffee, if you need it."

"No, thank you, ma'am," he said. "One cup's all I wanted. How much do I owe you?" He would have enjoyed another cup, but he had been right when he speculated that Ocilla might be the cook for the jail. And he didn't want to be there when the deputy came in to give her a head count for supper, preferring to let the sheriff think he had left town.

She paused a moment, then said, "Just forget about it. That coffee sat on the stove too long, anyway. Take care of yourself, Cord Malone." Then she spun on her heel and headed toward the kitchen before he could protest.

While Cord was enjoying a slice of Ocilla Bussey's apple pie, Dooley was being introduced to his place of confinement, which was the log building behind the jail. Not at all comfortable with the accommodations, and more than a little wary of the reason for locking him in the log enclosure instead of the jail, Dooley was inclined to complain. "What the hell are you stickin' me in here for? There ain't even no windows," he protested, looking at the narrow slits on the side of the building.

"Quit your bellyachin'," Fred told him. "They're tearin' up the insides of the jail to add more room for cells. This is the old jail, the first one they built. We've been usin' it for a storeroom, but we're holdin' prisoners in here again till the construction is done. You'll be just fine. There ain't but one other prisoner in here now, ol' Martin Boaz, so you've got the place to yourself."

"What's he in here for?" Dooley asked.

"Drunk and disorderly conduct," Fred replied. "He's still sleepin' it off."

As the deputy had said, Boaz was curled up on one of the half dozen cots in the dark room, close to a small stove. "Damn, man," Dooley protested to Fred, "it ain't humane to keep a man locked up in a place like this, 'specially since I ain't done nothin' to get locked up for."

"You'll get used to it," Fred said. "Look at ol' Martin over there. He spends about as much time here as he does in his own shack."

After Fred had closed the door and secured a huge

padlock on it, Dooley looked around him to see where he had landed. As his eyes gradually grew accustomed to the darkened room, he took inventory of what was available to him. There was a stack of firewood piled against a back corner, so he fed a couple of pieces into the stove. An examination of the log walls quickly told him that they were still solid and strong. There was a table in the middle of the room, a water barrel stood in a front corner of the room, and a foul-smelling bucket was opposite it, for depositing the water once it had gone through the prisoner. He tried the back edge of the door to see if the hinges outside might be weak. They were not. He was peering up at the roof when Boaz woke up. "Pine boards," he volunteered, startling Dooley, "with shingles nailed on top—pretty stout."

Recovering, Dooley asked, "You tried 'em?"

"Hell no," Boaz retorted. "What the hell would I wanna get outta here for? Warm place to sleep, and fine cookin' by Ocilla Bussey—it's a damn sight better'n what I've got when I'm sober. Matter of fact, it oughta be gettin' around time for supper." He drew up closer to the stove. "My name's Martin Boaz. What's your'n?"

"Bill Dooley," he answered. "I reckon you're right. Might as well settle down and wait for somethin' to eat."

The wait was not long, but it seemed long. By the time the deputy opened the door and stood back while the sheriff took a look at the prisoners, with the help of a lantern, Dooley was beginning to fear he and Boaz had been forgotten. "Stand back by the stove," Sheriff Draper ordered. Once Fred had placed a tray on the table holding two plates of food and two cups of coffee, the two lawmen backed out and locked the door again. After holding a wood splinter in the stove until it caught fire, Martin proceeded to light a candle on the table, and the two prisoners attacked the food.

After a few bites of the corn bread, Dooley was inspired to comment, "You sure weren't lyin' when you said the victuals was good. What did you say her name was?"

"Ocilla Bussey," Boaz said, "and I'd marry her if she'd have me."

Dooley paused, cocked an eyebrow, and took another look at the whiskey-soaked wreck of a human body with gravy dripping from his chin. "I can't understand why she wouldn't crave a fine-lookin' gentleman like yourself," he said. The sarcasm went unnoticed by Boaz.

Long after the supper was finished, Dooley waited impatiently for the sheriff, or his deputy, to come to tell him what they were going to do with him, but no one came. After using the bucket in the corner, emptying bodily contents from both ends, Martin curled up on his cot again to sink back into the stupor he had been in. Before resuming a steady drone of snoring, he made one final comment. "They'll be back in the mornin' with breakfast."

Resigned to a long night, Dooley tried to tell himself to relax and go to sleep, but he had no confidence that he would be able to. He wasn't fond of close confinement, and being closed up in the windowless cabin was like being in a hole in the ground. With the little stove glowing cherry red, the room was warm and snug against the cold night outside. However, the tiny slits for windows were not capable of providing proper ventilation, resulting in a smoky interior that made breathing difficult. Afraid to go to sleep then, fearing that he might suffocate before morning, he quit stoking the fire in the stove and attempted to stay awake. As the night deepened, and Martin's steady snoring droned on, Dooley's resolve to remain awake faded, and he finally gave in to the irresistible urge to close his eyes.

He awoke to lie tense in the darkness, pulled from his sleep by a noise overhead that he at first mistook for the sound of rain or hail on the roof of the building. He lay still for a moment, listening. Then suddenly he was startled by a sharp crack of splitting wood, and he rolled off the cot, thinking the roof was caving in. It was enough to awaken Martin as well and he sprang from his cot in alarm. "The damn roof is comin' down!" Boaz cried in panic, and backed away from the center of the room.

His warning was followed by one more crack like thunder and they both looked up to see a gaping hole in the roof and stars shining above. "Dooley?" a voice called in a loud whisper.

Astonished, Dooley answered, "Cord?"

"Yeah. Here, grab hold of this rope, and I'll pull you up. I think the hole's big enough to let you through. Did you hear me?"

"Yeah," Dooley replied, "I heard you." He hurried to take hold of the rope that dropped down to the floor. While he quickly wrapped it firmly around his wrists, he looked over toward the corner at a confused Boaz. "You wanna get outta here, too?"

"Hell no, I'm waitin' for breakfast," Martin said. "They'll let me out in the mornin', anyway."

"All right, Cord, I'm ready. Haul away!" He was immediately jerked off the floor and up he went through the hole and onto the roof. Unable to keep from giggling like a truant schoolboy, he had to be cautioned to be quiet. "I had a feelin' about you, boy," he chortled delightedly. "Right through the damn roof! Hot damn! How the hell did you break through?" he asked, seeing no tools of any kind.

"It's mostly rotten," Cord said as he quickly coiled his rope. "Let's get the hell down offa here."

Below them, inside the storeroom, Martin Boaz returned to his cot and curled up under his blanket. *I hope it don't rain before morning*, was his only concern and his last thought before falling asleep.

Cord's bay gelding was waiting behind the building and Dooley climbed on behind him. They rode down the street until entering an alley that ran behind Eddy Street. Once Cord was satisfied that no one had witnessed the bold escape, he pulled up and questioned Dooley. "You were slick enough to steal that buckskin the first time. Do you think you can steal him again? I know where he is, and I know where your saddle is."

"Hell yes," Dooley exclaimed, "just take me to him." He paused a moment then to say, "You can't steal a horse but once, so I'm just goin' after my own horse. Besides, I never stole that horse in the first place. I traded your old sorrel for him."

"I reckon that would make him mine, then," Cord couldn't resist saying.

Dooley grinned. "Maybe, but the saddle ain't. I stole that fair and square."

"They didn't even put him inside," Dooley observed when they pulled up behind the stables and found his buckskin in the corral with several other horses. "Gotta thank 'em for makin' it easy for us." He hesitated a moment when an ambitious thought entered his mind. "It'd be just as easy to steal the whole damn bunch of 'em. Ain't nobody here to stop us."

"You just worry about findin' your saddle. I ain't drivin' half a dozen stolen horses down the main street in the middle of the night," Cord told him.

"It was just a thought," Dooley said. "Kind of a habit, I reckon." He gave Cord another grin and asked, "You sure you're Ned Malone's son?"

It appeared that Dooley had been right when he said there was no one there, for there was a padlock on the front door and the back door was barred from the inside. This did not pose much of a problem, however, for the hayloft door was open a crack. Noise from a saloon some one hundred yards down the dark street could be heard clearly, but there was no one in sight as Cord led his horse under the hayloft door. Dooley stood on the saddle and easily reached the hayloft and, with a considerable amount of grunting and struggling, pulled himself up. "Damn," he swore, "I ain't as young as I used to be."

"Make it quick," Cord reminded him. "It ain't gonna stay dark forever." He led his horse back around to the back of the corral to wait for Dooley.

It seemed to take Dooley longer than necessary, but he finally came out the back door of the stables with his saddle on his shoulder and his bridle in his hand. "Lookee here," he said to Cord, "they left my rifle with the saddle." That struck Cord as rather curious. He would have thought the sheriff would take the weapon and lock it in his office. He told Dooley as much. "Oh, they had some feller sleepin' in the tack room, who was supposed to keep his eye on things, I reckon," Dooley replied.

"Somebody's inside?" Cord responded, immediately alert, confused by Dooley's lack of urgency.

"Yeah, he woke up when I went in the tack room, but he went back to sleep after I gave him a little tap on the head."

"Damn it, Dooley!" Cord reacted in anger. "You killed him?" He knew there was no chance a man could remain unconscious for any length of time unless Dooley had beaten his brains in.

"Ah, no, hell no," Dooley insisted. "I never killed him. I didn't have no reason to kill him. I just gave him a little tap with a pair of tongs and tied him up while he was tryin' to figure out which end was up."

Relieved, but still unhappy with the degree of crime that seemed to increase for him with every turn in the road, Cord hustled Dooley along. As quickly as they could manage, they bridled the buckskin and threw the saddle on him, and in a matter of minutes, they were loping along Eddy Street, heading out of town. As a matter of simple logic, they avoided the common stage road to Fort Laramie, hoping to fool the posse that was bound to be coming after them in the morning. Crossing Lodgepole Creek well west of the road, they headed north where daybreak found them about ten miles short of Horse Creek. With two tired horses needing rest, they stopped by a little stream to make some coffee and get a couple of hours' sleep.

Chapter 8

With half of one day taken up to hunt fresh meat near the Chugwater, the two desperadoes continued riding north, covering the ninety miles to Fort Laramie in three days' time. Levi Creed could have camped at any number of different spots on his way to the Black Hills, so all Dooley could offer as help was to take Cord to the usual places of refuge for outlaws. Steering clear of the fort, Dooley led them toward the somewhat famous Three Mile Hog Ranch. However, they did not stop there. Cord had heard of it, a place where soldiers took advantage of the services offered by a bevy of soiled doves. Because it was frequented by the soldiers, it was shunned by road agents and horse thieves such as Dooley and his ilk. "If Levi stopped here, it would be at Bug Eyed Alice's place," Dooley said. "It's a couple of miles past the Hog Ranch, and if you're lucky, there'll be one or two more women there, and you won't have to settle for Alice."

Following a narrow trail that led between two ridges, Dooley led them to a rough cabin beside a stream. There was a small corral and a lean-to behind the cabin with a wagon parked nearby. Two horses were tied out by the front porch. "Looks like Alice has got company," Dooley commented. He looked at the horses. "Don't look like Levi's rig, unless he's changed saddles since I've seen him. Course, that was quite a spell ago. I wasn't ridin' a buckskin then, either."

When they were about thirty yards from the cabin, a man stepped out on the porch holding a rifle in one hand. Cord figured that he had been watching their approach from a front window ever since they turned in between the ridges. "You know him?" he asked Dooley.

"Nope, never seen him before," Dooley said, then called out, "Howdy, friend, no need to get concerned. We mean no harm."

The man did not answer, but continued to eye them carefully. Cord felt certain that the slightest movement toward his own rifle would trigger an instant reaction that would no doubt result in his or Dooley's death. The door of the cabin opened then and a woman walked out on the porch to stand beside the man. She peered at the two riders approaching for a long moment before a sudden smile parted her painted lips. "Bill Dooley," she said. "Well, if you ain't a sight for sore eyes." She nudged the man standing next to her. "That ain't nobody lookin' for you, Charley."

"Howdy, Alice," Dooley responded. "Damned if you ain't pretty as ever."

"And you're as big a liar as ever," she returned, threw her head back, and chuckled heartily. "Come on in the house. It's cold out here. Who's that you got with you?"

"This here's Cord Malone," Dooley said. "We're ridin' up-country a piece, and I just wanted to stop by your place and let him meet one of the real ladies of the territory."

"Is that so?" Alice replied, still grinning from ear to ear. "Well, come on in, Cord, and be real careful not to step in any of that horse shit Dooley is talkin'." Remembering the grim man standing next to her, holding the rifle, she said, "This is Charley Patch. Him and his partner's been visitin' awhile. They just inherited some money and came to share some of it with me and the girls." She gave Charley a playful elbow in the ribs. It seemed to break him from his distrustful stance, but he still kept his eye on the two callers, especially the younger one with the scar across his forehead.

Cord was equally wary of the man she called Charley until he suddenly seemed to relax. Only then did Cord turn his attention to Alice. She was a tiny little woman of uncertain age, her most striking feature being the obvious reason for her nickname, for her eyes bulged noticeably as if coming out to greet you. He and Dooley dismounted and tied the horses to a porch post while Alice stood holding the door open for them. Before they stepped up on the porch, a female voice from inside shrilled, "Close the damn door before we freeze to death!" Alice ignored her, and held the door till all visitors had entered.

Inside, Cord saw the reason for the outburst. Sitting in a ladder-back chair in a corner of the small parlor, a young woman wore nothing more than a thin night shift. Seated at a table near the window, Charley Patch's partner studied Dooley and him warily. Sensing the tension between the men, Alice made some quick introductions. "Bill Dooley, and who?" She had to pause for Dooley to remind her. "Cord Malone," she went on. "Charley you met out on the porch. This is his partner, Ford Wilson. Him and Darlene here just had a little party in the playroom. Ruby's in there now, fixin' herself up a little. She'll be out in a minute."

"Well, we don't wanna interfere with you boys' little social thing here," Dooley began. "Me and Cord is on our way up toward Deadwood. We just stopped in to say howdy to Alice. We'll get right on outta the way in a minute or two." Seeing the look of disappointment in Alice's face, he confessed, "Me and Cord are flat broke right now, so it's just a neighborly call. We're supposed to meet somebody and we ain't caught up with him just yet." Both of Alice's customers smirked at his remarks.

Quick to recover her balance, Alice playfully remarked, "Dooley, you're too damn old to harvest my two girls, anyway. I didn't even have Darlene the last time you were here, but you might know Ruby."

"I wish we had the time and money to get acquainted," Dooley said, "but you know how it is." He turned to Wilson and repeated it. "You know how it goes in this business, don't you, boys?"

"What business?" Wilson replied sarcastically. "I don't know what business you're in."

Dooley gave him a knowing grin. "Oh, that's right. Alice said you boys inherited some money."

"That's right," Wilson said, and winked at his partner. "My uncle died suddenly. He was a prospector, and he left all his gold to me and Charley."

Alice saw in a hurry that the conversation had excellent prospects for building into a little trouble, so she was quick to butt in. "How'd you and Dooley get together?" she asked Cord. "You don't say a whole lot, do you?"

"Don't have to," Cord replied. "Dooley takes care of that." She laughed and nodded.

"Cord is Ned Malone's boy," Dooley told her. "You remember Ned Malone, don't you?"

She grimaced as she searched her memory. "Name sounds familiar, but I can't place him."

"He was one of the old gang," Dooley continued, "him and Levi Creed and the rest of us."

This got an immediate reaction from the bug-eyed little woman. "Levi Creed," she exclaimed. "I remember that son of a bitch, all right. That ain't who you're tryin' to catch up with, is it?"

"Matter of fact, it is. Have you seen him?"

"Yeah, I've seen him, all right. He was here three days ago. Ask Ruby. She's in there now, changin' the bandage on her nose." As if on cue, the door to the bedroom opened and a tall, lanky woman came out, a piece of cloth tied around her face, holding a bandage in place over her nose. "There," Alice said, "don't that look like that bastard's callin' card?"

"Let him show up here again," Ruby vowed. "I'll geld the bastard. I've got a .44 Colt revolver, and the only reason he's still alive is because I didn't have it handy when he left here." She touched her bandaged nose gingerly. Her deep-set green eyes, flashing with anger, were made darker by the bruises around them, already turning yellow.

Dooley looked at Cord and noticed the sudden

tightening of his jaw and the deep frown lines over his eyes. His tense young friend was anxious to get on Levi's trail. "Well," he offered, "don't sound like ol' Levi's changed much over the years." He turned back to Alice. "I don't reckon he gave you no idea about which way he was headin' when he left here."

"Who cares where he was headin'," Ruby answered for Alice, "just as long as it's away from here?"

Dooley shifted his gaze back to Alice, questioning. She responded much as Ruby had. "I don't know why you'd wanna do any business with that man. If he ain't the devil, he's his first cousin."

"But do you know which way he was headin'?" Cord finally spoke up.

"No, I don't," Alice replied. "He didn't say."

The conversation had gone on long enough to suit Charley Patch. He didn't know who Levi Creed was and he didn't care. What he knew for sure was that he and his partner were the only ones who showed up with money to spend, and he wasn't inclined to cool his heels any longer. "Well, she's told you what she knows, so why don't you boys get on your horses and get the hell outta here, so the payin' customers can get down to business?"

"Just hold your horses," Dooley said. "We'll be goin' directly."

"You heard him," Charley's partner interjected. "He said to get on your horse and scat."

Dooley glanced at Cord again, but there was no indication in his partner's face that he was inclined to respond. Dooley, however, didn't care much for Wilson's tone. "You know," he said, "we was fixin' to leave, but I don't cotton much to bein' told to leave, 'specially by some blowhard saddle tramp who's bushwhacked some poor miner up in the hills. So I reckon we'll stay awhile and visit with the ladies."

"Why, you old wore-out son of a bitch," Wilson spat, "somebody needs to teach you some manners."

Not about to back down now, Dooley replied, "And who would that be? One of you two jug heads?"

"Yeah, one of us," Charley Patch said as he leveled his rifle at Dooley. "Now get the hell outta here before I put a couple of air holes in you and your deef and dumb friend." When no one moved right away, he cranked a cartridge into the chamber, threatening.

As they had once before, in the Crystal Palace in Ogallala, Cord's instincts took charge of his body. Without conscious thought about what he was about to do, he launched his body into the startled Charley, his shoulder into the man's midsection, while grabbing the barrel of the rifle with one hand. Ruby screamed and just managed to jump out of the way of the hurling bodies before they crashed against the wall. The rifle fired, sending a bullet into the ceiling and causing the women to scurry for cover. It was the only shot Charley was able to get off. There was a brief struggle over possession of the weapon before Cord wrenched it out of his hands, pulling Charley up from the floor with it before he was slammed back down from a solid blow from Cord's left fist.

Like a lightning strike, it had all happened so fast that both Dooley and Wilson were stunned into a momentary paralysis. When they recovered enough to take action, Wilson lunged for the table and his gun belt, where he had left it before his visit with Darlene. He was not quick enough, for Dooley was able to act in time to pick up a chair and break it over his back, landing him flat on the floor. "Is this what you was lookin' for?" Dooley taunted as he drew the pistol from Wilson's holster and held it on him. Charley gamely tried to get up from the floor again before being met with another blow from Cord's fist. This time, he stayed down.

With the altercation under control to both men's satisfaction, Cord and Dooley backed away from their assailants while keeping a steady eye on them. Meeting back to back in the middle of the room, they prepared to take their leave. The decision was seconded by the trio of women standing near the bedroom door, with Ruby holding her pistol, and Alice a double-barrel shotgun. Darlene had no weapon, but was holding a broom in a menacing fashion. "I'm always happy to see you, Dooley," Alice said, "but I think it'd be best if you and Cord left now, and came back another time." She paused, then added, "When you got some money."

"I reckon you might be right," Dooley said. "It was nice meetin' you, ladies," he said to Ruby and Darlene. "Make sure they give you some money for that chair."

Cord cocked Charley's rifle continuously until all the cartridges were ejected, then tossed it aside. "Ma'am," he said to Alice, picked his hat up from the floor where it had landed during his tussle with Charley, and followed Dooley outside. When he got to the horses, he found him hurriedly rummaging through the saddlebags on the other two horses tied up at the porch. He held up a small canvas bag and grinned at Cord, then climbed into the saddle. There was no time for discussion, so Cord stepped up and followed Dooley, who was wasting no time in riding out of the yard toward the path between the ridges.

They held their horses to a hard gallop for about a mile before letting up on them. "I don't know if they'll come after us or not," Dooley said. "It might depend on whether or not one of 'em looks in his saddlebag for this little sack." He pulled it out of his coat pocket and hefted it in the palm of his hand. "Hard to tell. Might go five or six ounces." He chuckled at the picture he formed in his mind when it was discovered missing. "Might be a smart idea to try to cover our tracks."

"Might be at that," Cord agreed, still a bit uncomfortable at having stolen the gold dust. *Something else to add to horse thief and jailbreaker,* he thought.

Dooley, having come to know his young partner by then, sensed the guilt Cord felt. "Ain't no cause for you to trouble your mind about this little sack of gold dust. I figure they owed us this much for the trouble they put us to. Hell, they stole it from some prospector somewhere, and most likely left the poor soul dead or dyin'. Besides, gold don't really belong to nobody. You just hold it for a little while. Then you give it to somebody else to hold for a little while. You grab it when you get a chance, 'cause it'll be in somebody else's hand right quick. It don't belong to nobody, and sure as hell, not them two we just left behind us."

Accustomed to his partner's logic on nearly every subject, Cord figured it useless to argue. They walked the horses until reaching a wide stream, where they rode them into the water, hoping to lose anyone coming on behind. After a good quarter of a mile, they left the water and rode up a grassy bank. Dooley pulled up to let Cord come up beside him. "Partner, damned if you ain't a ball of chain lightnin' when somethin' lights your fuse. That ol' boy back yonder didn't know what hit him. I bet he thought a mountain lion had lit into him." Cord shrugged, but made no reply. Dooley didn't express it, but he felt a great sense of confidence knowing he was riding with a raging bull when the going got rough. Knowing what Cord was thinking, he continued talking. "We ain't got a helluva lot of daylight left, so we'll have to rest these horses before much longer. But we ain't but about twenty-five miles from Rawhide Buttes. That's the next place to look for Levi. There's a stagecoach layover there, and there's another place like Bug Eyed Alice's—Ol' Mother Featherlegs. Her place ain't as fine as Alice's—ain't much more than a dugout, but she's always been friendly with the outlaws."

Having seen for himself the reason for Bug Eyed Alice's name, Cord was curious enough to ask the origin for Mother Featherlegs. Dooley laughed. "Ol' Mother Featherlegs," he repeated. "I don't know who give her the name, but it was because of them bloomers she wears, makes her legs look like feathered chicken legs. But, anyway, I'll bet Levi stopped there. He won't get away with beatin' up on any of Mother's girls. He knows he'd have a passel of outlaws lookin' for him in a hurry."

The ride to Rawhide Buttes was uneventful, with no sign of anyone following them. Whether that was because they had been so efficient in hiding their trail, or the owner of the missing gold had not checked his saddlebag, was hard to say. The important thing was they arrived at Colonel Charles F. Coffee's Rawhide Ranch stage stop just as the stagecoach pulled in from the north in time for the midday meal. They decided to treat themselves to a good meal, since they now had

financial resources, thanks to the unintentional gener-
osity of Charley Patch and Ford Wilson. They had dust
to spare, but most of it was going to be used for necessary supplies, which were available there as well.

They tied their horses up before the main house,
which was called an inn, and followed the passengers
in the door to the dining room. "Got room for a couple
more mouths to feed?" Dooley asked cheerfully when
they met a stern-looking woman standing inside the
door.

Her stern features gave way at once to a warm, wel-
coming smile, and she greeted them cordially. "We
sure do," she said. "We've got room for a dozen more."
Their rough, trail-hardened appearance, in sharp contrast to that of the passengers on the stage, seemed not
to concern her. Or at least she did not show it. She had
not exaggerated about the accommodations, for the
passengers plus the two of them took up only half of
the long table.

"Much obliged, ma'am," Dooley said. "We're only
carryin' dust. All right if we pay you with that?"

"That's no problem," the lady said. "We have scales.
We deal with prospectors all the time."

Cord and Dooley sat down at the end of the table,
opposite the passengers, and waited for the food to be
brought in. A few disapproving glances from the passengers did not go unnoticed by Cord, but he allowed
that he and the shaggy-looking Dooley probably looked
as though they had not been housebroken, and they
both smelled like a horse—Dooley more than he, of that
he was certain. When the bowls and platters began to
arrive, his thoughts went immediately to the food. It

was pretty simple fare, but it looked like a banquet to Cord.

"If you two gentlemen would move a little closer to the other folks, it'll be a little bit easier to pass the bowls around," the stern-looking woman suggested.

"Why, sure," Dooley said. "I reckon it would make it a little easier at that." And he got up right away. "Maybe we'll leave a little space between us, though. Me and Cord are kinda dusty." The young couple closest to them looked relieved to hear his remark.

Once they were settled again, and the eating got under way, further interest in the two waned, but Cord was still mindful of the contrast. The young couple had captured his attention. They looked not much older than he, and he guessed that they had been married fairly recently. The young lady looked fresh and clean, considering that she had been riding in a stage-coach all the way from Deadwood or Custer. It was in sharp contrast to the women he had seen most recently, and whom he would see that afternoon when they went to Mother Featherlegs's parlor. She glanced up from her plate at that moment to meet his gaze. Embarrassed, he quickly averted his eyes, but not quick enough to miss a shy smile before she looked away. He could not help thinking of Eileen, someone he had not allowed himself to think about for a long time. The young woman here on this day reminded him very much of the precocious daughter of Mike Duffy. He wondered if she regretted kissing him so unexpectedly on that last day. Suddenly the thought struck him that he wanted to be like the young husband sitting across the table from him. He only allowed the thought to live for a few moments before reminding himself where he was and what he had come to do.

Dooley, who had been noisily absorbed in his eating, glanced at Cord and ceased his gnawing on a pork chop. Curious, he then followed Cord's gaze to stare at the young bride, then looked at Cord again. "Huh," he grunted, and resumed his noisy attack on the pork bone. "Ain't no use in folks like us thinkin' 'bout things like that," he told Cord in a whisper.

"Reckon not," Cord said, and returned his thoughts to his plate.

After their dinner was finished and paid for, they went to the general store there and stocked up on the basic supplies they needed to survive—coffee, dried beans, bacon, salt, and a little bit of sugar for Dooley. Any other food needed would be supplied by their rifles. With their purchases secured on the horses, they set out on the short ride to Ol' Mother Featherlegs's dugout haven for outlaws.

Dooley had not lied when he said Mother's place was not much more than a dugout. In fact, most of her dwelling was dug out of a slight rise in the ground near a spring, and a room had been built on the front of it. It was home, however, to four people at that time, Mother, her companion, and two prostitutes. One of them, a rawboned woman named Lucy, was filling a bucket at the spring when Cord and Dooley rode up. She straightened up and put her hand over her forehead to shield her eyes from the sun as she watched them approach. After a few moments, she turned toward the house and yelled, "Company!" She took a few steps back and placed her water bucket on the stoop at the front door, then turned to face the visitors again.

"Howdy, darlin'," Dooley greeted her as he pulled the buckskin up to the porch. "Won't be long before that spring will be froze."

"I thought it was froze this morning," Lucy replied. "It probably ain't water you two are looking for, I bet."

"Why, no, ma'am, it ain't," Dooley replied. "We was just cravin' the company of some charmin' young ladies who might be wantin' to entertain two fine gentlemen like ourselves—and maybe take a sip or two of whiskey if you have some on hand."

Lucy laughed, shaking her head from side to side, then called back over her shoulder again, "Ma, Bill Dooley has come to see ya, and he's as full of shit as ever."

"It's nice to be remembered so fondly," Dooley said with a wide smile parting his whiskers.

A short, heavyset woman with a shock of red hair walked out to greet them. She was followed by a slip of a younger woman with her hair cut off like a man's. "Bill Dooley!" Charlotte Shepard called out to him. Known only by the name of Mother Featherlegs, she knew practically every outlaw, horse thief, and road agent in the territory. And she enjoyed their trust, so much so that she was often trusted with the care of stolen jewels, money, and gold. "Where the hell have you been? I ain't seen you in I don't know when."

"I ain't been up in these parts for a spell," Dooley said, "else I'da sure been callin' on ya."

"Who's your friend?" Mother asked. "Don't recollect seein' him before."

"Cord Malone," Dooley answered, "Ned's boy."

"Ned, huh?" Mother responded. "Ain't seen him lately, but his sidekick, ol' Levi Creed, came by here day before yesterday." She paused to remember. "Ain't that right, Lucy? Or was it two days ago? Anyway, he ain't changed much. Kinda like you, lotta snow in his hair and beard, and a little more beef on the hoof. He ain't sweetened up any since the old days, but he knows better'n to show his ass around here. Dick would kill him."

"Where is Dick?" Dooley asked. "He ain't finally run off and left you, has he?"

"Hell no. You know I couldn't run him off. He's gone down to Cheyenne to do some horse tradin'."

"Ain't he afraid to leave you defenseless ladies here all alone?" Dooley asked. He nudged Cord and said, "Dick is Mother's . . ." He paused. "What is he? Are you two married yet?" When she responded with a "hell no," he went on. "He calls hisself Dangerous Dick Davis. He lies around the house most of the time. The only thing dangerous about him is you might trip over him and break your neck." Cord glanced at Mother, but she apparently didn't disagree with Dooley's assessment of her paramour.

"Well, let's don't stand out here in the cold," Mother said. "Are you fellers lookin' for some dinner?"

"We've done et," Dooley replied. "You ain't told us who this young thing with no hair is. She weren't here the last time I rode through."

"Her name's Birdie. She's Lucy's cousin, come to live with us awhile, since my other girls went down to Cheyenne for the winter."

"Howdy, Birdie," Dooley said. "You look a mite young to be in this business. What happened to your hair? Looks like you got your head caught in a threshin' machine."

Birdie responded with a scowl. "I ain't in this business, and I like my hair like it is," she told him curtly.

"Oh," Dooley cried, feinting fear, "she's got some bite. I best not mess with her no more."

Lucy laughed. "I guess you best not. Birdie ain't made up her mind what she wants to do yet." She reached over and playfully ruffled Birdie's shortened locks. "She got hold of my scissors and whacked off her hair after some cowboy grabbed her and tried to tote her off to the bedroom—thinks it makes her look like a boy." She smiled wistfully at her cousin. "I wish I was as young and pretty as she is."

Dooley, always the diplomat, hastened to tell her, "Young and pretty is sure nice, but it ain't always what a man wants in a horse or a woman. Sometimes a horse with a few more years on her is broke in to a more comfortable gait. I've always said that you've got a real comfortable gait, and that makes for a more satisfying ride." He looked at Cord and winked.

Lucy shook her head and laughed. "Dooley, you're so full of shit. It ain't gonna get you no discount on the price."

"Let's go in the house," Mother repeated. "It's cold out here."

As soon as the door was closed, Cord was eager to get the information they had come for, so the first thing out of his mouth was a question. "Did Levi Creed say where he was headin' when he left here?"

Mother Featherlegs looked surprised. "Well, bless my soul, he talks after all." She smiled at Dooley, then turned back to Cord. "No, Levi didn't say where he was headin', and nobody cared enough to ask him. Was you wantin' to catch up with him?"

Cord shrugged indifferently, feeling no reason to tell the women why he was trailing Levi. Her answer to his question told him that the only thing he and Dooley had gained by coming here was verification that Levi had been there. As far as he was concerned, there was no need to waste any more time with Mother Featherlegs and her girls. He knew, however, that he was going to have to give Dooley time to satisfy his desires. He was the one who stole the gold dust. It was his right to spend some of it foolishly.

Fully aware of what Cord was thinking, Dooley said, "Cord ain't much in the mood to do no partyin', but you're welcome to turn your full attention on me. He's got a lotta years to get his sap to runnin'. I ain't got that many more. So whaddaya say, Miss Lucy? Let's have us a little drink of likker and then go to the bedroom for a little tussle."

"Sounds like just what you need," Mother said, and got a bottle from the cupboard and a couple of glasses.

When she placed them on the table and started to pour, Cord held his hand over one of them. "Not for me, thanks, but I'd just as soon have a cup of coffee if you've got some. I'll pay you the same as I would the whiskey."

Mother looked at him as if unable to believe her ears. She glanced at Dooley. He just grinned and shook his head. "All right," she said. "I'll put on a pot of coffee." She returned her gaze to Dooley again. "How in the world did you two hook up? You ain't brought no preacher in my little home, have you? Him and Birdie would make a good couple. They wouldn't say more'n two words between 'em."

Lucy led a grinning Dooley off to her room, and Mother went into the kitchen to start a pot of coffee, leaving the two young people to wait out an awkward silence. After a few minutes, Mother came back to tell Birdie to keep an eye on the coffeepot to make sure it didn't boil over. "Why don't you two go sit at the kitchen table where you can watch it?" she said. "I was fixin' to wash my hair when you and Dooley showed up. I think I'll go ahead and do that now while Dooley is busy and my water's still hot. Birdie, you can entertain Cord." She threw a towel over her shoulder and led them into the kitchen, where she picked up a kettle of water that had been heating on the stove. Birdie held the door open while Mother carried the kettle out to the small porch.

"Watch you don't catch your death of pneumonia out there," Birdie said, and closed the door.

The big gray coffeepot was beginning to grumble by the time Mother came hurrying back from the porch. She paused long enough to set the kettle on the table, then went at once to her room to dry her hair. Alone again, the quiet couple sat at the table without exchanging a word of conversation until the coffeepot began bubbling rapidly and Birdie got up to move it to the edge of the stove. She returned to the table with two cups of fresh coffee and sat down. After another long silence, she could tolerate the vacuum no longer. "Why are you trying to find that fellow, Levi?"

"He took somethin' from me," Cord replied, "and I reckon I need to take it back." She wasn't curious enough to press him further on the subject, which satisfied him. When she got up to fill the cups again, he asked, "Why are you livin' here with your cousin? From what you said before, it doesn't sound like you're thinkin' about whorin' for a livin'."

"I'm not," she answered emphatically. "I'm just stayin' here for a while till I save up enough money to go to Omaha."

"What's in Omaha?" he asked.

"I don't know. It's a big enough place to find some work waitressing or tending some rich woman's children, something besides doing what Lucy does."

"How are you savin' up money, if you ain't whorin'?"

"Mother pays me a little something every month to do the cooking and cleaning. What about you? Are you an outlaw? Why don't you wanna be with Lucy like the fellow you're riding with?"

He shrugged. "I don't know. It ain't nothin' against your cousin. I just don't want to, that's all."

"How'd you get that scar on your forehead—in a barroom fight or something?"

"No, it happened when I was a kid." There was a few moments' pause while they stared at their coffee cups. Then he asked, "Do you really wanna look like a boy, like your cousin said? Is that why you cut all your hair off?"

"Huh," she snorted. "I cut it off because of that slimy rat that lives with Mother, that Dick Davis. He was always playing with my hair, telling me how pretty and soft it was and how he liked to feel it. I know what he had in his rotten mind, so I cut it off."

"Why didn't you tell Mother, or your cousin, about it?"

"I didn't want to tell Lucy about it," she said reluctantly. "She might have had words with him and Mother, and it might have caused her to get kicked outta here, and this is all she's got."

He felt for the girl's predicament, but it was not his affair to interfere with. He could understand her chances of being violated if she remained where she was, but he had his own problems to deal with. Still, he couldn't help feeling a sense of guilt for not trying to help her. Finally he offered. "Is one of those horses I saw in the corral yours?"

"That little chestnut mare is mine. Why?"

"Well, I was thinkin'. I've got some business I've got to tend to, but I could take you over to the stage station at Rawhide Buttes. They've got a dining room and a place for passengers to stay the night. I'll bet you could find some work there. Maybe it'd be better than stayin' here."

"I've thought about doing that very thing," she said. "I just never made up my mind to go ahead and do it. I'll think about it some more." She got up from her chair. "But right now I'd better get up and start fixing supper. I expect your friend will be hungry when he comes out of there. He's been in there long enough to work up an appetite." She started to go to the cupboard, but stopped and turned back toward him. "Thank you for your offer."

"Well, you two musta found somethin' to talk about," Mother commented, coming into the room just then, her hair still wrapped in a towel. "I expect you'd better get about makin' some supper, Birdie."

"Yes, ma'am," Birdie replied. "I was just fixing to."

Cord got up and started back to the parlor just as the door to Lucy's room opened and Dooley walked out,

looking pale and a little unsteady on his feet. "Hot
damn!" he blurted. "I need another drink of likker,
and a cup of that coffee." Lucy followed him out of the
room with a confident grin of satisfaction on her face.
Cord speculated that she would have been more
pleased with her performance only if she had killed
him. "I swear," Dooley said to Cord, "about one visit
like that every six months oughta take care of me, or
kill me. There ain't no better way to find out for sure
that you ain't as young as you used to be."

Chapter 9

Cord was anxious to get moving again, but since it was now crowding suppertime, he realized they would save very little time if they left before morning. Dooley was enjoying himself, so Cord didn't complain when he said he wanted to stay over for the night. Cause for worry, however, was the fact that Dooley was not confident that they would ever catch Levi since they had not overtaken him at Rawhide Buttes. "I know some places," he assured Cord, but he didn't seem as sure of himself. Maybe Levi went on to the Black Hills; maybe he didn't. Cord was feeling discouraged, but he knew that he had made a promise over his mother's grave. He had no choice but to keep looking. Events of the next couple of hours changed his plans drastically.

"Somebody's coming," Birdie said. Cord was aware of it, too. The horses in the corral told him. He got up from his chair at the table and went over to the corner of the room where he had propped his rifle.

"Hold your horses, Cord," Mother said. "Let's find out who it is before you go shootin' my customers." She got up and went to the front door.

Lucy went to the window. "It's just one person," she said.

Mother Featherlegs opened the door a crack, just enough to see outside. After a moment, she opened it all the way. "Who is it?" Lucy asked.

"Damned if I know," Mother replied. "I thought at first it was Dick comin' home, but this feller looks a little heavier than Dick." She stepped out on the porch and greeted the stranger. "Evenin'."

"Evenin'," the stranger returned, and stepped down from the saddle. He looked around him, seeming to be a little unsure of himself. "Uh, ma'am"—he stumbled over his words—"I was lookin' . . . that is, I was told . . ." That was as far as he got before she came to his rescue.

"Mother Featherlegs," she said, having witnessed the same scene many times before. "Is that who you're lookin' for? Did somebody send you lookin' for a place to have a good time with a female companion? Well, you're in the right place. Tie your horse up there and come on in the house. Most of my girls ain't here right now, but Lucy's here, so come on in."

All smiles then, the stranger did as she suggested. "I'm stayin' over at the Rawhide Buttes Ranch for the night, and a feller over there told me about your place."

"Well, this is the right place to be," she said, and held the door open. "What's your name, young feller?"

"Watkins, ma'am, Henry Watkins," he said as he stepped inside, only to pause when he saw several people in the room, two of them men. Wondering if he might have stepped into something he'd be better off without, he started to beg their pardon but did not have time to before Lucy stepped up and took him by the arm.

"Come on in," she said. "I'll introduce you to the guests here."

He glanced at Dooley in the corner, who nodded in return. When he shifted his gaze to the man sitting back in the other corner, he was met by a wide-eyed stare. "Slick?" Cord blurted.

"Cord?" Slick answered. "Cord Malone?"

The others in the room went stone quiet before Lucy asked, "You two know each other?"

Still with a look of astonishment frozen on his face, Slick said, "We sure do. We used to work cattle for the same outfit in Ogallala."

"Slick, what in the hell are you doin' here?" Cord asked as he got to his feet to shake Slick's hand. "Did you quit the Triple-T?"

"Yeah, I did," Slick answered. "I guess there ain't no way you coulda heard, but a feller moved in on the other ranches around Ogallala, and I reckon he picked the Triple-T to run out. He brought a small herd in and then satisfied himself to takin' over most of our range. There was a fight. You know Mike Duffy, he wasn't about to give up Mr. Murphy's range that he'd been grazin' for five years to some double-dealin' crook. Trouble is, that feller—name's Harlan Striker—ain't particular who he hires to run his cattle. Hired gunmen is what they are, and there was some cattle killed and brands changed. Half of our crew either got shot or decided to head for healthier country. Then Mike and a couple of the boys caught some of Striker's crew changin' the brand on some of our cattle, and a gun-fight started. Well, they killed Mike, and Blackie and Jake Scott said they were lucky to get outta there without gettin' killed theirselves."

Cord was shocked. "Mike's dead?"

"Shot him right in the chest," Slick said. "Stony and Blackie went back and got Mike's body and brought it home."

Cord immediately thought of Eileen and her mother. "What about Mike's wife and daughter? I hope Will Murphy is gonna take care of them."

"Maybe . . . " Slick hesitated. "Most likely, I reckon. Trouble is, Mr. Murphy ain't even in the country. Went back to Ireland to visit his relatives, and won't be back before spring. Lem Jenkins says he believes this feller, Striker, most likely knew that and figured he could move in while he was gone."

Cord was almost stunned. What Slick was saying seemed impossible. Mike Duffy gone? He always pictured the tough little Irishman to be indestructible. His thoughts went again to Eileen. What would she and her mother do without Mike to take care of them? He had to pause to think for a moment. Everyone else in the room watched silently while the two of them talked. Cord looked up again when another question occurred to him. "What are they gonna do? Who's in charge now?"

"I reckon you'd have to say Stony and Lem. They said they were gonna fight Striker's gang of gunmen. They said they weren't gonna have Will Murphy come home from Ireland to find everythin' he'd built over the last five years gone."

"What about you?" Cord asked then. "What are you doin' up here in Rawhide Buttes?"

Slick shrugged, a sheepish look upon his face. "On my way to Deadwood where the gold is. Hell, I didn't hire on to fight in no damn range war. I wasn't the first one that decided to take off. Stony and the others are crazy to think they can go up against those hired guns. You know me, Cord. I'd be right with 'em if it was a fair fight."

"Yeah, I know you," Cord replied, not surprised that Slick had run out on the others.

He didn't say more at the moment, and after a long pause in the conversation, Mother Featherlegs chimed in to save her opportunity for profit. "Well, sounds to me like a drink could help the bad news of your friends. I'll open a fresh bottle, and maybe Mr. Watkins would like somethin' to eat. Sounds like you could use one, too, Cord—hearin' such bad news and all."

Cord was already deep in thought. The news had been bad, all right, and he worried over the question of whether or not it should affect him. He planned to go back to the Triple-T someday, if only to return Lem Jenkins's Winchester, but it wasn't his business to concern himself with what went on there now. He was on a mission of revenge that was foremost in his mind, and he had to figure that he was getting closer and closer to Levi Creed. Then images began to form in his mind, not just of Eileen, but of Stony and Lem and Blackie. "I need to do some thinkin'," he said to Lucy when she offered the bottle. "I need some air." He then went out the door to the porch, leaving the others to do the drinking.

Outside, the cold night air struck his face like a splash of cold water, and he stepped down from the porch to stand in the middle of the yard, looking up at the clear nighttime sky. The decision was never really in question; he knew what he had to do. Lem and the others needed his help, and he needed to know that Eileen and her mother were taken care of. Levi Creed would have to wait; he was going back to Ogallala. Just then he heard the door open behind him, and he turned to see Birdie coming toward him.

"I need to talk to you," she said. "You're thinking about going back to that ranch, aren't you?"

"I think I've pretty much got to," he said.

"You're always on your way to do something you've got to do, aren't you?" When he failed to answer, she continued. "Well, I wanna go with you."

"What?" Cord responded, surprised. "You can't go with me," he started. "Why in hell would you wanna go with me? I don't even know what I'm gonna run into, but I guarantee you, if what Slick just told me is true, it ain't gonna be no place for a girl. I know I said I'd take you to Rawhide Buttes Ranch, and I'll still do that. I'll take you there before I start back to Ogallala. I promised and I'll keep my word."

"I know you would," Birdie said. "That's why I wanna go with you to Ogallala. I don't wanna go to Rawhide Buttes. And I'm afraid the longer I stay here, the more chance I've got for something bad to happen to me, so I wanna go with you. I know you're thinking about having a girl to look after and slowing you down, but I can take care of myself and you won't have to slow down for me. I'm pretty tough." She looked into his eyes and pleaded, "Cord, I can't stay here. I don't wanna be here when Dick Davis gets back from Cheyenne."

He averted his eyes to escape her intense stare. As much as he wanted to turn her down, he found he could not. Looking into her eyes again, he said, "All right. I'll take you. Can you be ready to ride in the mornin'?"

"I can be ready to ride tonight," she said.

"In the mornin' will do," he said. "I've gotta talk to Dooley now."

"Thank you, Cord. I promise I won't be a bother."

"I can't say as I'm surprised," Dooley said when told of Cord's decision to abandon his search for Levi Creed. "After that feller told you about the trouble back at that ranch, I could tell you were studyin' on it—looked like it was botherin' you more than a little bit."

"Those are good people I left back there," Cord tried to explain. "They helped me when I needed help. Now they need help. I'll get back on Levi's trail one day, but I'm headin' back to Ogallala in the mornin'. So I reckon you'll be goin' your own way. I 'preciate the help you gave me. I don't know how I got talked into it, but I told Birdie I'd let her go with me."

"Is that a fact?" Dooley reacted, surprised. "What's she wanna go to Ogallala for?"

Cord shrugged. "I don't think she wants to go to Ogallala as much as she just doesn't wanna stay here."

"I reckon I can understand that. She don't look like she's really cut out to work with Lucy and the others at a hog ranch. You think there might be a little some-thin' goin' on between the two of you? She wouldn't look half bad if she let her hair grow out and put on a dress."

"No," Cord replied emphatically. "She just wants to get shed of Ol' Mother Featherlegs, and she ain't got no place else to go."

"You know," Dooley said, tugging at his whiskers thoughtfully, "I can't say as how I ain't just as glad you're gonna give up trackin' ol' Levi. That's one son of a bitchin' evil man, and he's as quick with a gun as anybody out there, unless the last few years have slowed him down. Sometimes it don't pay to go after a snake like that. Chances are you're liable to get bit."

"I won't ever be satisfied until that man meets with what he's got comin'," Cord said. "I'm lettin' him get away right now, because I have to, but I'll find him one day, even if we're both old and gray by the time it happens." With that settled, he changed the conversation. "What do you think you'll do now?" Dooley shrugged, having had no time to think about it. "I reckon you could ride on up in the Black Hills with Slick where they're screenin' all that gold outta the streams," Cord suggested.

Dooley grimaced, which he always did when he made an effort to think really hard about something. "No," he finally said. "If I was of a mind to go up to Deadwood or Custer, I'd most likely go by myself. I don't cotton much to ridin' with a man who run out on his friends when the goin' got a little rough." He paused to think again. "You know, if it's all the same to you, I'd just as soon ride on down to Ogallala with you."

Almost as big a surprise as Birdie's request to accompany him, this, too, was something he had not anticipated, although he should have suspected that Dooley had become comfortable in their partnership. "Are you sure about that? We might be ridin' into the middle of a range war with a bunch of hired guns."

Dooley shrugged indifferently. "Hell, Cord, I ain't foolin' myself no more. I'm too old to raise hell like I used to. My days of robbin' and rustlin' are over and done. But I ain't dead yet. I reckon I can still steal a horse now and again, if I need one, and I can shoot at somebody who's shootin' at me. From what that feller said, you might need an extra gun, and I wouldn't run out on you."

Cord studied the contrite little man for a moment before commenting. It struck him that Dooley was seeing the end of his life in his mind's eye, and it scared him. He seemed to be pleading for an opportunity to avoid loneliness in the years rapidly approaching. "You ever think about an honest livin' workin' cattle?" he asked.

"I don't know . . ." Dooley hesitated. "It's been a helluva lotta years since I've thought much about anythin' but makin' money without workin'. But I've worked cattle. I came up to this country with a cattle drive outta Texas. But, hell, who the hell would hire me?"

"You never can tell," Cord said. "Sounds to me like the Triple-T is gonna need some men. Might be a job there for the both of us. Won't hurt to go find out— right, partner?"

"Right," Dooley replied, a wide grin parting the whiskers again.

They left early the next morning, the determined avenger, the sometimes reformed outlaw, and the short-haired waif, an unlikely trio of traveling companions. With

Dooley once again directing the line of travel, they set out to the southeast, planning to strike the North Platte River within a day and a half. They fell short of that goal, owing to a chance meeting with a herd of antelope. With no thoughts toward passing up the opportunity to gain a good supply of meat, they took half a day to hunt the lightning-fast animals. Each man killed an antelope, and any notions that the girl would be a burden on the trip were immediately dispelled when Birdie jumped right in to help with the skinning and butchering. She then assumed the responsibility for doing the cooking.

The third day found them riding along the North Platte, traveling a path beat out years before by covered wagons on their journey to Oregon, and that night was spent within sight of the formation the settlers called Chimney Rock. The next morning they awoke to find a thin covering of snow that hid all but the deep ruts left by the settlers' wagon wheels. It would be two more days before they reached range land that Cord was familiar with, prairie he had ridden for the Triple-T. They camped one more night by the river, planning to reach the ranch by noon the next day. While Cord and Dooley took care of the horses, Birdie set about gathering wood among the trees by the river, and soon had a warm fire blazing in a deep gully where there was some protection from the wind sweeping the prairie. In a short time, there was meat roasting over the flames and the coffeepot resting in the coals.

Bill Dooley settled himself as close to the fire as he comfortably could without setting his clothes on fire, watching Birdie tend the meat. "I swear," he declared, "it seems to me that the weather gets colder than it used to. I reckon my blood must be gettin' thinner the older I get. When I was your age, Cord, I used to be able to lay down on the prairie without no fire and sleep like a baby."

"Is that a fact?" Cord replied, somewhat skeptical. "Maybe your blood *is* gettin' thinner. I don't know, but I think your memory has sure as hell rotted away."

Dooley chuckled at Cord's response, encouraged by the fact that the always stoic young man had actually made a joke. His expression turned a bit sheepish then and he asked a favor of them both. "You know, when we get to that ranch you worked for, there ain't no use in tellin' everybody that I'm wanted by the law, is there? I mean, I'd sure like to maybe get a fresh start with folks who don't know about my outlaw days."

"I don't see why anybody needs to know about your past," Cord said. "I don't think anybody on the Triple-T has any business askin' any questions. You can tell 'em you're the president of the United States for all I care."

"Maybe I'll do that," Dooley said, and poured himself another cup of coffee. "Who the hell is the president, anyway?"

"Damned if I know," Cord replied, scratching his head. "Grant?"

"No," Birdie said. "Rutherford Hayes."

"I don't believe I ever heard that name before," Cord said. "Better remember that name, Dooley, if you're gonna be the president."

"If we're gonna do that," Birdie added, "let's don't tell them you found me in a whorehouse, either. We can tell them I'm the president's daughter." Her remark caused them all to laugh.

The joking caused Cord to try to remember the last

time he had experienced a lighthearted evening with friends. He could not remember one—maybe there were times with his mother when he was a small boy; he couldn't recall. That thought caused him to return to the somber vow of vengeance he had taken, and had now put aside, for how long he couldn't know. A sudden nickering from the horses brought his mind back to the present, and he became immediately alert. Hearing it as well, Dooley rolled over the edge of the gully into the shadows, a reaction formed after many years on the fugitive end of a deputy marshal's posse. Cord motioned for Birdie to get down near the narrow head of the gully. She did so at once, pulling the .44 Colt she had taken to wearing from her holster. Silently berating himself for becoming careless, Cord drew his rifle up beside him and hugged the side of the gully. There was something out there in the darkness—there always was—but this something had come close enough to make the horses inquire. A few more moments passed; then the silence was broken.

"Looks like we got us some squatters, Bo, or maybe some cattle rustlers. Whaddaya think?" Mace Tarpley walked up to the side of the gully to stand just outside the firelight, his rifle carried casually in one hand.

"Sure looks that way," Bo Denton agreed. "On Roman-Three range, too, after Mr. Striker said not to let no drifters camp on his land." He appeared on the other side of the gully. "Whaddaya reckon we oughta do with 'em?"

Trapped between the two men, Cord was not in a position to do much about it. They might have evil intentions in mind, or they might just be thinking about having some entertainment by rawhiding some drifters. The longer he could keep them talking, the better his chances of coming out of this alive, he figured. He hoped that Birdie would stay huddled down in the narrow head of the gully. A moment later, that thought was answered.

"Look up here at the top of this gully," a third voice said as Benny Sykes moved up to stand over Birdie. "Looks like a boy hidin' up here."

There was nothing left for Cord but to try to talk his way out of the situation. "This ain't nothin' but a little misunderstandin'," he said. "We thought we were on Triple-T range."

"Well, you ain't," Mace said. "You're on the Roman-Three, and Harlan Striker don't allow no riffraff on his property."

"That so?" Cord replied, getting madder by the moment, but trying to control his anger for fear he might get Birdie hurt. "Well, if you back off a little, we'll move on across the river."

"That ain't gonna do no good," Mace said. "The other side of the river belongs to the Roman-Three, too. So I reckon we're just gonna have to teach you and the boy a little lesson so you don't forget whose land this is."

"There's another'n here somewhere, Mace," Bo warned. "There's three saddles here."

Mace became alert at once and pulled his rifle up in both hands. "Where's the other one?" he demanded of Cord.

"Right behind you, you sorry piece of shit," Dooley informed him from the shadow of the trees, "with this Winchester aimed at the center of your back."

Bo's hand immediately dropped to the handle of his

Colt. "Pull it and you're a dead man," Cord warned him, his rifle now leveled at him.

"I've got the other one," Birdie announced, trying to make her voice as husky and deep as she could.

"Looks like there's a standoff," Cord told Mace. "That kinda changes things, don't it? I figure you've got two choices. You can take a slug in the back, and your two friends get one in the gut, or you can back outta here real slow and get offa Triple-T range. What's it gonna be?"

"Mister, I don't know who you are, but you're makin' a helluva mistake. Harlan Striker owns this range, and we'll hunt you down," Mace threatened.

"That's about the dumbest thing I've ever heard somebody say when we've got the drop on ever' one of you," Dooley opined from the deep shadows behind Mace.

Mace was smart enough to see that the advantage had been reversed, and chances were he and his partners would lose if he pushed a gunfight. The situation infuriated him, knowing that he had been careless in scouting the camp before walking in on them the way they had. They should have accounted for the third man. It was too late now for anything but threats. "All right," he said. "There ain't no need for anybody to get shot tonight. But if you know what's good for you, you'll get offa Roman-Three range first thing in the mornin', 'cause there'll be more'n three of us next time."

"You tell your boss that there won't be any more crowdin' in on Triple-T range and no more cattle missin' from Will Murphy's herd," Cord told him. "Tell him he's been warned and there won't be no more warnin's."

"Mister," Mace said, "you're talkin' like a man that don't know what he's up against."

"I'm tired of hearin' your mouth," Cord responded. "Get on your horses and get outta here." He raised his voice then. "Dooley, keep your eye on 'em. Make sure they don't change their minds."

"I'll watch 'em," Dooley assured him.

"Come on," Mace called to his two companions, and started to back away toward their horses. Benny Sykes, who was standing over the narrow end of the gully, had other ideas. During the standoff, he had been trying to get a better look at the "boy" huddled in the trench below him. He didn't look to be a very big boy. The hand holding the pistol aimed at him looked a little unsteady. He felt sure it was worth a try, but he hesitated to make the move. When Mace and Bo started backing away, he felt that the time was now, if he was going to do it. Suddenly he reached for the .44 at his side, setting off an explosion of gunfire. He never cleared his holster, doubling over when the bullet from Birdie's pistol tore into his side at the same time a slug from Cord's rifle smashed his breastbone. Almost in one move, Cord swung his rifle back in time to stagger Bo with a shot in the hip when the unfortunate man pulled his pistol. The pistol dropped to the bottom of the gully.

Not fool enough to try anything with a rifle already aimed at his back, Mace threw his hands up in the air. "Don't shoot!" he cried. "We're done! We're goin'."

"Drop that rifle and back outta here," Cord ordered as he climbed up on the side of the gully. "Birdie, you all right?" She said that she was, although her voice was shaky. Back to Mace then, he said, "Pick up that body and you and your friend get the hell outta here."

Down on his hands and knees, Bo called out to Mace, "Mace, I'm shot. I can't walk. You gotta help me!"

"Help him," Cord said.

Still burning inside by the total reversal of what had promised to provide some entertainment at the three campers' expense, Mace swallowed the bile rising in his throat and moved to help his wounded partner. He glanced down at his rifle lying on the ground, only to hear Dooley's words behind him. "I wish you would." It was enough to hurry him along to help Bo back to his horse. Standing by the horses now, Dooley pulled the rifle out of Bo's saddle scabbard and held the horse's bridle while Mace struggled to get Bo up in the saddle. "Now get over there and pick up the other one," he said.

With Cord following him and holding his rifle on him, Mace went over to the head of the gully where Sykes's body lay. Sykes was not a small man, and after a couple of attempts to pick him up, Mace complained, "I'm gonna need help to get him on his horse."

Impatient with the clearing of his camp, Cord handed his rifle to Birdie and said, "If he makes a move, shoot him." Then he grabbed the corpse by the shirtfront and jerked it to its feet, got his shoulder under his midsection, and hefted him up. "Come on," he barked, and walked over to Sykes's horse and dropped the body across the saddle. Taking his rifle back from Birdie then, he watched while Mace climbed in the saddle. "Now git," he said, and stood back. Mace didn't have to be told again. He rode up from the riverbank, furious and humiliated, vowing silently to avenge his defeat, holding the reins of Sykes's horse. Behind him Bo rode, lying on his horse's neck in an effort to ease the pain caused by sitting in the saddle.

Cord and Dooley followed their departing visitors on foot for a few hundred yards before turning back to their camp by the river's edge. "I reckon we'd best move from here," Cord said when they got back to the fire where Birdie was waiting.

"That's just exactly what I was thinkin'," Dooley replied. "Those fellers might come sneakin' back around here to take a couple of shots at us." There was no way of knowing if they had extra pistols in their saddlebags or not, or how far away their home base was. At any rate, it wasn't worth gambling on a peaceful night if they remained where they were.

Cord looked at Birdie. The young lady looked as if she was still shaken from the traumatic experience of shooting someone. He readily understood the shock to her whole system, for his adrenaline was still racing as well. "Are you all right?" he asked. "That was a pretty brave thing you did."

Her eyes seemed to get even wider as she grappled with her emotions over having shot someone. After a moment, she responded, "Yes, I guess so." She paused again. "I didn't even know I was going to do it. The gun just went off. It scared me, and now I can't seem to stop shaking."

"We're gonna move on in closer to the Triple-T," he told her, "and try to find somethin' a little safer. Why don't you gather up the cookin' utensils and see if you can pack up as much of that meat as you can. Dooley and I will saddle the horses and get ready to pull outta here." He figured she'd snap out of it a little quicker if she busied herself with something. She nodded and began kicking snow over the fire as he left to help Dooley.

In a short time, they were packed up again and ready to ride. What meat they could carry was wrapped in the two antelope hides and tied on behind Dooley and Cord. The cooking supplies rode with Birdie on her mare. They rode for close to an hour before they began to see numbers of cattle in separate bunches, which told them they were well within the boundaries of the Triple-T. So they began to scout out a campsite that would afford some protection in the event they had any more guests that night. They settled on a small island in the middle of the river where they could see the approaches from either side. Cord and Dooley decided to take turns keeping watch until daylight. Birdie insisted that she could stand a watch as well as they, but the men wouldn't hear of it.

Chapter 10

Harlan Striker was fuming when interrupted at breakfast to be told that one of his men had been killed and another wounded. His dark eyes seemed to throw sparks as Mace explained what had happened. "You mean to tell me you surprised three drifters camped on my range and you come limpin' back here with your tails draggin' and one less man? And now you're tellin' me that the three of them are still alive? What in hell do you think I pay you for?"

"We got bushwhacked," Mace said in defense. "We didn't know that one of 'em was hid back in the trees. He had the drop on us. There wasn't nothin' we could do."

"Three damn drifters," Striker repeated in disgust. "And you ain't ever seen any of 'em before?"

"Maybe they weren't just drifters," Mace said, remembering then. "The big one with the scar on his face said to tell you there wouldn't be no more cattle rustled on Triple-T range. They knew where they were and they knew the Triple-T. That sounds to me like they've hired on some new hands, and there ain't no doubt that feller with the scar is a paid killer. They were out there keepin' an eye on the cattle, just waitin' for us to show up."

Striker couldn't deny that possibility, but it still didn't excuse the report Mace offered on the prior night's incident. His crew of fifteen men had been hired for their toughness and their know-how with guns. With Triple-T's crippled manpower situation, he should have had no trouble rolling right over them. Will Murphy wasn't even in the country, so when Mace put a bullet into Mike Duffy's chest, there was no one left to lead the Triple-T crew—and more than likely nobody to hire on new hands. And yet they stubbornly held on. "Damn it!" he suddenly swore, and threw his coffee cup against the log wall, causing Mace to take a quick step back. The news was turning his breakfast sour. "I need every man I've got." The ranch house he had planned to have completed before winter was still only partially built, and would now have to wait until spring before the other bedroom and dining room were finished. He wanted a herd of at least two thousand to ship to the markets in the coming summer, and that meant changing a lot of Triple-T brands. "Rena!" he yelled. "Bring me some fresh coffee."

In a few moments, the seldom-speaking half-breed Crow woman came from the kitchen, carrying the coffeepot. Solidly built and just a shade shorter than Striker, she was accustomed to his angry outbursts, but unperturbed by them, however, because she knew he would have trouble finding a replacement for her. She stood silently there by the table, holding the coffeepot and staring at the table. "Where's your cup?" When he pointed to the cup lying on the floor near the wall, she looked at him and frowned. "You throw it down there again, I don't bring you no more." She picked up the cup, put it in front of him, and filled it.

"Don't you sass me," he warned. "I'll send your ass back to that stinkin' reservation."

"Ha," she scoffed, "who you gonna get to cook for you?" She fixed Mace with a dull gaze then and asked, "You want coffee?"

"No," Striker answered for him, "he don't want no coffee. Now get outta here. We're talkin' business." She shrugged and left the room. Mace stared after her, always amazed at how Striker tolerated the woman's impudence. Any of the men working for him would have been shot for such back talk. *Of course, none of the men came crawling in the old man's bed when he got cold in the middle of the night,* he thought, and would have grinned had he not been faced with Striker's angry countenance.

"How bad is Bo hurt?" Striker continued.

"Well, I reckon he'll live, but he ain't in no shape to ride anytime soon—shot in the hip. We put him in the bunkhouse. Smokey's lookin' after him, but there ain't a helluva lot he can do. It's pretty much up to Bo if he gets back on a horse or not."

"He'd better," Striker said. "He ain't no use to me if he can't ride."

"Yes, sir. There's one other thing," Mace said, reluctant to bring it up. "Those fellers took my rifle, Bo's and Sykes's, too. I'm gonna need another'n."

Striker's scalding look of disgust was enough to make Mace cringe. "Then you'd better see about gettin' it back," he snapped, and let him stand there under his fierce gaze for a long moment. "You can take one of the rifles against the wall, but it's only a loan till you get yours back. If you don't get it back, I'll take the cost of that one outta your pay."

"Yes, sir," Mace replied, humbly. "I 'preciate it. Ain't no problem. I'll damn sure get my rifle back, and I'll get the son of a bitch who killed Sykes."

"They've got to learn that they ain't gettin' away with killing any of my men," Striker told him. "By God, they want a war, I'll sure as hell give it to them. Take some of the boys and go find those three gunmen. You know what to do when you find 'em."

"Yes, sir," Mace said.

Striker watched his foreman take his leave, and stared at the door after it closed behind him, thinking about what had happened the night before. If what he suspected might have happened, he wondered if Mace was the man he needed to take care of it. The Triple-T must have imported some new gun hands to fight against his takeover. That could be more trouble for Mace than he knew how to handle. Mace and his boys would do any foul deed asked of them, but they were little more than back-shooting bushwhackers. And up to this point, that's all he had needed. Then again, maybe he was worrying too soon. The three riders they ran up on last night might be part of the same crew they'd been fighting all along, whether Mace had seen them before or not. *Before I spend any money on some high-priced specialist, I'll wait to see if anything's changed on the Triple-T,* he thought, but he had invested too much in the takeover to be scared off by some cheap gunslingers. If he had to send for a higher-priced

specialist, he would do it, although it was already cost-
ing him much more than he had anticipated to get the
cattle he wanted. It had taken him over five years as
vice president in a San Francisco bank to accumulate
his investment money, money he had embezzled, and
he was getting impatient to see his ambitions bear
fruit.

Mace and three men rode down to the river where
Sykes and Bo had been shot the night before, to find the
camp abandoned. "They musta got outta here pretty
early," Mace suggested.

"By the look of this fire, I think they musta left last
night," Lou Suggs speculated. "The ashes ain't even
warm."

"Right after we got away from here, most likely,"
Mace conceded. "They probably headed for the ranch
house." He hesitated for a few moments, not really sure
what he should do at this point. Striker had given him
specific orders to find the three riders, but if they had
gone straight to the Triple-T ranch house, he couldn't
very well follow them there. He wasn't sure how many
men were left on the Triple-T, but he suspected their
numbers had dwindled considerably. It seemed that
whenever he had spotted any of them, it had been the
same few faces. And if that was indeed the case, he
didn't understand why Striker didn't simply order all
thirteen of his men to raid the ranch house and wipe
them all out. He shared these thoughts with Lou. "Why
don't we just go on in that place and kill 'em all, and be
done with it?"

Lou Suggs was not an especially intelligent man,
but he was smart enough to see the reasoning behind

Striker's hesitation to make such a move. "I reckon Striker don't wanna take the chance of stirrin' up such a fuss that the law or the army will get wind of it. There's already talk in Ogallala about trouble between the Triple-T and the Roman-Three. As long as we just keep shavin' away at their cattle and thinnin' out their men, Striker probably figures won't nobody in town get riled up enough to stick their nose in it."

Mace considered Lou's comments for a few moments. "Maybe you're right, but he damn sure told me to take care of those three strangers. So let's ride on down the river a ways and see if we can pick up some sign of 'em."

The party Mace and his men searched for was approaching the charred remains of a line shack on Blue Creek. "Looks to me like this place was burnt down not too long ago," Dooley said as he stirred some ashes with the toe of his boot.

"Hard to say," Cord speculated, "but I'd have to agree with you." He recalled the first time he had seen the log shack. It had been on the first night he worked for Mike Duffy when Lem Jenkins took him around part of the perimeter of the Triple-T. Lem had told him that the shack was built on a spot where a large Lakota village had once stood before being destroyed by the army. This was over twenty years before that night and Lem said he had often found bits of metal and arrowheads half buried in the grassy prairie. Cord was about to pass that history on to his two companions when the first bullet kicked up ashes barely a few inches from his foot. "Get down!" he yelled when he realized what was happening, and another bullet whined as it passed between Dooley and him. All three hit the ground behind the burned timbers of the cabin. Several more shots rang out, thudding into the timbers shielding them. "Can you see where they're comin' from?"

"I think so," Dooley answered. "See that little knoll where the creek bends back to the right? I think they're layin' behind it."

Cord looked in the direction indicated. "I think you're right." He looked behind him to see if Birdie was all right. She was scrunched up against his back. "Well, we can't stay here," he decided. "Stay low and lead the horses back into the creek. We can get a little better cover below the bank. Use the horses for cover till we get there." He didn't have to encourage them further, for the bullets were beginning to land closer to them as the shooters found the range. Clambering to the creek on a dead run, they ran the few yards from the shack to the water, all three jumping down the bank, leading the horses behind them.

Once they were safely settled, Cord led them a dozen yards downstream to a group of trees that offered a little less exposure. "Well, our luck's holdin' out," Dooley said. "They ain't hit none of us or the horses, either. We can hold 'em off from here."

"That may be," Cord said, "but we ain't goin' anywhere as long as they've got that high ground. They can keep us pinned down in this creek for as long as they want to." In order to prove what he said, he put his hat on the barrel of his rifle and held it up over the edge of the bank. In less than a second, the hat was knocked off his rifle. "Well, I reckon they've got their rifles right on the distance now."

Afraid they'd shoot the horses if they tried to run,

Dooley said, "I reckon we ain't got no choice but wait till dark and sneak outta here then."

"It's a long time till dark," Cord replied, "and I don't cotton much to bein' holed up in this creek all day." He didn't express it, but he was fighting to control his anger over the thought of being shot at when he was well on Triple-T range. He edged up behind a tree trunk to look at the knoll that protected the shooters. There were no targets presented for him and Dooley to return fire. He followed the creek with his eye then and figured it was worth a try. "I'm gonna work my way down the creek to where it turns back toward those buttes," he told Dooley. "I just might be able to sneak outta there at the closest point to that knoll and get up behind 'em."

"And get yourself killed." Birdie offered an opinion.

"Not if I'm careful," Cord replied.

"Damn, Cord," Dooley complained, "I was countin' on you to help me get started makin' an honest livin' with your friends on the Triple-T. You go gettin' yourself shot and that leaves me in a tight spot. Hell, they ain't gonna hire me without your say-so."

Cord almost laughed. "I'm touched by your concern for my life," he said. "You ain't got nothin' to worry about. Just remember to tell 'em you're the president." He didn't wait to hear Dooley's response, but immediately started down the creek, running hunched over in an effort to keep his profile below the creek bank.

"Damn it!" Birdie called after him. "Be careful!" She had placed her faith in the tall young man to see her safely to Ogallala. Without him, she was not that confident in Dooley's commitment to her welfare.

As if aware of what she was thinking, Dooley tried

to reassure her. "Don't worry. He won't take no crazy chances. If anythin' happens to him, I won't leave you on your own."

"Thanks," she mumbled, still not comfortable with the idea. She turned to look after Cord, who was already close to fifty yards away, running in a crouch, and expected to see him knocked over by a bullet at any second.

After a long few minutes, with no shots fired in Cord's general direction of flight, Dooley stated, "I don't think they saw him."

Running until he was almost staggering from his hunched-over posture, Cord reached the point where Blue Creek turned abruptly toward a couple of buttes to the south. He paused to rest there and took a look at the situation. At the bottom of the back side of the knoll, three horses were tied to some mesquite bushes. When his eyes followed the slope of the hill, they came to rest on three forms lying near the top of the knoll. Flat on their bellies, all three were aiming at the creek bank some two hundred yards distant. Figuring that he should make his way about halfway up the slope to give himself the best chance of getting at least two of the three men before they had time to react, he left the creek and sprinted toward the horses.

The bushwhackers were too engrossed in their efforts to keep their adversaries pinned down in the ditch to notice the man coming up behind them. Even the inquisitive whinnies of the horses went unnoticed. Kneeling next to a clump of sagebrush, Cord brought the Winchester up to his shoulder and took careful aim at the man on the right. Suddenly he hesitated, unsure.

Then instead of squeezing the trigger, he pulled the rifle down and yelled at them, "Hold your fire!" As if someone had thrown scalding water on them, all three jumped to defend themselves from a rear attack, causing Cord to have to yell at them again. "Stony! It's me, Cord Malone! Don't shoot, damn it!"

"Cord!" Stony Watts replied, hardly believing his eyes. "Where the hell did you come from?" He paused to explain the obvious to Blackie. "It's Cord!"

"Damned if it ain't," Blackie replied. "Watch yourself you don't catch a bullet. We've got three rustlers pinned down in the creek."

"And they ain't stuck so much as a finger outta there," Stony said. "I'm afraid if we don't run 'em outta there, they'll hole up till dark and slip out when we can't see 'em."

Cord climbed on up to join them. "I swear, Stony, you've already run one of 'em out, you damn fool."

"We have? How do you know?"

"Me, damn it," Cord replied. "I was in that creek. Now I'll show you how to get the other two out." He stood up at the top of the knoll and yelled out toward the creek, "Dooley! It's all right. You can come outta there now. The shootin's over."

Totally confused for a moment, and still slow on understanding, Stony stared at Cord in disbelief. It took Blackie to state the obvious. "You mean that was you down there we was shootin' at?"

Cord nodded slowly. "You've got a strange way of treatin' folks who come to help you. That's for damn sure." He watched the creek until Dooley and Birdie appeared on the edge of the bank, leading the horses up.

"I swear," Link said, "it's a good thing ain't none of

us a better shot, ain't it? We thought you were the bastards that burnt the line shack down."

"I reckon," Cord replied. "And it's a good thing I recognized Stony's big butt just before I pulled the trigger because I thought you three were rustlers."

"Well, if that ain't somethin'," Stony crowed, finding the incident humorous now that no one had been shot. "I didn't think we'd ever see you again. Who's that you got with you?"

"That's Bill Dooley," Cord said. "He's a good hand with a rifle. He came along to see if he could lend a hand. The other one's Birdie."

Blackie turned serious for a moment. "You heard about Mike?" he asked.

"Yeah. I ran into Slick up at Rawhide Buttes in Wyomin' Territory. He told me, and that's why I came back—figured you'd need some help."

"That yellow dog," Stony slurred. "He didn't waste much time hightailin' it outta here when the shootin' started." His scowl turned immediately back to a smile then. "Boy, I'm mighty glad to see you, though, and that's a fact. This bastard Harlan Striker just showed up with a few head of cattle, figurin' he was gonna take himself a herd offa the Triple-T. He brought in a bunch of hired guns to rustle our cattle and change the brands. Calls hisself the Roman-Three, and it don't take a genius to figure out where that name came from." When Cord didn't appear to understand, Stony showed him. Using a stick as a pencil, he drew on the ground. "Here's our brand, the Triple-T." He drew the brand, TTT. Then he drew one horizontal bar across the bottom. "Burn one bar across the bottom and you've got III, a Roman three. That's his brand."

"It don't get much simpler than that, does it?" Cord remarked. "How are Muriel and Eileen gettin' along—you know—with Mike's death? Are they all right?"

"As well as anybody could be after their husband and daddy is shot down by a gang of murderers," Stony said, bristling with the thought. "And Striker's got us outnumbered pretty bad. Ain't but five of us, not countin' Slop, and Striker's got fifteen men, and all of 'em handy with a gun."

"I reckon he ain't got but thirteen now," Cord said. "Some of his men jumped our camp last night." Stony grinned when he heard it. "And with me and Dooley, you've got two more."

"I'm likin' it better all the time," Blackie said. "Maybe we've got a better chance of holding on to Mr. Murphy's cattle. He's over there in Ireland and don't even know somebody's trying to run him outta business."

"This feller, Striker, knows what he's doin'," Stony said. "Mr. Murphy hadn't been gone but about a week when Striker showed up on our north range. First thing he did was to go after Mike. We figure he thought if he rubbed out our boss, all the hands would just take off and leave him to take over the cattle. When we didn't run, he just tried to pick us off one or two at a time till we all got too scared to stay. They got ol' Art Hundley when he was ridin' night herd, but Slick is the only one that run off scared."

Cord looked back toward the creek where Dooley and Birdie were standing, holding the horses. Turning back to Stony, he said, "Get your horses, and come on down to the creek. I need to tell Dooley and Birdie what's goin' on."

* * *

"What in the hell did you do," Dooley asked when Cord came striding down from the knoll, "talk 'em into surrenderin'?" When Cord didn't answer right away, Dooley questioned, "You didn't tell 'em *we* surrendered, did you?"

"They'll be along in a minute," Cord said, "soon as they get their horses. Then you can meet your new partners, President . . ." He glanced at Birdie. "Who'd you say?"

"Hayes," she supplied, "Rutherford Hayes."

"Yeah, him," Cord said. Serious then, he told them how close he had come to shooting Stony in the back. "Maybe, if we quit tryin' to kill each other off, we'll have enough guns left to keep this fellow, Striker, from stealin' all Will Murphy's cattle." He turned to see Stony and the other two ride up and dismount.

"I reckon we didn't give you much of a welcome to the Triple-T, did we?" Stony greeted Dooley and Birdie.

"At least it was a warm welcome," Blackie added.

"Well, the only harm done was a lot of cartridges wasted," Dooley replied, grinning, "most of 'em yours."

"No matter," Stony said. "We're damn glad to get your help." He stepped forward and offered his hand. Dooley grasped it and pumped it up and down vigorously. When he let go, Stony turned and offered it to Birdie. He couldn't help wondering at the fragile complexion and soft hands of the boy. It caused him to look more closely into the frank open face staring back at him. "Dang, you're a girl. . . ." His voice trailed off. "I swear, I thought you were a boy." Remembering his manners then, he quickly tried to back out of the hole he was in the process of digging. "Excuse me, miss. I just wasn't payin' close attention."

"That'll be the first time Stony ain't paid close attention to a lady," Blackie commented. "My name's Blackie, and this other feller's Link. We're mighty glad to see you folks, and I'm sorry we tried to kill you, but things has been kinda touchy around here lately."

"That's right," Stony added. "Ever since Mike was shot, we've pretty much pulled the trigger first and asked questions later." He fixed his gaze on Cord then and motioned toward Birdie with his eyes. It took several times before Cord caught on and quickly shook his head. Stony nodded understanding, looked back at Birdie, and smiled. He was brought back to the problem at hand by Cord's next question.

"How are you handlin' the situation with the five of you against Striker's gang of outlaws?"

"The best we've been able to do is to have three of us watchin' the cattle as best we can durin' the day. We figured we'd better leave at least two men at the ranch in case Striker's men make a run at Mr. Murphy's or Mike's house. Lem Jenkins and Billy Atkins are stayin' there today. Of course, Slop's always there, so the three of 'em take care of the chores with Muriel and Eileen doin' a lot of the work."

Cord thought about that for a few moments, getting the picture in his mind, so he could decide how he could be most effective. It seemed obvious to him that the first concentration should be toward reducing the odds. "When are they doin' most of the rustlin', at night?"

"That's right," Stony answered. "So they don't make as good a target, I reckon, but they ain't shy about workin' in broad daylight, either. When they work in

daylight, they keep riders out pretty far for lookouts—
makes it pretty hard to sneak up on 'em to try to get a
shot at 'em." He shrugged and chuckled. "We thought
we'd caught some of 'em without their lookouts this
mornin' when we saw you."

"I kinda got an idea that they keep a lookout on the
ranch," Blackie commented, "see where we're goin' in
the mornin'. Then they go to some other part of our
range and work on our cattle without havin' to worry
about us showin' up."

"Yeah," Link piped up. "And if we all split up to try
to cover more of our range, it'd be one man against
however many they had in that place."

Armed now with a pretty complete picture of how
the attempted takeover had progressed since Mike
Duffy's murder, Cord would have to think about how
best he could be effective in the range war. The first
thing to be done, however, was to take Dooley and
Birdie to the ranch to get Birdie settled in with the
other two women, and make Dooley familiar with the
men he was to work with. Since the Triple-T was losing
stock every day, Stony decided they couldn't afford to
leave the section around the upper end of Blue Creek
unguarded, so he suggested that Cord should go on to
the ranch and get settled in while he, Blackie, and Link
continued on.

Chapter II

Eileen Duffy walked out to the porch when she heard Billy Atkins's shrill whistle from the hayloft in the barn announcing riders approaching the front gate. Nowadays it could mean a raiding party as well as guests calling. She shielded her eyes from the late-afternoon sun to pick out the three figures approaching the gate from the north. At first, she did not recognize any of the three, but as they came closer, she took a longer look at the one in the middle, and she was certain that she had seen someone who sat a saddle the way he did. Tall, but sitting easy and relaxed as his body rolled rhythmically with the lazy lope of the bay horse he rode, it could be only one person. Lem had told her that Cord would return, but she had found it difficult to believe that he actually would.

Behind her, her mother stepped out on the porch to see. "Who is it?" Muriel asked.

"Cord Malone," Eileen replied, taking care not to

show any emotion. "Looks like he's finished that important business he said he had to fix, and he's got somebody with him."

"I declare," Muriel said, "I never thought we'd see
him around here again, but thank the Lord he's back.
Stony and Lem need all the help they can get."

Standing at the corner of the corral, Lem Jenkins
peered out toward the gate, having also heard Billy
whistle. His eyes not as sharp as Eileen's, he squinted
in an effort to identify their visitors. In another minute,
he recognized the rider between the other two, and he
made no effort to hide his emotions. His face broke out
in a wide grin, happy to see the troubled young man
who had left the Triple-T on a trail of bitter vengeance.
He did not recognize the two with him, but two more
guns would surely be welcome. He walked out a few
yards in front of the corral to be sure Cord saw him.
Up at the house, Eileen saw the three riders turn
toward the corral and Lem, instead of coming directly
to the porch where she and her mother stood. Register-
ing slight irritation at that, she turned to her mother
and said, "I'm going to the barn. I wanna know if they've
come to help, or just blowing through like the useless
tumbleweeds most of them are."

"I'm going with you," Muriel said. "I want to know,
too." She followed Eileen down the steps. The two
women arrived at the corral to join Lem at the same
time Cord and his friends pulled up at the corral. Billy
Atkins joined them a minute or two later.

"Danged if you ain't a sight for sore eyes," Lem
greeted Cord.

"Heard you were havin' some trouble," Cord
replied, then immediately shifted his attention toward

Muriel and Eileen. "I'm right sorry to hear about Mike. He was a good man."

"I hope you've come back to help," Muriel said. "Lem and the boys are doing the best they can to keep the Triple-T from being stolen right out from under us, but they're up against a vicious gang of murderers."

"I have, ma'am," Cord said. "I've come back to do what I can to help, and I brought Bill Dooley and Birdie Summer with me." He glanced at Eileen to find her gazing intently at him, only to avert her eyes when they met his.

Lem didn't allow him time to think about Eileen's lack of a greeting. "Well, partner, I knew somewhere along the line you'd show up here again, and I'm mighty glad to see you."

"I had to return your rifle," Cord said.

"Well, step down," Lem said. "Did you take care of that thing you left here for?"

"No, but that can wait till we take care of the problem we have here right now." He and his two friends dismounted. Lem and Billy both stepped forward to shake hands with the new arrivals. "I reckon we'd best unload some of this jerky and supplies we're haulin' on our saddles. Dooley and I can go grab a bed in the bunkhouse." He turned again to Muriel. "I'd be obliged if Birdie could stay in the house with you and Eileen, ma'am."

His request was met with looks of astonishment from mother and daughter. Eileen responded, "Why can't he stay in the bunkhouse?"

"It wouldn't do," Cord replied. "Birdie's a girl."

His simple statement caused all four of the Triple-T to turn in surprise to stare at the now embarrassed young woman. Muriel, as shocked as the others, still managed to quickly respond, "Please excuse our rudeness, Birdie. We were so busy seeing Cord again that none of us took notice of you and your friend. Of course you can stay in the house with us, and welcome."

Dooley, seeing the awkward moment caused by Birdie's appearance, was inspired to ease the situation. "Yes, ma'am, and I'm really an old lady. Have I got to stay in the bunkhouse with these jaspers?" The comment served his purpose, and everyone laughed.

One in particular took a much closer look at the blushing young girl. Eileen berated herself for not noticing at once that Birdie was female. At first glance, she, like the others, had thought Birdie was a boy, maybe a little frail, but short hair and a boy's clothes were all she had noticed. Upon closer inspection, however, she now became aware of the fine, delicate features of her nose and mouth, her smooth face, and the soft blue eyes. *Damn!* she thought. *She's older than she looks and pretty, too.* She looked quickly back at Cord, interested now in his manner with the young girl. Exactly what was their relationship? she wondered. There was no way she could tell by his actions, causing her to complain to herself, *The same old blank expression on his face.*

"I reckon I shoulda told you right off," Cord said, feeling somewhat contrite for not pointing out something that he thought would be apparent, forgetting his impression the first time he had seen Birdie. "She's already showed me that she's handy with a gun, but it was just Dooley and me that figured on helpin' out with the trouble with the Roman-Three. Birdie's just thinkin' about gettin' to Ogallala, so she came along with us."

"I'm not in any particular hurry to get there, though," Birdie volunteered, "so I'd be glad to help out here any way I can."

"Good," Lem said, "Muriel and Eileen can probably use the help, and we're always happy to welcome pretty young girls." He hoped his comment would make up some for mistaking her for a boy.

"Here," Billy spoke up then, his interest having been immediately aroused, "let me take care of your horse for you." With a huge smile on his face, he stepped up to take the mare's reins. "You must be kinda tired if you've been ridin' all that way from . . ." He hesitated then, realizing no one had said where they had started out from.

"Rawhide Buttes," Dooley supplied for him, "and she ain't complained a whimper on the whole trip. Like Cord said, she sure came in handy with that six-gun she's wearin'."

She just sounds like the perfect little angel, Eileen thought, but to Birdie, she said, "I'll help you carry your things up to the house. You can use my old room. I'll sleep with Mama."

When Eileen and her mother left to escort Birdie back to the house, Cord turned to Lem to be brought up to date on the situation with the rustlers. "It's gotten to be pretty much a cat and mouse game," Lem told him. "What the bastards are doin' is splittin' up and hittin' the herd at night. Right now most of our cattle are feedin' along Blue Creek, along the northern boundary of our range. So the rustlers will come down off the Roman-Three and cut into the herd, and we have to drive 'em off. But there ain't been enough of us, so when we try to chase after 'em, some more of their gang rides in and cuts the tail end of the herd off, and so far we ain't been able to stop 'em from drivin' large numbers of our cows back to their range where they're waitin' to brand 'em." He shrugged helplessly then. "We don't know nothin' else we can do. We just need a lot more of us to match up with their gang." He nodded toward Billy. "Me and Billy will ride night herd up at Blue Creek tonight, when Stony and the others come in to get a little sleep."

"Just the two of you?" Cord asked.

"Like I said before, there ain't but five of us altogether, so some nights we have to ride shorthanded. With you and Dooley here, we'll have a couple more to watch the herd—still ain't as many as we're facin', but it'll help."

"Yeah, hell yeah," Dooley replied at once. "We're ready to go tonight."

Cord thought Lem's words over for a few minutes before deciding how best he should be used. When he was satisfied that he could be most effective riding alone, he told Lem and Dooley what he proposed to do. "If it's all right with you, take Dooley with you and Billy, and I'll ride alone to see if I can keep the bunch that tries to drive off the drags from the rest of the herd."

"I ain't sure that's the smartest thing to do," Lem responded. "You'd be in trouble up to your ass if they found out you were workin' all by yourself."

"Then I reckon I'd better be careful," Cord said.

"I reckon it's your neck," Lem said. He liked the sound of one man out there working alone while the rustlers' concentration was on cutting out part of the herd. He meant it when he told Cord it was a risky thing to do, but he had seen the determined man in action before. He might be successful in thinning out the rustlers, and that would greatly increase the Triple-T's chances of saving their herd. "Let's get you and Dooley settled in the bunkhouse. Then we'll get some supper and head up Blue Creek."

"That sounds good to me," Dooley commented, "especially that supper part." He was looking forward to working cattle on this side of the law, eager to see if he could successfully make the switch.

Halfway up Blue Creek, they met Stony, Blackie, and Link on their way back to the ranch. "Put you to work already," Blackie called out when they reined up to talk.

"Lem don't let new hires lie around the bunkhouse," Cord answered.

"That's a fact," Lem said with a chuckle. "Gotta make sure they earn their bacon."

They talked for a few minutes, Stony passing on any information of sightings of the raiding Striker gang. "Maybe you'll have a peaceful night," he said. "That sky don't look too good, like we might get some rain, or a little more snow. Maybe Striker's men won't take a chance on the weather turning bad. The only folks we saw today were three coyotes snoopin' around the old burnt-out line shack, and we pinned them down in the creek for a while before we let 'em go." He laughed then when Lem didn't get the joke at once, as evidenced by his frown of concern. In another second, Lem chuckled as well. "Like I said, maybe you'll have a peaceful night," Stony went on. "Ol' Striker mighta gave his boys a night off to go into town."

"I doubt that," Lem said. "We'll see you boys in the mornin'." He gave his horse a little nudge with his heels and started out again.

Riding up the western side of Blue Creek, they came to a wide valley, bordered on one side by a low mesa and a low line of hills on the other. This was where they found most of the cattle. "It'll be gettin' dark before much longer," Lem speculated. "Might as well build us a fire near the head of this valley. It's as good a place as any. Then we'll start takin' turns ridin' night herd. That's the way we usually do it."

When Billy and Dooley left to look for firewood on the bank of the creek, Cord told Lem what he planned to do. "I know it'd be good to have four of us to watch for rustlers, but I'm thinkin' I'll do more good if I ride on off alone. I'll find a place across the valley in that line of scrubby hills where I can hide my horse and see what happens. Maybe I can catch some of 'em when they ain't lookin'."

"You be careful, Cord," Lem warned. "These boys are playin' for keeps."

"So am I," Cord replied as he turned the bay's head toward the already darkening border of trees along Blue Creek. He asked the bay for a gentle lope after he crossed over the creek and began to search the rugged hills beyond for a spot that suited him. The place he picked was a narrow ravine that sloped up to the top of a ridge. The light snow that had fallen the night before was still evident in the shadow of the ravine, having been shaded from the day's sun. It caused Cord to apologize to the horse for not building him a fire. "We're both gonna have to stay outta sight for a while." Leaving the horse tied to a clump of sage, he climbed up the ravine to the top of the shallow ridge, where he had a pretty good view of the valley in both directions. He expected the unwelcome visitors to come from the north since that was the direction of the Roman-3. *Nothing to do now but wait,* he thought as he pulled the collar of his heavy coat up around his neck. Shortly after darkness set in, the rain started, a cold, miserable rain that prompted him to break out his rain slicker and pull his hat down low over his forehead. Stony's comment came to mind then, and he wondered if there was really much chance of the rustlers showing up on this night. On the other hand, he considered, it might be the perfect night to steal someone's herd.

"Same place they was this afternoon," Lou Suggs reported when he rode to the back side of the first of a chain of three buttes on the western side of Blue Creek and dismounted.

"I figured they would be," Mace replied. "How many men?"

"Three," Lou answered, "just like always. They've got 'em a fire built, and right now they're just settin' around tryin' to stay dry, and most likely tryin' to decide which one of 'em has to risk his neck ridin' night herd." His remark brought a few chuckles from the eleven men standing around Mace.

"Three," Mace repeated. "Reckon it was that scar-face son of a bitch—the same three that shot Sykes and Bo?" He was still smarting a bit from having reported to Harlan Striker that he had not found the three that afternoon.

"Hell," Lou said, "I couldn't tell who it was. Couldn't see that good in the dark and the rain and whatnot."

"All right," Mace directed. "It's time to do a little cattle drivin'. Bart, take five men and go on down along that line to the last hill yonder. You know what to do. Get in behind the cattle and start the whole damn herd runnin' toward the head of the valley. The rest of us will take care of those three settin' by the fire." He was tired of picking away at small portions of Willard Murphy's cattle. It was time to go to war now, since they had brought in that hired gun, and time to kill the drovers and finish the Triple-T for good. In spite of Striker's concerns about attracting the attention of the law, Mace was of the opinion that nobody really knew or cared if there was a range war going on in the empty prairie north of Ogallala.

In the saddle then, seven of the thirteen men started out along the base of the hills, circling around to come up from behind the three seated around the campfire. When within one hundred yards of the herd, Mace started the shooting, aiming his rifle at one of the three men around the fire. Because of the difficulty of aiming accurately while riding a galloping horse, he missed all three, but his aim was good enough to kick up a double handful of burning branches in the fire, sending the three men scrambling. There followed an explosion of gunshots as every one of the outlaws fired their weapons, starting an instant stampede.

Diving into the gully to take cover, Lem and his partners strained to see from whence the shooting came. In the chaos of the initial moments of the stampede, with the air filled with thunderous gunfire, it was difficult to determine the point of attack as all three tried to hold on to their frightened horses. But soon they saw the line of riders cutting into the terrified cattle, and they began to return fire. "They're pushin' 'em up the valley!" Billy cried out.

"Get after 'em," Lem yelled, "or we'll lose the whole damn herd!" But the rifle fire kicking up dirt around the gully made it suicide to even think about climbing in the saddle. The best they could do was to take what shots that were presented by the rustlers darting back and forth as they pinned the drovers down.

"By God, they ain't just after the cattle. They're out to kill us," Dooley shouted. "If you're gonna steal the whole herd, you ain't gonna want no witnesses left to talk about it!" Unnoticed behind them, a line of six riders moved up from the rear of the frantic cattle—unnoticed except for one lone man.

Scrambling down the ravine to get to his horse, Cord thought the same as Dooley. He could see that the Roman-3 gang had split in two, with half driving the cattle, and the other half intent upon murdering the drovers. The thought hit him hard at that moment, one that had not occurred to him before. Although he had not known either for any length of time, two of those pinned down in that gully were the closest friends he had, Lem Jenkins and Bill Dooley. In the saddle then, he raced after the riders circling the gully, formulating his plan as he rode. In the chaos of dust kicked up by the startled cattle mixing with the now steadily falling rain, combined with the dark, it was difficult for one rider to identify another, so he would use that to his advantage. Selecting his first target, Cord pulled the bay up beside Lou Suggs.

"Keep throwin' lead at that gully!" Lou shouted to him. "Don't give 'em a chance to aim!"

"Right," Cord answered and, with his rifle leveled

at Lou's gut, pulled the trigger, knocking the rustler out of the saddle. He kicked his horse hard then to catch up with another of the riders.

Bart Smith pulled up short when he saw a riderless horse gallop past him. He looked around him from left to right to see if he saw anyone on foot. "Who's on the ground?" he called out to the rider catching up to him in the swirling cloud of mixed dust and snow.

"I don't know," Cord answered as he closed the distance between them.

"It's damn hard to tell who's who in this mess," Bart complained. "You couldn't recognize the devil himself if he was to ride right up to ya." A few seconds later, as Cord drew up close to him, Bart was suddenly startled. "Who the hell are you?"

"The devil," Cord replied as he pulled the trigger with his rifle leveled at him. He turned the bay's head then and cut through the swirling mass of cows to the other side of the herd. He worked his way clear of the stampeding herd just as the leading cows reached Blue Creek. Circling back the way he had come, he almost ran into another rider, who was firing his pistol into the air in an effort to prevent the cows from veering away from the water. The rider yelled at him for help in steering the wild mass of beef into the shallow creek. It was the last sound he made on this side of the divide between the living and the dead.

Hunkered down in the gully, Lem, Billy, and Dooley fought to hold out against the circle of Roman-3 riders assaulting their position. The gully offered adequate protection from those shooting at them, but they were helpless to stop the theft of their cattle as long as they remained pinned down in the gully. Of the three, only

Billy had been hit, having caught a rifle slug in his shoulder. Not so fortunate, all three had lost their horses to the outlaws' bullets. Their plight was not all one-sided, however, for Lem and Dooley had each emptied one of the saddles. Both of the victims had been hit as the last of the crazed cattle had swept past the gully, leaving Mace and his assassins more easily targeted.

Realizing he was more vulnerable now that he could not use the swirling cattle for cover, Mace shouted for his men to go after the cattle and forget the three men in the gully. As he dug his heels into his horse's sides, he encountered two riderless mounts trailing off behind the herd, casualties that had to have been caused by someone other than the men trapped in the gully. A new sense of alarm gripped him now, since he and his men had been unsuccessful in killing the three he had pinned down in the gully. There was someone else moving in behind his men, and the thought that he had ridden into a trap leaped to his mind. Maybe the Triple-T had hired on more than the three he had encountered at the line shack to fight the Roman-3. It came back to his memory that he had not remembered having seen any of the three before that day. He was sure he would have remembered the one with the scar across his forehead. How many more had Willard Murphy's foreman hired? And how many of his own men were left? At this point, he had no way of knowing. Suddenly the thought of a band of avenging killers working their way up behind him and his men took precedence over taking a herd of cattle for Harlan Striker. Maybe it was time to think about staying alive and to hell with the cattle.

He whipped his horse mercilessly as he fled past the

rear half of the stampeding cattle when they were
slowed by the creek crossing, straining to see clearly in
the cloud of dust, snow, and water swirling about him.
Off to his left, he saw one of the riderless horses, which
caused him to flog his rapidly tiring horse even more.
Then all of a sudden a form took shape in the darkness
before him, heading straight for him, appearing to cut
him off. Mace didn't hesitate. Whipping his rifle around,
he fired, and the rider doubled over in the saddle as his
horse bolted to miss Mace's. In the confusion of the
moment, while he struggled to control his horse, and
attempted to cock his rifle, he almost collided with the
other horse. As it veered away, so close that he could
see the wounded man holding on to the saddle horn
with both hands, he recognized Johnny Dukes, one of
his own men. Stupefied, Mace hesitated a split second
before pumping another slug into Johnny's chest, preferring not to chance any of the others finding out who
had shot him. His senses told him now that the raid on
the Triple-T herd had gone wrong and saving his life
was now the number-one priority. There was no need
for further speculation. He wheeled his weary horse
away from the cattle and fled along the tree line that
bordered the creek. They had ridden into a trap. He
was convinced of that now. There was nothing for them
but to escape while they could, every man for himself.
Striker was going to need more men to fight the added
numbers of the Triple-T. A few dozen yards behind
him, Ben Cagle saw him head toward the creek, and
being of like mind, he set off after him.

The cattle were well up in the northernmost portion
of what was considered Triple-T range by the time
Cord caught up with the leaders. Keeping well within

the body of the herd to keep from being seen by the rustlers, he worked his way up to overtake the outlaws attempting to guide the leaders. *If I don't turn them pretty soon, they're gonna be off our range,* he thought. *I'd better work fast while nobody can see very far in this mess.* With that in mind, he kept pressing forward until he finally caught sight of the point men. There were two of them, one riding alongside the lead cattle, the other about thirty yards behind him. Both men seemed inclined to follow the direction already taken by the frightened beasts, firing an occasional shot in the air to keep them moving.

Cord slowly closed the distance between himself and the rearmost of the two rustlers. With the air not so congested from the swirling dirt and snow as that in the tail end of the mass of churning hooves, darkness was the only cover he could count on. He was bent upon surprising the outlaw as he had the others, but the man turned to see him when he was almost even with him. "Ben?" he called.

"Yeah," Cord answered.

"The hell you are!" the rustler exclaimed a moment later when Cord drew closer. With his pistol already drawn, he quickly aimed it at Cord and pulled the trigger to discover he had been careless in counting his shots while discharging his pistol into the air before. The last sound he heard was the dull click of a firing pin on an empty chamber before Cord's rifle slug knocked him out of the saddle. Cord looked quickly up ahead at the man's partner, but he did not look back at the sound of the rifle, evidently thinking it just another shot to keep the cattle moving.

The trick now was to get the lead rider to help him
turn the herd back upon itself. Cord figured it would
be a lot easier than trying to turn them alone, and he
had already seen that the sound of a gun would not get
the man's attention. So he closed the distance between
them slightly and began to yell at him. After almost a
full minute of yelling, the rustler finally looked back at
him. When he did, Cord immediately started waving
his arm toward the right, yelling, "Turn 'em!" Without
thinking to question the signal, the rider pulled up to
the lead cow's nose and began shooting around its
hooves. Behind him, Cord did the same on the cows
following close behind. In a short time, their combined
efforts proved effective to turn the stampeding herd
and head them back the way they had come.

Once the cattle turned back on themselves, they
were further slowed down when they came to the
creek again, this time heading in the opposite direction. It finally occurred to the rider ahead of Cord what
had happened. He turned to shout at the shadowy
rider behind him, "What the hell are we doin'? We're
drivin' 'em back the way we just came!" When there
was no answer from his *partner*, he pulled up short to
wait for Cord to catch up. It was then that he realized
that the two of them appeared to be alone, and there
should have been at least five or six bringing up the
rear of the drive. "Where the hell is ever'body? Is that
you, Mace?" He didn't wait for an answer, for in the
next instant he saw Cord's face. His automatic reflex
was to shoot, but Cord's rifle was already trained on
him. He rolled out of the saddle as the .44 slug ripped
into his midsection. Suddenly the valley was quiet,

Striker's remaining men having fled in the opposite direction from that taken by Mace, convinced that superior numbers had overwhelmed them.

Back at the gully, the three Triple-T cowhands realized it was safe to come out of their defensive position. The tidal wave of crazed cattle had swept past them and the shooting had ceased altogether. Even the rain tapered off. Lem did what he could to tend to Billy's shoulder wound, while Dooley took his .44 Colt and put the two horses still alive out of their misery. "That's just a damn shame," Dooley lamented. "I was gettin' to where I was kinda fond of that horse."

"Well, we're on foot now," Lem said, "and I ain't sure if we lost the herd or not." He paused then to peer out into the darkness. "It ain't gonna be too much longer before daylight. I wonder how Cord made out. There was a helluva lot of shootin'. I hope he didn't get shot."

"That boy has a way about him," Dooley said confidently. "He'll show up directly. Then we'll find out what happened after we drove those bastards off." It was a little while yet, but his prediction finally proved to be valid, for Cord called out to them from the darkness.

"Dooley! Lem! Can you hear me?"

"Yeah, we hear you," Dooley answered. He turned to give Lem a wink.

"I'm comin' in, so don't go shootin' at me," Cord called again.

"We ain't makin' no promises," Dooley joked, greatly relieved to hear his young friend's voice again.

In a few minutes' time, a large form materialized out of the darkness as Cord walked his bay gelding into the shallow valley, leading four riderless horses. He pulled up before them and looked around their embattled gully and the carcasses of three horses. "Damn," he muttered quietly, then observed, "Looks like you fellers need some horses. I reckon it's a good thing I rounded up these strays. We've got some cattle to drive back home, and I don't know how good you fellers would be on foot." Noticing Billy's empty sleeve, he asked how bad it was.

"Ain't nothin' in it broke," Billy replied. "The bullet musta just hit meat, but Lem made me stick my arm inside my shirt till we get back to the ranch where he can give it a better look. I can ride, if that's what you're wonderin'."

"Good," Cord said, "'cause we need to get those cows movin' back down Triple-T range. What's left of those rustlers musta took off, 'cause there ain't no sign of any of 'em I can see right now. But I don't advise us to wait around to see if they decide to take another turn at us." He released the reins of the four rustlers' horses. "Pick you out a horse and we'll go get our cattle."

After following Blue Creek, which ran roughly north and south for half a mile, Mace veered sharply to the north, heading in the general direction of the Roman-3. It was not until he left the tree line that he became aware of someone on his tail. At once alarmed, he pressed his already tired horse for more speed, a command the horse could no longer obey. Instead of increasing its speed, the horse began to falter, finally slowing down to a weary walk, no matter the flogging and cursing it endured. Mace was forced to dismount, and he could hear the sound of hoofbeats drawing

steadily closer. Frightened now, with the image of
the man with the scarred forehead seared on his brain,
he drew his rifle from the saddle sling again. Using the
weary horse for protection, he laid the rifle across the
saddle, stood behind it, and waited. In a few moments,
the rider appeared out of the fading darkness, riding
head-on into the fatal ambush. When the rifle spoke,
the rider was hit in the chest, causing his horse to run
out from under him, dumping his body heavily to the
ground.

"Ha!" Mace shouted gleefully. "You chased after the
wrong man this time." To be sure of his kill, he pumped
another round into the motionless corpse. Still not certain, he hurried to stand over the body, only to draw
back in alarm when he discovered the lifeless face of
Ben Cagle staring up at him in eternal shock. Shocked
as well, Mace felt his knees go weak for a moment. He
had killed two of his own men on this ill-fated night.
His first impulse was to look quickly around him to
see if anyone had witnessed his latest assassination,
even though he was sure there was no one else.

It's his own damn fault, he thought, anxious to excuse
his acts of cowardice. *Come riding up on me in the dark
like that, he should have had better sense.* The problem facing him now was what to do next. The night sky was
even then melting away to a lighter shade of gray, and
looking back over the way he had run, he could see no
sign of anyone else trailing him. While deciding what
best to do, he took a look at Ben Cagle's horse. A sorrel
with white markings on the legs, it was not in much
better shape than his own. Both horses needed rest. He
took another long look back behind him, wondering
just how many men might be scouring the prairie on

both sides of the creek with the notion of finishing the job they had started. "I can't stay here," he decided aloud, but he was not sure which way he should go— back to the Roman-3 to face Striker's wrath—or strike out for parts unknown? It occurred to him that he had no idea how the rest of the men had fared, or how many had survived. Two he had done for himself, and he had seen two other empty saddles. *Of course,* he told himself, *those two might have been casualties for the other side.* It was all perplexing to the simpleminded outlaw, and for want of a better alternative, he decided to go back to the Roman-3 and hope their casualties were not as severe as he feared. He took the time to relieve Ben Cagle of his gun belt, which he hung on the saddle horn. Then he searched his pockets for any money he could find. Lastly, he took a hard look at his late partner's hand-tooled boots, but decided they were too small for his feet. Feeling a little more secure, since there was still no sign of anyone pursuing him, he took the reins of both horses and started walking toward the Roman-3.

Far behind him the large gang created in Mace's imagination had thoughts only of moving their cattle back to a safer location near the Triple-T headquarters. It was a task not easily accomplished by four men— one of them wounded. Events of the night just passed would be remembered and referred to by local ranchers as the Second Battle of Blue Creek. While not on a scale of the first, when army troops attacked a village of two hundred and fifty Sioux over twenty years before that date, the nine bodies found later were hardly insignificant.

Chapter 12

The folks at the Triple-T Ranch awoke to find the leading cows of a herd numbering in the neighborhood of two thousand, five hundred head moving into the range close about the ranch headquarters. Already up and about their chores, Stony, Blackie, and Link were preparing to ride back out to Blue Creek to ride herd right after breakfast. "Looks like the cows came to us, instead of the other way around," Blackie observed casually.

"Looks that way, don't it?" Stony allowed. "I don't know why in hell we didn't move 'em back down this way before. I reckon we just liked gettin' shot at."

"I expect we oughta ride out and help 'em move 'em on in," Blackie said.

"Best tell Slop we'll be back a little later for breakfast," Stony said. "Else he might throw it all to the hogs."

At the house, Muriel came into the kitchen to find

that Eileen had already built up the fire in the stove and had coffee on to boil. "Well, you're up bright and early," she said to her daughter. "I didn't even hear you leave the room."

"I didn't see any sense in waking you," Eileen replied. She had no intention of telling her mother that she was up earlier than usual strictly as a point of pride. She wanted to make sure she was up and stirring about in the kitchen before Birdie got up. This even though she told herself she had no reason to be competitive with their guest. "They drove the cattle in around us last night," she went on to say. Muriel moved to the window to see for herself. At almost the same time, the door to the other bedroom opened and Birdie came to join Eileen at the stove, seeking its warmth.

"Good morning. Did you have enough quilts last night?" Muriel asked.

"Yes, ma'am, I did," Birdie replied, still shivering a little.

"I see you put on a dress this morning," Eileen commented.

Birdie laughed. "I just wanted you to see that I had one. I was getting tired of everyone thinking I was a boy." She laughed again. "But I've still got those long pants on under this skirt."

Muriel laughed with her. "I don't blame you for that. It got cold last night. When it really starts getting cold, maybe you'd better crawl in with Eileen and me."

"Maybe I'd better," Birdie joked. "I don't have much meat on my bones. Can I get in the middle?" Her reply evoked another laugh from Muriel, but no more than a polite smile from Eileen.

Being very much a woman, Birdie sensed the slight

chill toward her, coming from Eileen, but she could not understand the reason for it. *Hell, I haven't been around long enough to make her mad at me,* she thought. *Maybe she thinks I'm a slut because I was riding with Cord and Dooley. Well, she can think what she wants, it's no skin off my . . .* Another thought occurred before she finished that one. *Maybe that's the problem—Cord.* She smiled to herself then, understanding. Turning to Eileen, she favored her with a warm smile and said, "Can I help you with breakfast? I'm a decent cook."

Stony and his two partners rode out to meet the four riders following along behind the herd. Catching sight of Billy's bloodied coat, he pulled up at once. "Trouble?"

"Well, I reckon," Billy answered. "But we brought the herd back home with us. I just got a little nick in my shoulder, but it was a whole lot worse on that bunch of bushwhackers from the Roman-Three. You'll notice ain't none of us ridin' our regular horses but Cord. They shot ours, so we came home on their horses, since they didn't have no use for 'em anymore."

"I see you even brought back an extra horse," Stony said. "Does that mean you killed four of Striker's riders?"

"I ain't sure how many were killed, 'cause Cord got most of 'em, workin' on his own while me and Lem and Dooley were holed up in a gully." Obviously getting more and more pumped up over their successful clash with the Roman-3 crew, Billy went on. "They had the three of us pinned down, but we got two of 'em. Cord got the rest." He turned to Cord then. "How many did you kill, Cord?" Lem looked quickly at his young friend, immediately concerned about the nature of his response.

Cord didn't answer right away, uncomfortable with Billy's apparent boastful accounting of the night's violent results. When his words finally came, they were quiet and without emotion. "I don't know. We were all shootin' at everything that moved in the dark. I reckon we'll see how many of Striker's men show up durin' the next few days."

Disappointed that Cord didn't share his triumphant high over such a victory against superior odds, Billy complained, "Come on, you tellin' me you don't know the number you killed? Hell, man, you were a damn killin' machine."

"It ain't nothin' to brag about," Cord said.

"Cord's right," Lem interjected then. "It ain't nothin' anybody should wanna brag about. Best to not talk about it too much." He knew that it would not do for talk to get around about the number of deaths Cord had accounted for.

Equally aware of the problem that could be caused for Cord, Dooley spoke up when Billy seemed not to understand. "Cord did what he thought he had to do to keep all of us from gettin' killed. It ain't gonna do him no favor to go around braggin' about how many men he shot—give him a reputation he don't need and set him up for every two-bit gunslinger who wants a reputation for hisself."

The light of understanding shown in Billy's eye and he nodded soberly. "Let's take care of the horses and get us somethin' to eat before Slop throws it out," Lem said, satisfied that everyone understood the problem that could have been caused for Cord. Turning back to Billy again, he suggested, "Maybe you'd rather have Muriel take a look at that shoulder first."

"I'd rather eat first," Billy said without hesitation.

Lem rapped lightly on the back door and waited for one of the women to answer. In a minute, the door opened and Muriel was standing there. "What is it, Lem?"

"I come to ask you if you wouldn't mind takin' a look at Billy's shoulder," Lem said. "He got hit in the shoulder last night and the bullet's still in there. He ain't hurtin' real bad, but I'm afraid if Slop or one of us other men goes diggin' around in that wound, we'll just make it a bigger mess."

"Why, of course I'll look at it," Muriel replied. "Where is he?" She was accustomed to being called on for the more serious doctoring.

"Down at the bunkhouse."

"Bring him up to the house," she said. "It'll be easier to tend to him here where I've got everything I need."

Eileen and Birdie, both in the kitchen, overheard the conversation taking place at the back door. Still feeling a slight chill coming from Eileen, Birdie had made every effort to try to help out, but there was little that she had been able to contribute so far. She saw this as an opportunity, so when Lem left to get Billy, she offered her help. "I can tend to Billy's wound for you. I've got small hands, so I won't make too big a mess of the wound, and I've got a little experience tending bullet wounds." She hoped they would not ask how she came by her experience, for she had no intention of admitting that it was two occasions when she had helped Mother Featherlegs remove lead from a couple of the madam's outlaw customers.

"Why, that would be very nice of you, Birdie," Muriel said. "Are you sure you don't mind doing it?" Birdie assured her that she did not, and Muriel chuckled as she added, "I'm sure Billy would prefer it."

"I'll heat up a pan of water, if you'll show me where some clean rags are," Birdie said.

"I've already put some water on the stove," Eileen said. "I'll get you some rags." She went at once to the pantry.

Eileen pulled some scraps of old shirts from the top shelf of the pantry and turned to find Birdie confronting her. "I wanted to say something to you," Birdie told her. "I wanted to make sure I wasn't stepping on your toes when I volunteered to take care of Billy." Eileen met her statement with a puzzled expression. Birdie continued. "I think Billy's kinda cute, but I don't want to make you mad if you've got any notions about him."

Eileen's puzzled expression transformed suddenly into one of pleasant surprise. "Billy?" she responded. "No, I've no notions about Billy one way or the other." Still astonished to find that Birdie apparently had no designs upon Cord Malone, she sputtered for a moment before giving Birdie a genuinely friendly smile. "You're right. Billy is cute, but don't give it another thought. I'll not be in your way." She gave her a little squeeze on the arm. "Now, let's get you all set up to take care of your patient." Birdie returned Eileen's warm smile and followed her back to the kitchen table, smug in the knowledge that she had thawed Eileen's frosty demeanor toward her. Maybe Billy was cute, but she had no particular interest in him. As far as Cord was concerned, she hadn't made up her mind. In the short time she had known him, she had to admit that she naturally looked to him for her protection. It was hard not to.

Within a few minutes, Billy showed up at the kitchen door. As Muriel had suggested, he seemed very pleased to find out that his doctor was to be the sprightly young lady with the short hair. Birdie sat him down at the kitchen table, close to the stove, so he would not be too cold with his shirt off. She made short work of the procedure, probing quickly with a kitchen knife until she felt the nick of the blade on the slug, then grasping it with her slender fingers, extracted it and held it up for him to see. With nothing for the pain except one long pull from a bottle of rye whiskey and a splash on the wound after the extraction, Birdie soon had the wound dressed. Through it all, Billy, although experiencing considerable pain, did his best to remain silent in an effort to impress the ladies. As a reward for his valor, Birdie sat down at the table with him for a cup of coffee.

"Have a cup of coffee with us," Birdie offered when Eileen walked back in the kitchen. "I was just about to ask Billy if he and the others were heading back out tonight to watch the herd." She was confident that the question would interest Eileen.

"Not all of us," Billy answered as Eileen poured herself a cup of coffee and sat with them. "Just Cord—he's plannin' on watchin' the trail down along Blue Creek to see if they're thinkin' about tryin' anything tonight."

His comment provoked Eileen's attention. "He was out last night with Lem and the new man and you," she said. "Shouldn't it be someone else's turn tonight?"

"That's what Lem told him," Billy replied, "but it

was his idea. He said he'd catch a little sleep this afternoon and head back out tonight."

Damn, she thought, wondering how she was going to accidentally bump into him if he was going to be sleeping most of the afternoon. *Oh well, he'll have to wake up to eat before he goes. I'll think of some way to talk to him.*

"I'm going down to the barn," Eileen announced casually. "I believe those chickens are finding some new nesting places." She could think of no other excuse.

"I've got to go down to the smokehouse," Birdie said. "I can go by the barn and check for you."

"No, I'll do it," Eileen said. "I wanna get outside for a few minutes to get some fresh air. Why don't I cut the ham for supper, as long as I'm going anyway?" She had been beginning to fear that Cord was never going to come out of the bunkhouse. So when she had finally seen him walking down to the barn, carrying his rifle in one hand and a cloth bundle that Slop had undoubtedly given him in the other, she had hurriedly picked up her shawl and headed for the door.

"You're gonna need this," Birdie said, holding out a butcher knife.

"I guess that would be handy," Eileen replied as she paused to take it, flushing slightly, hoping Birdie didn't make anything of her apparent rush to get out the door. Hurrying through the chilled afternoon air, she went straight to the barn, passing the smokehouse on the way. Inside the barn, there was no sign of anyone, so she went to the last stall on the right, where Cord had sometimes kept his favorite, the bay. The stall was empty. "Damn!" she murmured, and thought, *Where the hell did he go?*

"Whaddaya fixin' to do with that knife?"

Startled, she jumped, and turned to see him coming from the tack room with his saddle over his shoulder. "Use it on you, if you come up behind me like that again," she informed him.

"Sorry. I didn't mean to scare you."

"You didn't scare me," she immediately came back, reverting to the stony disposition she usually reserved for him. "I just didn't know you were there."

"Sorry," he repeated. "I'm fixin' to get out of your way right now." He turned toward the door, then paused and turned back to her. "Is there somethin' I could help you with?"

"No. Some of the chickens are building nests somewhere I haven't been able to find, and I thought they might be in some places I haven't looked."

He cocked his head and attempted a smile. "What were you gonna do when you found 'em, kill 'em?"

"No, Mr. Smart Aleck, this is to cut some ham for supper," she replied. When he nodded and started to leave again, she stopped him once more. "We haven't seen you up at the house since you came back—Lem and Billy, but not you."

"Well, I reckon I didn't have any business up at the house," Cord said.

"I think I should tell you that Mama and I appreciate the fact that you came back to help the other men. I didn't think to tell you yesterday."

"I figured I owed your daddy that much," he said. Tiring from holding his saddle while they talked, he

dropped it to the ground. "How are you folks gettin'
along with your daddy gone? Are you gettin' along all
right with Birdie?"

"Of course we are," she answered quickly. "Birdie's
just fine, and she seems more than willing to take care
of Billy." Her earlier jealousy flared slightly in spite of
Birdie's professed interest in Billy. She couldn't help it.
"Is that your main concern right now, Birdie?"

He studied her intently for a few moments, wondering why she always seemed to be angry about something he said or did. Why, he wondered, did she even
bother to talk to him if she was uncomfortable around
him? He thought of the kiss she left him with when he
had taken his leave to go after Levi Creed. He couldn't
explain it when considering her almost militant attitude toward him from the first day they met. Finally
he answered her question. "I hope Birdie's doin' all
right. She's a fine little lady, but she ain't my main concern."

"What is, then?" Eileen asked as he took a step
toward her.

Without answering, he reached out for her, pulled
her up toward him, and kissed her hard. Her body,
rigid at first, relaxed as she responded to his embrace.
He released her and stepped away. "Those rustlers
tryin' to steal our cattle, that's what," he said, answering her question.

"Why, you brazen jackass," she fumed indignantly,
"you've got your nerve!"

"I figured you gave that kiss to me when I left here
before, so I figured I'd return it to you." He gave her a
genuine grin. "I brought Lem's rifle back, and I brought

your kiss back, so I reckon I'm all square with everybody." Without waiting for her retort, he picked up his saddle and headed for the door.

She hurled it after him anyway. "Don't you ever think you can do something like that again," she cried. "If I'd wanted a kiss from you, I'd have let you know." He continued on his way, never looking back. "You're lucky I'm going to let it pass this time, instead of telling Lem and Stony. They mighta had something to say about how you treat a lady."

"'Preciate it," he said, still without looking back. He climbed over the top rail of the corral and called the bay to him. When he slipped his bridle on the patient horse and proceeded to saddle him, he was careful to keep his back turned toward the perturbed young woman, lest she read the indecision in his eyes. *Well, that ought to just about take care of that for good and all,* he thought. At least now he would know why she always seemed angry with him. *But why did she kiss me the first time?* Maybe it was because she figured never to see him again. That seemed as good an explanation as any, so he decided to attribute it to the mysterious mind of a woman, a phenomenon that God had created most likely to forever confuse man.

Eileen stomped into the kitchen, trying to be angry at the same time she was still feeling the strength of his kiss. Seeing Birdie standing there expectantly, she told her, "I didn't find any new nests. Maybe I was wrong."

Birdie waited a little while for her to continue, but she didn't, so Birdie asked, "Where's the ham?"

"Oh, fiddle!" Eileen exclaimed angrily. "I forgot. I'll go back right now and get it."

"I can get it," Birdie called after her, but Eileen was already storming toward the smokehouse. *She forgot it*, Birdie smiled to herself. She, like Eileen, had noticed the broad-shouldered young man when he went toward the barn as well. *Big ol' good-looking fellows will make you lose your memory, even the ones with big scars across their foreheads.*

Out by the corral, Bill Dooley approached Cord, who was tightening the bay's girth strap. "What's wrong with the little missy? She got away from here like somebody slipped a hornet in her underdrawers."

"Don't know," Cord claimed. "Just a woman thing, I reckon."

"I'm thinkin' I'll go with you tonight," Dooley said. "Maybe keep you from stickin' your neck out too far."

"You'd be welcome," Cord said, "but I thought you might wanna hang around here in case we get some more folks showin' up to visit Mr. Murphy's cows. I ain't plannin' on stickin' my neck out. I just thought I'd try to take a look to see how many men Striker's still got. We mighta cut him back enough so he'll give it up and move on to somewhere else."

"I don't know," Dooley said. "This feller might not be used to gettin' his ass whipped like he did last night—might not like it. I doubt he's finished with us yet."

"Well, we'll go see," Cord said. "It'd help to see what we're up against."

In contrast to the triumphant return that morning at the Triple-T, it was a different scene at the Roman-3. Harlan Striker walked out on the front porch of his partially finished ranch house, a cup of hot coffee in his hand, and looked out across the prairie to the south. Troubled, because he had expected to see his drovers bringing in a sizable addition to his herd by this time of morning, but all was quiet. "Where the hell are they?" he demanded. "Rena!"

In a few minutes, the imperturbable half-breed woman came to the front door. "What you want? I busy."

"I don't give a damn if you're busy or not," Striker replied gruffly. "Get me some fresh coffee. This is cold."

She came out on the porch and took his cup, dumped the cold coffee off the edge of the porch, and said, "You don't stand out here in the cold, your coffee don't get cold." She held the cup up and added, "I put it on the table. You want hot coffee, you come inside to drink it."

He didn't retort as he usually did, for his mind was occupied with the matter of his missing crew, and the lateness of the hour. But a thought flashed briefly through his mind as he followed the belligerent woman inside, that he had had enough of her abrasive attitude, and he was reaching the point where she had outlived her usefulness. She was not that good a cook, and he felt he was ready to find a younger woman to take her place. *It'll be a pleasure to cut her sassy throat,* he thought.

It was midmorning when Sam Plummer, Tom Tyler, and Robert Marsh straggled back to the Roman-3, looking for some breakfast. They dutifully reported to the ranch house to face Striker's wrath. Furious to hear the results of a planned raid designed to finish Will Murphy's grip on the range below Blue Creek, he railed against the three stragglers. "Where are the rest of the men?" Striker demanded.

"We don't know," Sam replied when the other two declined to answer. He was about to suffer another blast from his outraged employer when Mace finally showed up, leading Ben Cagle's horse, and diverting Striker's wrath toward him.

Like the other three, Mace suffered his boss's rage meekly, and when his explanation was demanded, he tried to excuse his and his men's lack of success. When Striker asked him where the other men were, Mace admitted what he now knew to be true. "There ain't no more. The four of us is the only ones left."

His answer almost staggered Striker. "How can that be?" he demanded. "Are you telling me that we sent thirteen men down there, thirteen supposedly experienced gun hands, against five common cattle drovers, and they killed all but you four?"

"Yes, sir," Mace replied, "and Bo." This reminder of the wounded man lying in the bunkhouse seemed to intensify Striker's irate frustration. "But it ain't all like it looks," Mace was quick to implore. "Most of our men were killed by that hired gun they brought in this week. Our men didn't have a chance. That devil ain't like a real man. He's a high-priced killer, and they brought him in here to rub us all out. Scar-faced feller—I don't know who he is, but I don't know of but one other man that could do what he did, and I've seen him. So it ain't him."

"Who paid him?" Striker demanded, unable to understand. "Murphy's not even in the country, and Mike Duffy's dead, so who paid for a hired killer?"

"I don't know," Mace answered meekly, "but somebody did."

Striker didn't say anything for a long moment, unable to think clearly in the face of the devastating and unbelievable facts presented him by gunmen he had hired for the purpose of wiping out the Triple-T. Finally he seemed to have settled down, for he spoke calmly and under control. "If it's a contest of assassination they're playin' now, then two can play that game. Who is this other famous gunman you referred to, and how can I get in touch with him?"

"Well," Mace replied, "I ain't sure if it's his real name, but Strong is the only name I've ever heard him called. I met him one time in Custer City, up in the Black Hills, but I think he spends most of his time ridin' outta Cheyenne, over in Wyomin'. Another feller I rode with then, and that was a year and a half ago, said anybody wantin' to hire Strong left him a message at the telegraph office in Cheyenne. I don't have any idea if you could still get in touch with him there."

"Well, I intend to find out," Striker decided. "I'm gonna send you to Cheyenne to find this Strong fellow. You tell him I've got a job for him here that'll pay him five hundred dollars just to kill one man." Then, considering the dependability of the man he was sending on this errand, he offered an incentive for Mace to complete it. "I want you to leave for Cheyenne today and I'll pay you a bonus of one hundred dollars when you bring Strong back here to do the job."

"Yes, sir," Mace responded immediately, thinking it was better than hanging around the Roman-3 for the next few days, waiting to see if that gunman with the scar was going to show up there to finish the job. "What if he ain't there when I get there? He might be outta town. I can leave him a message at the telegraph office, but I ain't got no way of knowin' when he might get it."

Striker considered that possibility for a moment. "I'll give you two weeks to get back here with Strong. After two weeks, the deal is off. So you'd best get goin'."

"Yes, sir, I'll get goin' right away, but I ain't got no money to buy supplies and feed myself while I'm lookin' for this feller."

"All right," Striker conceded. "I'll give you twenty dollars to take care of what food you'll need. When that runs out, steal what you need. You're a damn out law, ain't you?"

"Look yonder," Dooley said, and pointed toward a stand of willows on the bank of Blue Creek. Grazing peacefully on the grass between the willows, Cord saw four saddled horses. The two men reined their horses back for a few minutes while they scanned the creek bank carefully, looking for riders, but it was plain to see that the horses were not tethered or hobbled. "Looks like there ain't nobody ridin' 'em." He glanced at Cord. "Some more of them saddles you emptied last night," he said.

"Or some of 'em you and Lem emptied," Cord replied.

"Shit," Dooley scoffed. "Between the three of us in that damn gully, I only know of two men we shot."

"I didn't shoot that many," Cord said. "Somethin' don't add up. We brought four horses back last night, and now we find four more. I know for a fact that I didn't shoot but five men, and if you're sure you and Lem and Billy got two, then that's two that somebody else did for. You sure you didn't hit but two of 'em? It

was awful hard to see what was goin' on in the middle
of all that shootin'."

"I'm damn sure," Dooley stated emphatically. "I got
one and Lem got one. Billy didn't hit nothin'." He stared
perplexed at Cord for a few moments; then his face
broke out in a wide grin. "They musta been shootin' at
each other." He shook his head, chuckling. "It was so
damn dark in that mess that they was helpin' us out."

"Maybe so," Cord said. "It was hard to tell who was
who." There was no other way to explain it. "I reckon
we just picked us up four more horses."

"And four saddles and whatever's in those saddlebags," Dooley reminded him. "And we need to scout
out that whole trail from here back to where the stampede started. I'm thinkin' we oughta find some extra
rifles and handguns if we find the bodies—kinda like
goin' over a battlefield, ain't it?"

They stretched a length of rope between two cottonwood trees on the creek bank and tied the four stray
horses to it to make sure they wouldn't have to round
them up after scouting the area for weapons. Riding
about forty yards apart, they swept the area over where
the attempted stampede had taken place. Three sweeps
of the prairie along the creek turned up seven bodies
and four rifles. Relieving the bodies of anything of
value, they then tried to wipe the mud and moisture
from the weapons before taking them back to fit in the
empty saddle scabbards on the horses. As a matter of
habit formed many years before, Dooley kept a running account of the value of the spoils. By the time they
were finished, the sun was sinking low on the western
horizon, so Cord suggested that Dooley should take

the horses back to the Triple-T. "What are you gonna be doin'?" Dooley asked.

"Well, like we said when we rode out here, it'd help to know what's goin' on up at the Roman-Three after last night's try at our cattle. So I think I'll take a ride up that way and see what I can see."

"Don't you think it'd be a good idea if there was somebody with you?" Dooley asked.

"I ain't gonna get close enough to run into any-body," Cord assured him, "just close enough to put an eye on the ranch, in case they're fixin' to mount up another gang of men and head this way. Maybe I'd have a chance to hightail it back to let everybody know they're comin'.'"

It was only a four-mile ride west of Blue Creek to the ranch Harlan Striker had built on a nameless creek that flowed down to the North Platte. Cord reached a pair of low buttes overlooking the barn and partially built ranch house just as dusk settled upon the valley. He decided he couldn't find a better place to keep an eye on the ranch, so he dismounted, tied his horse to a clump of sage, and settled down to watch. His inten-tion was to see how many men he and his friends at the Triple-T might be facing if Roman-3 was preparing to make another attempt at Triple-T cattle.

There was almost no activity around the barn, bunk-house, or house, with only an occasional person mov-ing between the buildings. It was almost like a ghost town, so much so that Cord had to wonder if most of the men were off on another raid. He had seen no one during his ride from Blue Creek, so if rustling was the plan for this evening, they must have taken a different path. The longer he sat and watched, however, the more he became convinced that Striker had no more than a handful left of his original crew. Sitting cross-legged, Indian fashion, in a dry wash that gave him some protection from the cold wind, he ate the biscuit and ham that Slop had given him, wishing he had a cup of hot coffee to wash it down with.

He remained on his perch at the top of the butte until all signs indicated that the Roman-3 was settled in for the night. During the entire time, he had counted no more than three or four men. No one had ridden out, and no one had come in. *If he still has a gang of men, they're sure as hell somewhere else,* he thought. He decided then that he and his friends had successfully ended the threat from the Roman-3. He got to his feet, untied the bay, and started back to the Triple-T.

Chapter 13

While peace returned to the Triple-T, and the small victorious crew settled back into the routine of keeping the cattle alive during the coming winter, Mace Tarpley rode into Cheyenne on a matter that would impart great impact upon the late Mike Duffy's cowhands. He wasted no time in going directly to the telegraph office to learn if the operator had had any communication with a man known simply as Strong. "That man," the operator responded, "yeah, he comes in here from time to time—scary-lookin' man—told Polly over at Strutter's place that he's a lawman workin' for the government."

When told that Strong had been in the day before to inquire about his messages, Mace was afraid he might have been a day too late. "Probably not," the operator told him. "He didn't have any messages, but he likes to stay a couple of days at Strutter's when he comes to town. I expect you might find him there playing cards."

Curious, the operator asked, "What line of business is Strong really in? He doesn't ever say much, just picks up an occasional message somebody's left him and walks out. I'd ask him what he does, but he doesn't look like the kind of man who likes questions."

Mace grunted in response. "Huh, he's the kind of man that minds his own business, which I reckon we all oughta do." He turned and went out the door.

Mace was very familiar with Strutter's Gentlemen's Club across the tracks from the depot. He had spent time there himself when he had some money in his pocket. It was the middle of the afternoon when he looped his reins over the hitching rail before the large two-story house and stepped up on the porch. He walked into the front hall and was met almost immediately by a large woman named Polly, who greeted him cordially, even while eyeing him skeptically from head to toe. "Hey, honey," she said with an obvious lack of enthusiasm, "you look like you might be lost. You lookin' for a drink, or a card game, or something else?"

Mace flashed his tobacco-stained grin for her, oblivious of her look of disdain. "I might be lookin' for a drink or two at that, but first I'm lookin' for a feller that usually stays here when he's in town—feller name of Strong. I've got some business to talk over with him. Is he here?"

"Maybe, maybe not," she said. "What kinda business have you gotta talk over with him? You'll have to take off that pistol you're wearin' and park it in the closet before you can go into the parlor. The owner don't allow any weapons in the parlor."

Mace snorted a chuckle. "Hell, lady, I ain't lookin' to

shoot him. I just wanna talk some business." He unbuckled his gun belt and held it out to her.

"Put it in there," she said, and pointed toward the closet, preferring not to take it herself. When he had dropped it on the floor, he followed her to the parlor. She held the door open for him, but when he stepped inside, she disappeared.

Mace stood near the door and looked the room over. There were four tables at one end of the room. Three of them were in use with poker games in progress. Two of the three tables had the usual spectators, while the other had no lookers standing around. This was the table that attracted Mace's attention, for he recalled something that he had been told by someone—he didn't remember who. Strong did not tolerate spectators hovering around the table when he played poker, especially the women who worked at Strutter's—with their subtle signs; the raising of an eyebrow, the tug of an ear, the wink of an eye, and any number of signals employed to separate the unwary stranger from his cash. The soiled doves that hovered over the tables at Strutter's were well aware of the man's violent temper, so there was little need to warn them to give him space.

Ignoring the players at the other two tables, Mace sidled over closer to the one with no spectators and four players. He had seen the man once before, but even had he not, Strong would have been easy enough to pick out. Big, even sitting down, he dwarfed the other three cardplayers at the table. A seemingly permanent scowl upon his face relaxed only slightly whenever he won a hand, as deep-set eyes, dark as coal, watched every movement made by his opponents. It was hard to guess the age of the time-weathered face, but the gray in his mustache was testimony that he was not a young man. It also told Mace that whatever the number of gunfights he had been engaged in, he had obviously come out on top. He seemed to take no notice of Mace standing there until he declined to call the bid and tossed his cards in. Then he fixed his cruel eyes upon Mace and growled, "Find you someplace else to stand gawkin'."

Mace's initial impulse was to withdraw immediately, but the promised payment of one hundred dollars made him stay to deliver his message. "I need to talk some business with you," he said.

This caught Strong's attention. "Is that so?" He took a moment to give Mace another looking-over. "Who sent you lookin' for me?"

"I met you once up toward Custer City," Mace said, hoping it would jog his memory, but there was no indication of it in the eyes glaring at him from under bushy black eyebrows.

"What's your name?" Strong demanded.

"Mace Tarpley," he replied. There was still no recognition apparent in the impatient face. "I got some important business to talk over with you, but it needs to be done in private."

Strong glared at him then, trying to decide. After glancing at his modest stack of chips on the table, he figured it wouldn't hurt to hear what the scruffy-looking jasper had to say. "After this hand, and one more, I'll hear what you've got to say. But, damn it, don't stand there gawkin'. Go over to the bar and wait."

"Right," Mace replied dutifully, and retreated to the bar. The bartender said nothing, but stared at him, awaiting his pleasure. "Gimme a shot of whiskey,"

Mace demanded, trying to regain some measure of bravado. He finished his first drink and ordered another before Strong threw his hand in after five more had been dealt.

He got to his feet so abruptly that he knocked his chair over, and without bothering to set it upright again, he strode over to the bar. "Buy me a drink," he ordered. Mace immediately nodded to the bartender. When Strong had his drink, he picked it up and moved down to the end of the bar, out of earshot of the bartender. "Now, what's this business you're talkin' about?"

Mace told him of the range war over near Ogallala and the paid killer the Triple-T had brought in to kill off his boss's ranch hands. Strong had gotten propositions similar to that before, so he was only mildly interested until Mace told him the payoff was five hundred. That got his complete attention. "Five hundred, huh?" Strong responded. "Cash money or gold coin?"

"Whatever way you want," Mace said, even though he didn't know how Striker was going to give it to him, and he figured it didn't matter. That would be Striker's problem.

Strong nodded thoughtfully to himself. The timing was right. He was running out of money fast, and had considered heading back up in the Black Hills. "This feller you want me to take care of, what's his name?"

"I don't know his name," Mace answered. "Tall feller, almost as big as you, has a scar runnin' across his forehead from here to here." He indicated on his own forehead. "But I ain't heard what his name is." He shrugged indifferently. "That sound like anybody you know?"

Strong thought for a few moments before replying,

"No, don't call to mind anybody I've ever run across. If he was anybody worth worryin' about, I'da heard of him." He nodded confidently to assure Mace. Then he asked, "Five hundred, right? Just for killin' one man?" When Mace guaranteed him that was the deal, he nodded again, satisfied that it was going to be an easy way to make a payday.

"I'm gonna need some supplies. I expect you'll be buyin' everythin' I need, cartridges and so forth."

"Hell, man," Mace replied. "Ain't you got a cent to pay for your own supplies? I ain't got no money. My job was to bring you Mr. Striker's offer. He didn't give me enough money to buy food for myself, let alone give you money for supplies." He was already tiring of Strong's money-grabbing ways.

Strong didn't say anything for a long moment while he fixed his gaze upon Mace, much as a bobcat measures a rabbit. "A man has expenses in this business," he said in a low, calm voice. "And he expects to be paid for those expenses. The five hundred is for the job. I'll need money for my expenses. That's money above the price for the job."

"I expect you can take that up with Mr. Striker," Mace said. "I ain't got nothin' to do with that part of it."

Strong took another minute to study this messenger from Harlan Striker. Judging from the appearance of the man, Mace was the typical outlaw, thief, or gunman Strong had ridden with over the years. His curiosity was aroused. "Just this one jasper? Why don't you shoot him?"

Mace wasn't prone to tell him that he had no desire to meet face-to-face with the man who had almost single-handedly rubbed out almost all of Striker's

gang. He wouldn't say that he hadn't given the idea
some thought, but the memory of that dark, stormy
night when his men's saddles kept coming up empty
had etched an image on his brain of a demonic killer
straight from hell. To answer Strong's question, however, he tried to show his indifference with a casual
shrug of his shoulders. "I offered to, but Mr. Striker
had this notion that it would be best to hire it done by
an outside man, who would do the job and be gone the
next day in case the law came nosin' around."

"Is that a fact?" Strong replied with skepticism.
"Well, I'll go shoot this gunman for your boss." He had
an idea as to why Mace didn't do the job himself, and
it was considerably different from the way Mace told it.
This problem that Mace's boss wanted eliminated
must be a genuine hell-raiser of a gunman. Striker might
be ripe for money over and above the five hundred.
After all, that was his initial offering, so it was important to make him know that he wasn't dealing with
any ordinary assassin. "Here's the way this deal is
gonna be handled," he told Mace. "There's a lot of folks
wantin' my services. I ain't just settin' around here
playin' cards. I've got a job I'll have to take care of
before I leave town." He didn't, but it was the picture
he wanted to paint for Harlan Striker. "I'm not gonna
waste my time on somebody's promise to pay me, so
when your boss wires me one hundred dollars, I'll be
on the next train to Ogallala, ready to get the job done."

"I thought you'd ride back with me," Mace replied.

"When I get an advance on the job is when I'll know
for sure your boss is a man of his word," Strong told
him. "He might as well know that if he wants the best
professional, it'll cost him more than the piddlin'

amount he has to pay a common bushwhacker. And
from what you're tellin' me, this jasper's too much for
the common back-shooter to handle, and I'll guarantee
your boss that I'll get the job done. If I don't, it won't
cost him nothin'. Now, that's the way I work, so you'd
best jump on your horse and get back to your boss. I
ain't gonna waste my time around here for long."

"Hell, it's a three-and-a-half-day ride back to the
Roman-Three from here," Mace complained.

"Then you'd better get started."

Lem Jenkins, as the eldest of Will Murphy's ranch
hands, called a meeting of the remaining crew, thinking it a good idea to see where they stood now that
they had apparently defeated Harlan Striker's move to
consume the Triple-T. The past week had brought no
new attacks on the men or the cattle, so everyone was
in attendance, even Muriel, Eileen, and Birdie. "I ain't
tryin' to take over Mike's job," Lem started out, "but I
thought we oughta see what's what before Mr. Murphy
gets back in the country. If somebody else wants to do
the talkin', that's fine by me." There was quick and
unanimous agreement by all present that he was the
logical choice to assume the position as foreman until
Murphy returned. This was due primarily to the reason that, at thirty-eight years of age, he was by far the
oldest and most experienced, with the exception of Bill
Dooley and Slop. Dooley was older than Lem, but he
was just newly arrived at the Triple-T. He was hardly
likely to accept such a position at any rate, even had it
been offered. And nobody knew exactly how old Slop
was, but he already stood slightly bent over because of

what he said was rheumatism. "All right, then," Lem
continued, "let's get started."

The first issue to be discussed was the shortage of
manpower. They were far short of the number of hands
needed to take care of a herd as big as theirs, which was
no doubt the reason Harlan Striker had thought he
could overrun them. "We're in a lot better shape than
we were before Cord and Dooley came to help." He
turned aside to comment directly to Muriel, "Except for
the loss of Mike, ma'am." She nodded with a sad smile
for his courtesy. He went on then. "We're just gonna
have to take care of the herd with the seven of us."

"I can ride," Birdie interrupted. "Muriel and Eileen
don't need me at the house, anyway. I'm just one more
in the way. I can work in the barn, too. That would give
you eight riders to watch the cattle."

Her suggestion sparked a reaction from everybody.
"I don't know . . . " Lem hesitated, caught by surprise.
"Tendin' cattle's a cold, hard job this time of year," he
said, "not exactly right for a slim little lady."

"I can ride and I can shoot," Birdie insisted. "Ask
Cord and Dooley."

"That's a fact," Dooley quickly verified. "We've seen
her in action. She didn't back down when the shootin'
started."

"I reckon I might be more help in the barn, or ridin'
herd, if one of the women wanted to do the cookin' for
the hands," Slop volunteered as he carried his big gray
coffeepot around the room, filling each outstretched cup.

All eyes shifted then to see Muriel's reaction. It was
Eileen who responded, however. "I can do the cooking," she quickly agreed. "Mama can help, if I need it."

Lem was astonished by the positive attitude exhibited by everyone. "I don't know if we need to go that far," he said. "Slop's already got the rheumatize so bad he's stove up pretty much, especially on these cold mornin's we're into now." He looked around the room to judge their reaction. "I think with Birdie helpin' out, the eight of us can handle it. Whaddaya think?" He saw nods of agreement from everyone. "Good. I'm sure we'll get more help when Mr. Murphy comes home. He'll most likely be hirin' on some more men."

The meeting had appeared to be over when Slop brought one more thing to their attention. "If I'm gonna keep feedin' you boys, I'm gonna need somebody to go to town. I'm gettin' mighty low on supplies, especially coffee, flour, and sugar. Mike usually sent one of you in with a wagon to pick up what I needed, but I reckon with him gone, we all forgot about it."

"Well, we sure don't wanna run outta grub," Stony sang out. "I reckon we'd best send somebody in to town tomorrow."

"I can do that," Birdie popped up again. "I can drive a team of horses."

As before, everyone looked at her in surprise. Then they shifted their gazes toward Dooley, who had vouched for her before. "Don't look at me," he said. "I ain't never seen her drive a wagon, but if she says she can, I sure as hell wouldn't doubt it. I'll ride in with her," Dooley volunteered. He was thinking that it had been a little while since he had had a drink. And he had a couple of extra rifles he had gained from the battle with the Roman-3's crew that he felt sure he could sell or trade. "I can give her a hand if she needs it, and it wouldn't hurt to have a little extra protection along in case somethin' comes up."

"That sounds like a good idea to me," Lem said. It would be a help if the young lady could pick up the supplies, and he was a lot more comfortable with someone along in case she needed help. "Let Slop make you a list to give Homer Tisdale at the general store. He'll put it on Mr. Murphy's bill." He looked around then and noticed the look of dismay in Billy's eyes, and couldn't resist japing him. "We'da sent you, Billy, but you ain't much good with just one arm."

"This don't slow me down none," Billy immediately refuted. "It's just about ready to come outta this sling, anyway." He blushed when Birdie gave him a smile.

Outside, after the meeting, Cord had a quiet word with Dooley. "You sure you wanna be walkin' around town carelessly? You know it ain't been long since there were likely notices sent out about your little set-to with the army. I expect they might still be glad to have you show up."

Dooley chuckled at the thought. "You're startin' to sound like an old mother hen," he joked. "Don't worry. I ain't lookin' to make any noise in town. I might have me one drink, but I'm just goin' along to make sure Birdie's all right." Changing the subject abruptly when something caught his eye, he said, "Look yonder." Cord turned to look in the direction Dooley indicated to see Birdie driving a team of horses toward a small farm wagon on the other side of the barn. Cord started to go help her, but Dooley caught him by the elbow. "Wait a minute. Let's see if she can hitch 'em up to that wagon." Cord humored him and they stood by while the frail-looking young lady backed the team on either side of the wagon tongue. "I swear," Dooley marveled, "ain't she somethin'?"

"She's just full of surprises," Cord said. The young lady did seem to know a little bit about damn near everything. He was beginning to wonder if she might be many years older than the sixteen years she claimed, and the thirteen years she looked. "Look after her," Cord said, "and stay outta trouble."

"Yes, ma'am, mother hen," Dooley answered as Cord untied the reins and prepared to climb in the saddle.

They had gotten a later start than they would have liked, because of the meeting, but Dooley figured they could still get to Ogallala, get their supplies, and start back home in time to make supper—and this was with time to let him visit the Crystal Palace for a couple of snorts. Birdie insisted on driving the horses, intending, Dooley supposed, to demonstrate to him that she was capable of the task. It was all right with him. He contented himself to sit on the seat beside her and make sure she kept the wagon heading in the right direction, since she had never been to Ogallala. They pulled into the town after a two-and-a-half-hour drive, and went directly to the general merchandise store owned by Louis Aufdengarten. Homer Tisdale greeted them from behind the counter. "Howdy, folks. What can I do for you?"

"We've come to pick up some things for the Triple-T Ranch," Birdie told him. She reached inside her coat pocket and produced the list Slop had told Muriel to write for him. "Lem Jenkins said you could just put it on Mr. Murphy's account."

Homer studied the note carefully, especially Muri-l's signature. He had seen her name on lists before, ʙut he had never seen either of the two standing at the ounter this day. "You folks must be new at the Triple-T," ʜe said.

"That's a fact," Dooley answered. "Me and Birdie ʌin't ever been in your store before."

"How's Mike gettin' along these days?" Homer asked ʌs he pulled a flour sack from beneath the counter.

"Well, we hope he's doin' just fine," Dooley replied, ʹsince he's been dead for a couple of months now, but I ɘxpect you already knew that."

"Yes, I knew," Homer sputtered. "No offense meant, ɪt's just that—"

"None taken," Dooley interrupted. "You don't know ᴜs from President . . ." He paused, trying to remember.

"Hayes," Birdie prompted with an impatient shake ɔf her head.

"Dog bite it," Dooley snorted. "I can't never get that ʄeller's name in my head."

Homer had to laugh. "I reckon you folks are getting ᴛhis list for the Triple-T, all right. I won't have no molas-ses for a couple of days."

"You wouldn't happen to be in the business of ʙuyin' guns, would you?" Dooley asked then. "I've got ᴛwo fine Winchester rifles in the wagon that I'd like to ʂell."

"Tell you the truth," Homer said, "this is a bad time to be trying to sell 'em. Right now there ain't that many folks around looking for rifles. Now, it'd be a different story come spring and summer."

"I ain't lookin' for much," Dooley said, the disap-pointment evident in his tone. "Maybe just enough to buy a little whiskey and some new britches. These is gettin' wore down till they're a mite breezy."

Always interested in a bargain, Homer said he'd take a look at the weapons. So the three of them grabbed some sacks of supplies and went out to the wagon. While Birdie went back in for a second trip, Homer and Dooley looked at the Winchesters. "They're in fine shape," Dooley commented while Homer checked the action of one of them.

"If I had to guess, I'd say you came by these in that little war Triple-T had with Roman-Three," Homer said.

"Maybe," Dooley said.

Homer took a cautious look up and down the street to make sure no one was watching. "Tell you what. Let's bring these inside and I'll see if we can strike a deal. I know I can fix you up with a pair of new britches, maybe trade for some other things and a little cash money." He took another look up toward the Crystal Palace, where there were three horses tied to the hitching rail. "You might wanna get all your stuff loaded and get on out of town, 'cause there's three of Harlan Striker's boys up at the saloon now. It wouldn't do for them to get a look at these rifles. I don't see anything on 'em that would identify 'em, but they might get an idea where you got the rifles if they know you're from the Triple-T. And I'd hate to see you folks get into any trouble." He didn't mention it, but he didn't think Striker's men would look kindly on him for trading for the rifles, but it was too good a deal to pass up.

This was not good news to Birdie and Dooley. It was especially disappointing to Dooley because the main reason he volunteered to accompany Birdie was that

ıe wanted to have a couple of drinks of whiskey. The
Crystal Palace was the only saloon in town that remained
ɔpen during the winter, and the possibility that he
couldn't get the whiskey he desired only made him
want it more. "Dang," he muttered, "I've had my mouth
set for a shot of whiskey for quite a spell now."

"Well, it doesn't sound like a good idea to get one
ıow," Birdie advised.

The craving for strong spirits took hold in Dooley's
mind, and he started reasoning with himself, down-
ɔlaying the potential hazard of a quick couple of shots.
'Hell," he suggested, "them fellers don't know me
from President What's-his-name. All that shootin' and
killin' that went on happened in the dark. They ain't
gonna know me any more than I'd know them."

"What if it's one of those three that jumped us when
we got here that first night?" Birdie asked, aware that
Dooley was letting alcohol do the thinking. "They saw
us, all three of us, you, Cord, and me—came right up
to that gully we were camped in."

"Well, yeah . . . " Dooley hesitated. "Maybe they
did. But, hell, we shot two of them jaspers, and the
other'n mighta been one of 'em that got shot in the fight
with the cattle."

It was plain to see that Dooley's desire for a drink
had grown into a genuine necessity, and Birdie was
convinced it was due to the fact that it was denied him.
"Why don't I just go in the saloon and buy you a bottle?" she suggested. "They might not remember me,
since I was scrunched down in the head of that gully."

"No, I don't want you to do that," Dooley said
emphatically, realizing that he was making noises like
some liquor-craving drunk. "I ain't sendin' you in no

damn saloon." Growing more and more angry with himself and reluctant to turn tail and run to avoid contact with riders from the Roman-3, he decided a couple of shots of rye were all he had wanted right from the beginning, and he would get them if he wanted. "You put the rest of that stuff in the wagon," he said. "I'm gonna walk up to the saloon and get me a drink of whiskey, and I'll be back in fifteen minutes." That said, he didn't allow time for further discussion, turning at once and striding purposefully toward the Crystal Palace, leaving Birdie to shake her head in frustration.

Mace Tarpley, Sam Plummer, and Tom Tyler sat at a back table, working on a bottle of rye whiskey and whiling away a couple of hours before starting back to the Roman-3. Striker had sent them into town to meet the noon train. But the train had come and gone with no sign of the hired killer from Cheyenne. There was a telegram, however, that told them that Strong would be on tomorrow's train instead of today's. "Striker ain't gonna like this," Sam said for at least the third time since the train left Ogallala.

"There ain't nothin' he can do about it," Mace said. "The man wired him and said some unfinished business set him back a day. Ain't no skin off our backs. Just means we get to come to town again. Beats doin' chores back at the ranch." He picked up the bottle and poured himself another shot, then held the bottle suspended for a few moments when something caught his attention. "Well, I'll be damned. . . ." His voice trailed off as he tried to recall having seen the man who just came in the door and walked up to the bar. "You ever see that man before?" Neither Sam nor Tom had. "I have," Mace continued. "I can't say for sure whether it was in some other town or someplace, but I know damn well I've seen him before, and I'm thinkin' it mighta been with some of that Triple-T outfit. I aim to find out."

"What'll it be, partner?" Clyde Perkins greeted Dooley when he approached the bar.

"I'll just have a drink or two of some rye if you've got it," Dooley said.

Clyde turned to select a bottle from the shelf behind him and poured the drink. "Ain't seen you in town before. Just passin' through?"

"Yeah, that's right," Dooley replied, tossed his drink back, and set the empty glass on the counter. With a slight flick of his hand, he indicated a refill, his throat having been rendered too hoarse to speak by the scalding liquid. "Whew!" He exhaled and reached for his glass, suddenly aware of the three men who had now walked up behind him.

"I think I smell a stink like the Triple-T," Mace said. "What about it, boys? You smell that stink?"

"I do, now that you mention it," Sam said, moving up to the bar on one side of Dooley, while Tom moved up on the other.

"How 'bout it, mister," Mace asked, "you ridin' for the Triple-T?"

Painfully aware that his stubborn desire for a drink had resulted in placing his behind in imminent danger, Dooley continued to face the bar. After a few moments when he could think of no way to extricate himself from the situation he had gotten himself into, he answered, "Triple-T? Don't believe I'm familiar with that outfit. You got me mixed up with somebody else. I'm just passin' through on my way to Cheyenne."

Mace's brain was working fast, putting scraps of memory together, and it came to him then. "Mister, you're a damn liar. The last time I heard you talk, you was aimin' a rifle at my back and tellin' me you was gonna shoot me."

"Nah, that couldn'ta been me," Dooley maintained. "I never been through here before. I'll just finish my drink and be on my way."

"Like hell you will," Mace said, and grabbed the back of Dooley's collar.

Knowing there was very little chance he would survive the confrontation, Dooley spent only a split second to rue his foolish decision before acting. One hand picked up the shot glass full of whiskey. With the other, he grabbed the nearly full whiskey bottle and in one swift move, he turned to splash the whiskey in Mace's face and landed a blow to the side of Tom's head with the bottle. The bottle bounced off Tom's skull unbroken, sending him to his knees. Dooley turned as quickly as he could to swing the bottle at Sam, now behind him, but Sam stepped back out of reach, drawing his pistol as he did. With no option but to charge, Dooley did so in a desperate attempt to save his life. As he closed with him, Sam pulled the trigger, doubling Dooley over and dropping him to the floor.

Frantic, Mace grabbed Clyde's bar rag and tried to wipe the burning alcohol out of his eyes. Furious, he drew his handgun and put another bullet in Dooley's back while the wounded man lay helpless on the floor. Then he quickly turned to Clyde, who had backed away from the bar in fright. "You saw it," Mace bellowed. "The son of a bitch attacked us. We didn't have no choice." Clyde showed no sign of protest. "So you just remember the way it was. You saw him try to kill me and Tom." He glanced at the man holding his head and struggling to get up off his knees. "Come on, Tom. We're done here. Ain't nobody to blame. The bastard tried to kill us and got hisself kilt instead." They walked out of the saloon, climbed on their horses, and left town, leaving the bartender to stand staring down at the still body of Bill Dooley.

Down the street, where Birdie was inside the store waiting, they heard the two gunshots. Immediately alarmed, she ran outside, looking toward the saloon, Homer Tisdale right behind her. Knowing the shooting had to involve Dooley, she started up the street, running. When halfway there, she saw the three Roman-3 riders hurrying from the saloon to jump in the saddle and hightail it out the end of the short street. She was not close enough to shoot with accuracy with the pistol she wore, even if she was sure who fired the shots and whether or not Dooley was the target.

Bursting through the door left open by the three riders, Birdie discovered Clyde Perkins still standing over Dooley, staring down as if deciding what he should do about him. "Dooley!" Birdie exclaimed, and ran to him. "Is he alive?" she demanded of Clyde.

"I don't know," he answered. "I don't reckon. He ain't moved."

"Go get the sheriff!" Birdie ordered. "They're getting away!"

"Sheriff Gillan ain't here," Clyde told her. "He's gone huntin'—said he'd be gone till tomorrow."

"Damn!" Birdie swore, frustrated. "What good is he if he's not around when you need him?"

"There ain't much call for him to do much sheriffin'

this time of year," Clyde answered. He didn't bother to tell her that Barney Gillan had not been on the job for very long, anyway.

Birdie bent down over Dooley, calling his name over and over, but there was no response from the still figure. Rolling him over on his back, she pulled his coat open and unbuttoned his shirt, which was already soaking in blood. She put her ear down on his chest and listened. After a long moment, she exclaimed, "He's alive! I hear his heart beating." She looked up at Clyde then. "He needs a doctor. Somebody needs to go get the doctor."

Clyde just shook his head sadly. "There ain't no doctor here, either, miss, not in the winter. Everette Hodge will be back in the spring, but he ain't no real doctor. He's a barber, but he can do a little doctorin' and pull teeth."

"Well, I don't believe Dooley can wait that long," Birdie said, making no effort to hide her irritation. "Isn't there anyone here who can help him?"

"I'm sorry, miss," Homer Tisdale answered as he came in to see what had happened. "There ain't much anybody here now can do for him. He looks pretty far gone, anyway. There ain't much a doctor could do for him from the look of it. You might just as well let him pass on away."

"The hell I will," Birdie retorted. "I'm taking him home. Somebody there will know how to help him." She could think of nothing else to do for him. "I'll bring the wagon up here and you two can help me get him in the back." She quickly got to her feet and ran toward the door, not waiting for their response.

She was back in a short time with the wagon, and

Clyde and Homer picked Dooley up and placed him in the bed. "Don't die on me, Dooley," she ordered as she spread a horse blanket over him that Clyde got from his back room. With still no sign from Dooley to indicate he was alive or dead, she climbed up on the wagon seat and started her horses back the way she had come.

It was well after dark when Birdie drove the wagon into the barnyard of the Triple-T and pulled right up to the bunkhouse door. Ignoring the usual practice of no women in the bunkhouse, she jumped down from the wagon and burst through the door. "I need help!" she exclaimed. "Dooley's been shot!"

The response was immediate, as every man responded to her call, even Link and Blackie, who were lying on their beds in nothing but their long underwear. They gathered around the wounded man in the wagon bed, who was lying still and now half frozen from the long ride back from town. Last to come out was Slop, carrying a lantern, and those gathered around Dooley made way for him. The doleful cook stepped up to the side of the wagon and, holding his lantern close over Dooley, took a long, intense look at the wounds, before issuing instructions. "Couple of you boys slide him off the wagon and carry him in and lay him on his bed." He held the lantern up a little higher, so they could see, and watched the process. "Take it easy," he cautioned. "He ain't no sack of corn. Couple of you other fellers unload them supplies and pile 'em in the pantry." They followed his orders without hesitation. When it came to most minor wounds and injuries among the men, Slop was the doctor. The more serious cases usually wound up under Muriel Duffy's care. After his first look at Dooley, however, he was not confident that he would be able to do anything for him. Dooley was gut-shot. Slop could probe for the bullet in Dooley's back, and sew the wound up, if need be, but the gut wound was beyond his expertise. "Somebody better go get Mrs. Duffy," he said.

While Cord and Stony carried the wounded man inside, Lem asked Birdie what had happened. Worrying over Dooley as they carried him in, she tried to tell Lem and the others how he happened to get into it with three men from the Roman-3. "I wasn't there to see it," she explained frantically, "but the bartender said they jumped him when he was minding his own business. All he wanted was a drink of whiskey, and then we were going to head back here."

"Did you see the three riders?" Cord asked.

"I didn't get there in time to see their faces," Birdie replied. "But the bartender said they rode for Harlan Striker. He said he heard one of them call the one that shot him in the stomach Sam."

"Sam," Cord repeated, staggered mentally for the moment, angered by the violent attack upon his friend, but not sure what he could do to punish those responsible—but punish them he must. Looking down at Dooley, he felt helpless. Desperate to do something to save his friend's life, he didn't know what to do to help him right now. Dooley looked near death, his eyes closed and not a sound from his lips, as Cord and Stony laid him on his bed as gently as they could.

Watching Cord's reaction closely, Birdie placed her hand on his arm. "I know what you're thinking, and you need to hold off a little before you do anything.

Right now let's see about doing what we can for Dooley. All right?"

Cord paused to think about what she had said, then nodded to her when he realized she was right. "Whaddaya think, Slop?" he then asked anxiously. "Can you do something for him?"

"Let's get his shirt off," Slop said, "so I can get a better look at him." Cord helped him peel the shirt away, exposing the ugly hole in Dooley's abdomen. There was blood coming from the bullet hole, but not as much as one would expect from a wound in that location. Much of the initial bleeding had been slowed by the cold ride from town in the wagon. "I ain't got no way of knowin' what that bullet's done to his insides," Slop said. "I know I can't do nothin' for it. We'll see what Mrs. Duffy says." He looked up at the concerned faces gathered around and shook his head, then continued. "I'll do what I can with the shot in his back, but I reckon we'll just have to wait and see what happens after that." He rolled Dooley on his side to look at the wound.

"He's got two wounds in his back," Blackie blurted, pointing to a second hole lower down near his side. It had not been apparent before Dooley's shirt had been removed. "They shot him twice in the back."

While it would have come to the others after a few minutes, Birdie realized it right away. "No, they didn't," she exclaimed. "That's where they shot him in the stomach. The bullet went straight through him and came out the back."

"That's a good thing, ain't it, Slop?" Stony asked.

"Maybe," Slop allowed, "hard to say. Leastways,

won't do no good to go diggin' around in his gut—do
more harm than good."

"Well, we oughta do something," Birdie said as
Eileen and her mother came in the door, just having
been informed what was going on in the bunkhouse.

"We will," Muriel said. "How bad is it?" When Birdie
told her what had happened, and that the question now
was how to treat Dooley's wounds, she offered her
opinion. "I think you're right to leave the stomach
wound alone. He's not bleeding from the mouth, is he?
Maybe he was lucky, and the bullet went on through
without hitting any of his organs."

"Has he showed any signs of coming to?" Eileen
asked.

"Ain't nobody give me a chance." The feeble response
came from the patient, startling all those hovering
over him.

"Dooley!" Birdie exclaimed. "You're alive!"

"Well, I reckon," he rasped weakly, grimacing now
with the pain he had just become aware of, "but I wasn't
sure for a long time when I heard you folks talkin' 'bout
what to do with me."

"Thank goodness you woke up," Birdie said. "I was
afraid you were dead."

"Me, too," Dooley answered, barely above a whisper. "But when you folks didn't start talkin' 'bout diggin' a grave, I started feelin' better."

"Can you drink some water?" Slop asked, and drew
an immediate reaction from several of the observers.

"Slop, you oughta know better'n to give a man water
that's been gut-shot." Blackie spoke for the crew.

"That's what they say," Slop replied. "But if he takes
a drink and it don't hurt him, then we'll know he ain't

really gut-shot, just lucky as hell. Then we'll just have to wait and see what happens when he goes to the outhouse, and see if everythin' else is workin'. He might make it all right if that bullet that went through him didn't cause his insides to fester. We'll just watch him awhile before we go to gettin' the shovels out. Don't you think so, Mrs. Duffy?"

"Cord," Dooley rasped, and his young friend bent low to hear him. "I'm hurtin' like hell. I wanna go back to sleep. Don't let 'em stick me in the ground without you makin' sure I'm dead."

"Don't worry, partner," Cord assured him. "I won't. Go ahead and go to sleep if you can. Mrs. Duffy will help you get well." Dooley's talking indicated a positive sign to Cord. The wiry old outlaw was tough enough to pull through as long as his insides weren't torn up. And it looked as though Slop was right when he said there was nothing they could do for him but wait to see if he came through on his own. A doctor could probably do no better. He would have told Dooley as much, but he had already gone back to sleep by then. Muriel and Slop talked about digging the bullet out of Dooley's back, and decided it could wait until they knew for sure the stomach wound wasn't going to kill him.

With Dooley asleep, Muriel decided it best to leave him where he was, and the Triple-T settled in for the night once again. The women returned to the house, and Cord drove the wagon down to the barn and unhitched the horses. There were a lot of thoughts running through his mind as he put the harness away—the question of what retaliation he should take out on the men who shot Dooley. There had been no

contact with any of the crew at Roman-3 since the deci-
sive battle at Blue Creek. Right at this particular time,
Triple-T seemed to control the activity over all the
range they formerly grazed. He felt strongly that Dooley
should be avenged, but if he set out to do so, would he
be dragging the Triple-T back into another range war,
where more of the crew would be killed? These were
the things that were troubling his mind when Lem
found him.

"I was wonderin' why it was takin' you so long to
take care of the horses," Lem said.

Cord shrugged. "I wasn't in any particular hurry,"
he said.

"Helluva thing about Dooley," Lem remarked.

"Yep, bad luck, all right," Cord replied. He knew
Lem well enough to know he didn't really concern
himself with how long Cord took to unhitch the horses.
"What's on your mind?"

"Well, I reckon I really wanna know what's on *your*
mind," Lem answered. "I know you and Dooley are
pretty close partners, and I was afraid you were down
here saddlin' up to go lookin' for some revenge for
what they done to him." He didn't mention the conversation he had had with Birdie and her concerns that he
was on the verge of setting out for the Roman-3. "I
don't blame you none for thinkin' that way," Lem continued. "And I say, hell, I'll help you. I'm sure the rest
of the boys feel the same way, and if you set out for the
Roman-Three, it wouldn't be just me followin' you.
Some of the others, Stony and Blackie for sure, would
be right behind. What I'm hopin' you'll understand is
that it wouldn't be a good thing to do right now. We
ain't got enough men to take care of the cattle as it is,

and now we've lost another one if Dooley don't pull through. If we get some more of us killed off, what's gonna happen to Mr. Murphy's cattle—the women up at the house—all of us? We'll have Triple-T cattle scattered all over the high plains."

These were questions that Cord had already been struggling with in his mind. His initial impulse had been to saddle up, load up his Winchester, and ride into the Roman-3, shooting everyone he saw. He knew that would be the wrong thing to do, just as Lem was now trying to tell him, but it was his natural inclination. In view of that, he decided that he would agree to do as Lem requested for the time being, but he would exact the vengeance demanded from the ones responsible for trying to kill Dooley. He considered it his debt alone, however, and would make sure none of the other men were involved. "I see what you're sayin'," he told Lem. "Don't worry. I ain't gonna go off half-cocked."

Chapter 14

The eastbound Union Pacific train pulled into Ogallala shortly after noon. Robert Marsh and Tom Tyler got up from the bench at the station, where they had been lolling around, waiting to meet the special passenger scheduled to arrive. Striker had ordered Marsh and Tyler to meet the train instead of sending Mace and Sam Plummer again, thinking it best to keep the two involved in the shooting at the Crystal Palace out of Ogallala for a while. He had prepared his men to expect retaliation from the Triple-T, but the attack never came. After a couple of days had passed with nothing from the Triple-T, Striker came to believe that the fight might have died in Murphy's men, and the possibility of overrunning their range might not be lost after all. That possibility looked even stronger if Murphy's hired gun was eliminated. After Strong did the job he was contracted to do, there should be little opposition left to impede Striker's plans to build a cattle dynasty to rival that of the Boslers. Then there would be time to make efforts to make his peace with the people of Ogallala.

Out of habit, the dark, brooding man inside the passenger car did not get up from his seat as soon as the train stopped in the station, taking a moment to take in the scene outside his window. There were no other passengers getting off in Ogallala, so the two men he saw standing by the track had to be his reception committee from the Roman-3. He took another moment to make sure they did not appear to be lawmen instead. Satisfied, he got up then and proceeded to the door. A big man, he seemed to fill the steps down from the passenger car, and he dwarfed the conductor waiting for him to detrain.

"Damn," Tyler swore. "The son of a bitch is big enough, ain't he?"

"I reckon," Marsh agreed as they waited while the ominous-looking man said something to the conductor before approaching him.

"Strong?" Tyler asked when the conductor left him and walked toward a cattle car farther back in the train.

"You from the Roman-Three?" Strong responded.

"That's right," Tyler replied. "I'm Tom Tyler. This is Robert Marsh." He waited for Strong to introduce himself, but there was no sign of interest from the imposing man, indicating that he cared not at all who they were.

Saying nothing more, Strong turned to follow the conductor. Tyler and Marsh exchanged puzzled glances, but saw no choice but to follow him. On a signal from the conductor, the engineer pulled the train a few feet forward to line the cattle car up with a stock ramp.

When the door was opened, Strong walked up the ramp into the car. Moments later, he led a dappled gray horse down from the car and climbed in the saddle. "Let's go," he said, sending the two men running for their horses.

The only words exchanged during the three-hour ride to the Roman-3 were "How far?" from Strong—and the answer, "'Bout three hours," from Marsh. The baneful stoic astride the dingy gray horse positioned himself so as not to have his back toward either man as they rode a worn trail across the plains. By the time they reached the ranch, Marsh and Tyler were halfway convinced that they were escorting a man less than human, simply by his demeanor.

Striker walked out to meet them, less intimidated by a man he paid to do a job. "Well, I see you finally decided to show up," he said.

"I showed up when I said I would," Strong replied. "Where can I find this gunman you want killed?"

"I know where you can find him," Striker responded, "but I don't think it would be a good idea to go ridin' into their ranch lookin' for him. You'd most likely get shot on sight. Besides, I don't want this killin' to look like a planned assassination. I plan to build this ranch after Triple-T goes under, so I don't want the town of Ogallala against me. I'd druther you make this a gunfight just between the two of you, so nobody thinks I ordered it done."

"I ain't plannin' to set around on a damn rock somewhere waitin' for the son of a bitch to ride past me. Sounds to me like the best way to get at him is in town. He goes to town sometimes, don't he?"

Striker shrugged. "Hell, I don't know—like anybody else, I reckon."

"Well, I'd rather bide my time in town. He's bound to show up before too long, and when he does, him and me will have a little problem, and we'll settle it in the street." Striker looked undecided, so Strong continued. "That way, ain't nobody got any complaint, even if the sheriff's in town. He drew on me, so I killed him."

Striker still wasn't sure. He finally gave in. "I reckon you know your business." When he thought about it, what Strong said might, in fact, be the better plan. If Strong provoked the man into a gunfight in town, there would be no reason to think Striker had anything to do with it, and no reason for the Triple-T to retaliate against the Roman-3.

"Damn right I do," Strong said. He had already decided he'd rather spend his time waiting in town where there was a hotel and a saloon to pass his time comfortably. "Now, what's this feller's name and what does he look like?"

"We don't know his name," Striker replied, "and I ain't ever seen him." Strong jerked his head back, impatient with Striker's reply, but before he had time to make the caustic remark he was thinking, Striker turned to Tyler. "Go get Mace." Back to Strong, he said, "I'll let the man who *has* seen him tell you."

"He's comin' now, Mr. Striker," Tyler said, and gestured toward the barn when he saw Mace already striding their way.

Mace could not mistake the look of contempt that Strong bestowed upon him as he joined them. He tried to convey an attitude of indifference to the assassin

Striker had seen fit to hire. "Well, I see your high-priced gunman finally got here," he slurred to his boss. "I coulda saved you a lot of money if you'd just gave me the word."

"Is that a fact?" Strong retorted. "Maybe we can settle that right now." His hand dropped to the handle of the .44 Colt he wore. Mace stiffened, surprised by the immediate challenge to his bluster.

"Just hold it right there," Striker ordered. "I didn't pay all that money just so you two can kill each other. Damn it, I ain't got enough men now."

"Whatever you say, Mr. Striker. You're the boss," Mace was quick to reply, thankful that Striker stepped in. He had no honest desire to face off against a man that looked like the devil's agent. Strong only smiled at him, already thinking about another killing after he was done with the one he was being paid to do.

"Tell him who he's looking for," Striker ordered.

"Yes, sir," Mace replied. "Tall feller, almost as tall as you, maybe not as big, hard to tell with that heavy coat he was wearin' when I saw him. But ain't no mistakin' his face, 'cause he's got a scar across his forehead above his left eye, runnin' across, all the way up in his hair. Wears a flat-crown hat, pretty much like the one Tyler there is wearin'. You won't have no problem knowin' him."

Strong nodded, satisfied. "Then I reckon I'll ride back into town and wait for him to show up," he said to Striker. "Soon as he does, you'll need to have the rest of my money ready, 'cause I won't be hangin' around after I'm done."

Striker couldn't help the feeling that he might have acted too quickly when he contracted with the sullen man, but he felt he was too heavily invested in him to change his mind now. "I hope to hell I ain't made a mistake," he said. "Hell, that son of a bitch might not come into town before spring. How the hell do we know? If you hang around that damn saloon all winter, you're gonna have to pay for it yourself. You ain't gettin' another cent outta me till he's dead."

Strong showed no concern over his remark. "He'll show up. I'd bet on it. I've seen a hundred like him. They all show up in the saloon sooner or later to brag about how many men they've gunned down. That's how they get a reputation and have people like you pay 'em to do the killin' for 'em. If I'm wrong, and he doesn't come into town before long, then I'll do it the other way. Ride out to the Triple-T and kill him. One way or another, you'll get what you're payin' for."

That seemed to placate Striker's doubts for the moment, and when Strong told him he would start back to Ogallala right away, he called for Rena to fix the assassin some food to take with him. "It'll be a little late to get supper by the time you get there," Striker said.

Dooley surprised them all, including himself, when he began to pull through by the morning of his second day after his frosty ride in the back of the wagon. Muriel and Slop were amazed that he felt well enough to take a little food, and was able to hold it down. There was no sign of blood other than a little still seeping from the wounds. Lem pronounced it a miracle. "I ain't never seen anybody get gut-shot before that didn't cough up all kinds of bloody mess. You must have somebody lookin' out after you, for a fact." He gestured toward the ceiling.

Dooley managed a weak grin for the folks hovering over him. "I reckon it's because of my saintly ways and the good life I've always led," he murmured.

Stony, Muriel, and Eileen laughed at his remark. "I believe you must have led an honest life, all right, for those bullets to have missed anything fatal," Muriel said. Only Cord and Birdie realized the irony of Dooley's comment, knowing the man had lived outside the law for a good part of his life. There was enough good in the man, Cord figured, that the good Lord saw fit to give him a little more time.

"Well, I ain't got time to stand around this bunkhouse and watch you women make a fuss over Dooley," Stony announced. "Slop said he ain't gonna cook no more if I don't go into town and get that molasses and cornmeal he needs." He turned to Cord. "How 'bout it, partner? You wanna go along? I might need some help with those barrels."

"I reckon so," Cord said. "I was fixin' to ride over to the lower range to see if I could pick up any strays that mighta wandered off toward those buttes again, but I reckon Blackie and Link don't need my help. Let me pull the saddle off my horse and turn him in the corral. I'll meet you by the barn."

He walked outside, pulling his coat collar up around his neck when the chilled air of the morning met him in the face. He heard the bunkhouse door open and close behind him. Thinking it was Stony, heading for the wagon, he didn't bother to turn to see. "It won't be so bad a day when that sun gets up a little higher, so maybe we won't freeze our behinds off."

"No clouds to amount to much," a feminine voice replied.

Surprised, he looked around then to discover Eileen following him. "I thought that was Stony behind me," he said, clearly embarrassed.

"I guessed as much," she said. "But I wouldn't want you and Stony to come back without your behinds." He started to apologize, but she stopped him. "Don't let it worry you." She caught up to him and walked with him to the barn, where he had left his horse with the reins looped over a rail of the corral.

"Somethin' I can help you with?" he asked.

"Nope, I just wanted to talk to you without everyone else around, that's all."

"Oh? If it's about that kiss in the barn that night, I reckon I owe you an apology." He got no further than that before she interrupted.

"Well, maybe it is about that kiss a little bit," she said. "But first, I want to know what your plans are as far as the Triple-T is concerned. Now that Dooley's been shot, are you planning to ride off after the men who shot him? Or are you going again in search of whatever that big important mission is you think you have to do? And I want to know about that kiss, too. What did you kiss me for? Did you think I was like one of those whores that work in the saloon in town—that you can just have your way with, and no commitment at all?"

"Why, no, ma'am," he sputtered, completely disarmed by the unexpected verbal assault. "I don't think you're like any of those women. I'm sorry if I—"

"Then why did you kiss me?" she interrupted.

"I don't know," he replied, unable to give her any plausible reason. "I just wanted to, I reckon."

"You just wanted to," she echoed, continuing to

scold him as if questioning an irresponsible child. "So you're trying to tell me you have feelings for me?"

"I guess so, maybe," he answered honestly.

"Well, let me tell you, Cord Malone, I would never allow a man to court me unless he had decided he was going to settle down in one place, and not go riding off to chase after some chore he can't even talk about."

Her blunt statement caught him completely by surprise. Courting Eileen Duffy was something he had never given thought to. Dumbfounded, he opened his mouth to speak, but nothing came out. Words failed him. Even his thoughts were tangled in a web of uncertainty, for he didn't know what his proper response should be. Deep down, he knew that she occupied a special place in his heart. But it had always been a fantasy place, like a fairy tale that had no connection to reality. It was too complicated for him to understand, but one thing he had assumed from the beginning was that she was much too good for someone of his station in life—a twenty-five-dollar-a-month cowpoke. And her almost abrasive attitude toward him had seemed to confirm that impression. She stood now, hands on hips, apparently waiting for him to say something.

After a long moment while he was trying to decide what he could say to her, he finally responded, "Are you sayin' you wouldn't be insulted if I was to ask you if I could court you?"

"I'm more likely to be insulted if you didn't," she shot back. "Are you asking?"

"I'm askin'," he said at once, still in a minor state of shock to find himself in this unlikely conversation, and still uncertain about the possibility.

"What about this secret mission you set off on

before?" she asked then. "Are you done with that, or are you going to ride off to who knows where again?"

Soaring moments before, he was abruptly dashed to earth again by the reminder of his solemn vow. He had taken an oath to avenge his mother's murder, and he knew he could not forsake that vow. As much as he was astonished by Eileen's frank confession, he could not stay here and let Levi Creed ride free, unaccountable for his evil sins. "I don't have a choice," he tried to explain. "There's a man I've got to find. I've got to settle somethin' with him before I can do anythin' else."

She shook her head impatiently and said, "Then the answer is no, you are not welcome to call on me. I've no intention to play second fiddle to some secret thing you think more important than me." She turned on her heel then and headed toward the house, leaving a mesmerized young man to wonder what had just happened. She allowed to herself that she might have been far too abrupt. But it was imperative to her to know that nothing would be more important to him than she, because she intended to give that devotion to him in return.

"What's ailin' you? I thought you was gonna turn your horse out in the corral, and you ain't even took the saddle off yet."

Cord was only then aware of the wagon pulling up behind him and Stony in the seat.

"What did you say to Eileen?" Stony went on. "She took off for the house like a scared antelope—just cold, I reckon."

"I reckon," Cord said, after a long moment. "I won't be but a minute." He pulled his saddle off the bay and turned the horse out. Then he headed for the barn to put his saddle away, wondering if the preceding moments with Eileen had been a dream, and wishing it was so. He was struck with the realization that he might have destroyed the one chance of happiness he was likely to have. It left him with an overbearing feeling of indecision, for he was not sure where his heart lay. He was not confident that he would know if he was in love or not; he frankly didn't understand the term. All he knew for sure was that he was suddenly staggered by the awareness of a deep longing to be with someone, a mate to share his life with. Was Eileen that woman—the self-confident girl who had seemed to distance herself from him before? He shook his head, trying to shake the melancholy thoughts from his brain. *It's over and done now,* he thought, resigning himself to what might possibly have been the biggest mistake of his young life. "I'm comin'," he called out when he heard Stony yell for him to hurry up.

He was bad news. Flo knew that from the moment he walked into the saloon and pounded on the bar for a drink. A huge brute of a man, who looked to need a bath more than a drink, he looked around him at the nearly empty room, confident that it was his for the taking. Intimidation was his specialty, and he wasted no time in applying it. "Gimme a bottle of whiskey," he told Clyde Perkins, and continued to look the saloon over while Clyde got a bottle of whiskey from under the counter. His eye paused, then fixed on the large woman standing by a table talking to Ralph McConnell, the telegraph operator at the train depot. Flo swore she could feel his gaze settle upon her before she turned to look at him.

"You can have that one," Betty Lou whispered. Seated at the table, facing the bar, she had seen the stranger walk in. "You're big enough to handle him. I'm afraid he'd kill me."

"I'm more your size, ain't I, darlin'?" Ralph asked playfully.

"You sure are, sweetie," Betty Lou responded in kind. Ralph was like most of the few men who wintered in Ogallala. He liked to talk and steal a touch of skin whenever he could, but was tight when it came to laying some money down. She and Flo realized that they had made a poor choice when they changed their minds about leaving for the winter. They had been all set to go to Cheyenne, but decided they might make out all right if they stayed after they found out that none of the other girls were staying. They hadn't counted on the men in town being so reluctant to part with their money. If it were not for the occasional trips for supplies from the ranchers, the two prostitutes would have been hard-pressed to survive.

"He doesn't look like he's housebroke, does he?" Flo commented.

Ralph turned to see who they were referring to. "Hell, he don't even look saddle-broke," he remarked. "He's the feller who got off the train from Cheyenne yesterday. A couple of Roman-Three boys met him."

"Look out, Flo," Betty Lou warned with a giggle. "He's headed this way and he's got his eye on you."

"Looks to me like there ain't no need for one man to have two women," Strong declared when he walked up to the table. "I'll take one of 'em off your hands. That's all right with you, ain't it, partner?" He fixed Ralph with a maleficent stare that served as a challenge.

"Yes, sir," Ralph quickly replied. "Take your pick."

"I was goin' to." Strong smirked. He undressed the somewhat skinny Betty Lou with his eyes, then grabbed Flo by the wrist. "What's your name, honey? You come on over here and set with me."

"My name's Flo," she told him. "And take it easy on that wrist. I ain't fixin' to run." With her other hand, she casually felt her hair to make sure her hat pin was in place, in case it became necessary to use it.

He led her over to another table before releasing her, placed the bottle of whiskey in the center, then stood over her until she seated herself. "We'll have us a few drinks before we go up to your room to have a little tussle," he said, favoring her with a wicked grin.

"Is that so?" Flo replied. "Well, you'd better have some money, 'cause this business ain't a hobby for me."

"Ha," he snorted. "Is that a fact?" He reached in his coat pocket and came out with a twenty-dollar gold coin. "You think you're talkin' to some shit-kickin' saddle tramp? You'd better be thinkin' how you're gonna earn this money."

Flo's scowl disappeared when she saw the color of the brute's money, replacing it with a honey-dripping smile, for she was certain she had heard the jingle of other coins in the coat pocket. In better times she might have told the crude beast to spend his money somewhere else. But in this slow winter season, she needed the money badly, so she did the best she could to hide her disgust for him. If she could keep him there at the table long enough, maybe there was a chance he would get too drunk to cause her much of a problem when she took him upstairs. She had used that ploy before, but Strong downed shot after shot, without so much as a blink of his eye. After consuming over half of the bottle, he got up from the table, picked up the bottle, and said, "Let's go. I'm drunk enough now that you're startin' to look pretty."

"Well, thank you, kind sir, for the compliment," she replied sarcastically. As she got to her feet, she cast an impatient frown at Betty Lou, who was watching with obvious interest, thinking it not worth any amount of money to subject herself to the rough experience her sister prostitute was bound to endure. Flo was a bigger and stronger woman, however, so she would probably have a better chance of controlling the brute.

Three-quarters of an hour passed, long enough for Betty Lou to become concerned, before Strong appeared at the top of the stairs again—this time alone. He paused there for a moment to tuck his shirttail in and put his coat on before coming downstairs. Betty Lou noticed a scratch on the side of his cheek and was at once alarmed for her friend, who had still not made an appearance. "Where's Flo?" she asked.

"Upstairs," he said, smirking, "cleanin' up, or doin' whatever you whores do when you've finished earnin' your money." Fully distressed then, Betty Lou got up from her chair and started for the stairs. Strong paused to look her over, grinning as he told her, "Maybe I'll have a turn with you next time."

"Not on your life," she responded, causing him to chuckle.

"Sassy little bitch, ain't she, partner?" Strong said to Ralph. "They're all like that."

"If you say so," Ralph replied, hoping to avoid saying anything that the huge man might take the wrong

way. He remained seated, relaxing only after Strong
had walked out of the saloon. Then he headed for the
door as well with a "See ya later, Clyde" as he walked
past the bartender.

Upstairs, Betty Lou hurried past a couple of doors to
Flo's room at the end of the hall. She found her friend
on her knees beside the bed, struggling to pull herself
up to sit on the bed. "Flo!" Betty Lou cried out when
she saw Flo's swollen eye and bloody face. "Oh, you
poor baby, are you all right?" She rushed to help her up
on the bed.

"Yeah, I guess so," Flo managed to respond. "The
son of a bitch hit me without so much as a warning. I
reckon he thought he didn't get his money's worth. I
didn't even have time to get to my hat pin, 'cause I didn't
see it coming." She sat still while Betty Lou cleaned
some of the blood from her face. "I guess he knocked
me out, 'cause, I swear, I don't remember anything
after he told me I cheated him till when I found myself
on the floor trying to get up. He's older than he looks.
I think he just can't cut the mustard like he wants to. I
reckon it was part my fault. I shouldn't have said that
maybe he was a gelding."

"We shouldn't have let you take him upstairs," Betty
Lou went on, fretting over their failure to acknowledge
the warning signals. "Here, let me wet a cloth and
clean you up a little better." She shook her head, distressed. "Your eye is gonna swell up something awful.
It looks like it's almost closed already—that low-down
son of a bitch."

"If I'd had my pistol out of the drawer, he'd have
never walked out of here," Flo swore.

"Did he hurt you anywhere else?" Betty Lou asked,

concerned then that Flo might have suffered damage on her body, especially in the parts with which she earned her living.

"No, not much," Flo said. "But if you're asking what it was like, it was about as close as I ever wanna get to wrestling with a horse." She came close to forcing a chuckle, but her split lip made her pause. "He's even got little round spots all over his back like a bunch of scars or something. I ain't sure he's human."

"Well, I'll take care of you," Betty Lou assured her. "I need to go outside and scoop up a handful of snow to put on that eye. Then maybe we oughta go tell the sheriff what happened."

Flo grimaced painfully. "If he ever comes back," she said. "He stays gone most of the winter." As soon as she said it, the realization of the town's problem sank in—Strong could pretty much do whatever he wanted to unless someone shot him.

Chapter 15

Harlan Striker was not in a good mood on this chilly winter morning as he permitted himself to consider the events of the last couple of weeks. The cache of money that he had brought to this valley to commandeer a herd of cattle for himself was rapidly draining away, and he still had no herd. And now he was second-guessing himself over his handling of the situation with Strong. His high-priced gunman was enjoying his leisure in the hotel and saloon in Ogallala, apparently in no hurry to complete the job he was hired to do. Reconsidering now, Striker believed he should have charged Mace with the job of simply waiting in ambush near the Triple-T until he got a shot at Murphy's hired gun. It would have cost him a great deal less money, and the problem might have already been solved by now. He had worried too much about his future relationship with the people of Ogallala. *Well,* he thought, *it might not be too late to fix it.* "Rena!" he yelled.

He had to yell a second time before the belligerent half-breed came into the parlor where he sat drinking coffee. "What you yellin' about?" Rena demanded. "I wash your dirty clothes."

"Go down to the barn and tell Mace I wanna see him."

"I wash clothes," she replied. "Why don't you go? You not doin' nothin'." It was the wrong thing to say, for on this particular morning he was not of a disposition to tolerate her usual insolent attitude.

Infuriated, he glared at her, saying nothing for a full minute. She met his gaze with one of obstinate defiance. He smoldered for a long moment more before uttering the threat "If you don't go down to that barn right now and get Mace, I swear I'll kill you."

She continued to gaze at him, her dark eyes narrow and challenging, but his eyes told her that this time it was no idle threat. Finally she shrugged and said, "I go." Shaking with rage, he watched her go out the door.

Having been told by the dispassionate Indian woman that Striker was in no mood to be kept waiting, Mace dropped the harness he had been in the midst of repairing and hurried up to the house. He found Striker standing out on the porch waiting for him. "You wanna see me, sir?"

"Yeah, I got a job for you, one that oughta be to your liking, and I'm willing to pay you a little extra if you get it done proper."

Mace was anxious to show his total attention as he stepped aside to let Rena pass when she went up the steps to the porch. She favored Striker with a sullen look when she walked past him to the door. "Yes, sir," Mace said. "You can count on me."

Striker continued. "I want you to saddle up and take a little ride over to the Triple-T. I made a mistake hiring Strong to do a job you could have done just as easily. I don't care how it's done, but I wanna get rid of that son of a bitch I brought Strong in here to kill. The only problem I have with Strong is that he's lookin' to enjoy himself on my money for as long as he can. I want him out of the way right now. So if you should happen to get a chance to put a bullet in Murphy's hired gun before Strong does, then I think I'll owe you the money and Strong can go to hell."

"What if I put a bullet in that bastard's back, and Strong starts to bitchin' about it—wantin' you to pay him anyway?" Mace asked. "I might have to put one in his back, too."

"Might at that," Striker replied. "I don't see any problem with that. And if that happens, why, I think I ought to owe you full payment."

The dollar signs began to swirl in Mace's mind when he thought about the possibilities, especially since Striker had placed no restrictions on him as he had with Strong—namely that the killing should appear to be a fair gunfight. He was still reluctant to test his skill against Strong face-to-face, but back-shooting was right up his alley. "Consider the problem took care of," he said. "I'll head out in the mornin'."

"Lem wants me to swing over by the south range to see what kinda shape that grass is in after that last snow," Stony said as he popped the horses' croups with his reins. "Take us a little out of the way, but won't take us but a little bit longer to get to town. So I hope you ain't in a hurry."

"I wondered where the hell you were headin', but I didn't care. I got all day," Cord said, his mind still occupied with his conversation with Eileen. There was another decision waiting for him, and that was when his search for Levi Creed should begin again. There had been no more raiding in days now, but he didn't think he could consider the problem solved. Besides that, there was still the matter of a shortage of cowhands to work the ranch.

Five hundred yards northeast, on a rocky mesa overlooking the main trail, Mace Tarpley lay in wait. Lying flat on his belly where he had scraped out a shallow gully in the light coat of snow, he rested his rifle upon the ground, ready to fire. Having stiffened considerably from the cold, he began to rub his hands together vigorously when he saw the wagon finally leave the barn. At that distance, he could not be sure it was his intended target, but he would soon know, for the trail passed right below his perch. At the closest point, he would have a shot of no more than seventy-five yards. It would be hard to miss at that range.

"What the hell?" he suddenly blurted when the wagon veered off at the ranch house gate and headed straight down the river. "Where the hell are they goin'?" He got up on one knee, straining to see if the wagon was going to change direction to again return to the main trail, but it continued on, following the river. "Son of a bitch!" he swore, undecided what he should do. He was still not sure the man with the scar was one of the men on the wagon. *What if he ain't?* he thought. Looking back at the barn, he saw no sign of anyone else about, and the wagon was getting farther away while he tried to decide what to do. *It's a fifty-fifty chance he's one of the men on the wagon,* he thought, and hustled back down the slope behind him to get to his horse. Even if the hired gun was not one of those on the wagon, it would help square things if he bushwhacked two of Murphy's hands.

The problem facing him at this point was the difficulty in following the wagon without being seen, a problem made tougher by the flat, snowy prairie. Mace figured his best bet was to take a wide circle around to the east, in an effort to get ahead of the slower-moving wagon, and move back to the river bluffs ahead of them. So he whipped his horse into a steady lope away from the back slope of the mesa. He loped recklessly over the stark white prairie until satisfied that he was well ahead of his intended targets. Then he cut back to the river when he came to a line of high bluffs that promised cover and protection. Leaving his horse to paw in the snow for grass on the riverbank, he positioned himself where he could aim his rifle along the line he figured the wagon would probably take.

About a quarter of a mile short of the bluffs where Mace lay in ambush, Stony turned his horses east, away from the river in order to take a look at the part of the range they were planning to move the cattle to. He and Cord agreed that the snow was not too deep on the grass, so they could go ahead as planned. Continuing on, on a more direct line to Ogallala, they rode only a short distance before they crossed the line of tracks left by Mace in his effort to get in front of them. Curious, Stony pulled up and both he and Cord jumped down to take a look.

"Now, who do you suppose left those tracks?" Stony

wondered aloud. "We ain't got nobody workin' out this way. Hell, that's the reason we had to come over here to look things over." He looked back the way the tracks had come, then turned to look where they headed. "Kinda looks like they're running right along beside us. Reckon it's an Injun?"

"Ain't but one horse," Cord said, "and he was movin' pretty fast." He got down to take a close look at a hoof-print that had landed solidly on a frozen patch. "I doubt it's an Injun. He's ridin' a shod horse."

"You reckon it's somebody tailin' us?" Stony asked. "'Cause if it is, what's he doin' over here? If he'd followed our trail, he'da done caught us a ways back."

"Unless he didn't want us to see him tailin' us," Cord said. "And it looks pretty much like he was high-tailin' it like he wanted to get ahead of us." Both men arrived at the logical conclusion.

"Son of a bitch," Stony swore softly. "Somebody's tryin' to get up ahead to bushwhack us, sure as hell." He looked at Cord and gave a shake of his head. "I reckon we figured wrong when we thought Striker was done with the fight. If we hadn't turned off when we did, we mighta drove right into an ambush."

"Looks that way," Cord agreed. "Maybe our luck's holdin' out this mornin'." He took a moment to think it over. "If we're right, then this back-shooter is most likely up ahead somewhere, waitin' for us to show up. After a while, it's gonna dawn on him that we musta turned off, and he's gonna backtrack to see where we went. I figure I'll just wait for him while you drive on in to town."

"What are you talkin' about?" Stony responded. "It's five miles from here to Ogallala and you ain't got no horse. Why don't we both just hold up here and see if he comes after us?"

"'Cause if he sees us waitin' for him, he ain't gonna keep comin'," Cord said. "Best you go on toward town—give him a trail to follow. Then I'll know for sure he's out after us. I'll be better off findin' a place to hide on foot."

"Yeah, but it's five miles to town," Stony repeated.

"I reckon I can walk five miles if I have to." He climbed back onto the wagon. "Let's get goin' now." He pointed to a low ridge about half a mile distant. "I'll jump off by that ridge yonder, and we'll see who's so interested in where we're goin'."

When they approached the ridge, Cord spotted a gully at the foot that appeared to be the perfect spot for what he had in mind. He directed Stony to drive the wagon close by it, then told him to pull up long enough to let him jump off. When Stony began to object to his strategy again, Cord said, "We may have this thing upside down and plumb backward. If that's the right of it, then the worst is I'll have a little walk to town. Now, get goin' before he catches sight of the wagon."

He stood watching Stony drive away for a moment before looking around the spot he had picked for his ambush. Satisfied that he was not likely to be seen by anyone riding a horse, he stepped carefully up to the narrow head of the short gully, trying to leave as few tracks as possible in the light snow. *Nothing to do now but wait*, he thought as he squatted on his heels.

"Where the hell are they?" Mace grumbled. He was sure the wagon should have caught up to him thirty minutes ago, but there was no sign of it for as far as he could see. Knowing they had to have changed direction, he got to his feet and brushed the snow off his clothes. They had either turned around and headed back to the ranch or cut over to head for town. Either way, he had to hurry to catch up to them if he was going to get a shot before they reached town. He hurried down the bluff to get to his horse.

Riding warily back along the riverbank, he kept a sharp eye for the first sign of the wagon until he finally found what he was looking for. "They're headin' for town," he announced aloud as he took only a brief moment to verify it by the tracks where the wagon had turned away from the river. He set off after it immediately, hurrying to overtake the two men, while still keeping a cautious eye ahead to make sure he wasn't seen by them. Knowing the distance from there to town was not that great, he couldn't ignore the sense of urgency to get the job done before reaching the settlement. It barely registered in his mind when he crossed over the tracks he had left before, when he had raced to get ahead of the wagon—such was his desperation to catch his intended victims.

Up ahead, it appeared the trail he followed turned at the foot of a low ridge. With no way of determining how fast he was catching them, he deemed it best to slow to a walk until he could get a look beyond the turn around the base of the ridge. Reining back on his horse, he leaned forward in the saddle in an effort to see what might lie ahead, oblivious of the form that rose silently in the gully just passed. "You lookin' for somebody?" Cord asked.

Shocked, Mace jerked around in the saddle to discover the scar-faced demon standing in the snow with his rifle trained upon him. Terrified, he jerked his pistol from his holster and fired frantically, his shots spraying wildly on either side of the man calmly aiming his rifle and squeezing off the round that knocked him out of the saddle.

Ejecting the spent cartridge, Cord walked cautiously toward the body lying still in the snow. With his rifle aimed at the body, he stood over him, watching for any sign of movement. Cord remembered the face. It was the one who did all the talking when three of Striker's men jumped Dooley, Birdie, and him on the night they arrived on Triple-T range. By all appearances, the man was dead, but Cord discharged his rifle once again to be sure. Then after stripping the body of arms and ammunition, he proceeded to approach Mace's horse in an attempt to calm the nervous animal. Once aboard, he rode the sorrel toward town, where he saw the wagon standing in front of the general store.

"Damn," Stony said when Cord walked into the store. "You walk fast."

"Didn't have to," Cord replied. "I had a horse."

"I wasn't sure, but I thought I heard gunshots when I was still a little ways from town." He didn't express it, but he could have also told him how relieved he was when he turned around just then to see him walk in. "Roman-Three?"

"Yep," Cord answered. "If I ain't wrong, I believe it was Striker's foreman. I reckon he was set on gettin' the two of us."

"He was after us," Stony said. "Then maybe there's some of the rest of his men plannin' to hit the ranch. But, hell, he ain't got no men left but two or three. I reckon it'd be best if we load the wagon and head on back home." He flashed a broad smile and added, "Course we can take a minute or two to have a drink and say hello to Flo. She'd be irritated to find out I was in town and didn't bother to stop by."

"Yeah, I reckon," Cord allowed. "But like you say, we'd best not hang around too long. So why don't you go on over to the saloon and be gettin' your visitin' done while I get Slop's list of supplies? Homer can give me a hand with the barrels." He gave Homer a questioning look.

"Be glad to," Homer immediately replied.

Grinning sheepishly, Stony said, "Well, if you insist." He handed Cord the list and headed for the door.

Clyde Perkins busied himself over a dozen shot glasses in a pan of water, drying each one nervously while keeping a cautious eye on the sullen brute seated at his back corner table. He had hoped the man called Strong would not return to his establishment again after the incident with Flo the other night. But there he was, bold as brass, sitting there as if he owned the town, and Clyde guessed he pretty much did as long as Sheriff Gillan was away. If Ogallala ever needed a full-time deputy, it was on times such as this. He hoped the women had sense enough to stay upstairs until Strong left. He had no sooner given birth to the thought than Betty Lou appeared at the top of the stairs. She happened to glance over toward the bar before starting downstairs and saw Clyde shaking his head in warning. Looking over the barroom then, she saw Strong seated at the corner table, and immediately pulled her foot back from the top step, then hurried back down the hall to alert Flo.

Clyde exhaled a sigh of relief, and looked again at
the unwelcome guest at the back table. Patiently waiting, for he had nothing else to do, Strong drank straight
from the bottle on the table, taking long pulls of the
fiery liquid. In between, he amused himself with a
twenty-dollar gold coin. Propping it up on edge with
one finger, he gave it a thump with the index finger of
his other hand, then watched the coin spin. He figured
the women would show themselves before long, even
though it was still a little shy of noon. He counted on the
sight of that twenty-dollar gold piece to overcome any
hesitation owing to his last visit to the saloon. This
time he had Betty Lou in mind for his amusement.

Clyde turned to stack the clean shot glasses on the
shelf behind him. When he turned back to the bar, he
recoiled, startled to see Flo on her way down the steps.
The look on her face told Clyde that she had murder on
her mind, even as she cocked her head to one side to
see clearly, one eye having swollen shut. Clyde quickly
shifted his gaze back to the corner table. Strong saw
the angry woman also, but seemed amused by the sight
of her obvious rage. He continued to play with the gold
coin until she descended the steps. "You look like you
mighta fell off the bed," he remarked sarcastically,
"and landed right on your face."

"You son of a bitch!" Flo charged, and brought up a
two-shot derringer from the folds of her skirt.

His eyes suddenly wide as saucers, Strong came out
of his chair and pulled the table over to protect himself. The tiny weapon fired twice, ripping two bullet
holes, spaced wide apart, into the table. Furious now,
his initial fright over, he lunged to his feet and charged
toward her. "You just dug your grave, bitch!" She tried

to back away, her face still twisted in defiance, but he was on her too quickly. He grabbed one of her wrists, but she snatched her hat pin from her hair and sank it in the back of his hand, causing him to roar out in pain. In quick retaliation, he slugged her with his fist, driving her to the floor. While she struggled helplessly to regain her senses, he went to her and grabbed her arm, preparing to drag her to her feet.

"Let her go!"

Strong turned to see Stony Watts standing in the doorway, his hand resting on the handle of his Colt .44. Pulling Flo up before him, Strong took a good long look at the man threatening him. He saw no scar that would proclaim him to be the gunman he was here to kill. "Or you'll do what, cowboy?" he spat at Stony. "This ain't none of your affair, so you'd best take yourself outta here while you still can, and go stick your nose in somebody else's business."

"Let her go," Stony repeated.

Strong drew Flo up closer in front of him, using her body as a protective shield. Confident now that Stony would hesitate to chance hitting the woman, he snarled, "You ready to die for this bitch's honor? Well, I'll be glad to accommodate you." He reached down with his free hand and pulled his pistol from his holster, taking his time in the process, enjoying the sudden look of desperation on Stony's face. Stony pulled his Colt, but still hesitated to use it for fear of hitting Flo. "This is the end of the line, cowboy. You shouldn'ta never drawed on me," Strong said as he raised his pistol and took dead aim, failing to notice the gradual returning of awareness in the injured woman. Just then realizing what was about to happen, Flo kicked backward as hard as she could manage, bringing her heel up sharply between Strong's legs just as he squeezed the trigger. The surprised brute recoiled, emitting a painful grunt, as his shot missed his mark, catching Stony in the leg and dropping him to the floor.

Staggered by the kick that caused him to double over in severe pain, Strong released Flo and strained to straighten up again to finish Stony, who was trying to reach the pistol he had dropped when shot. Cursing the woman still at his feet, Strong managed to recover enough to gain control again—only to find himself facing a tall man with a scar across his forehead and a rifle leveled at his belly. "You!" he blurted.

Cord was almost staggered by the confrontation as well. Many years had passed, but the image was close enough to the one carried in his brain to make him certain. "Levi Creed," he pronounced solemnly, causing Creed to hesitate. A long moment followed when the two men stared at each other. Cord became aware of a feeling of numbness throughout his entire body, from his boots to his brain, unaware that he had pulled the trigger until he felt the rifle buck in his hands. Creed grunted when the .44 slug ripped through his insides and he sank slowly to his knees, a look of profound disbelief etched upon his face. Rendered shocked and helpless by the bullet's damage, he was unable to resist when Cord walked up to him, pulled the pistol from his hand, and said, "Lottie Malone sends you her greetings." Still on his knees, Creed attempted to speak, but could not. His wide, staring eyes seemed to be trying to ask a question, but the ribbon of blood that seeped from the corner of his mouth prohibited his ability to talk. Sensing his intent, Cord answered his unspoken question. "Cord Malone," he said, "Ned's son, the one you left for dead when you put this scar on my head." Levi's eyes seemed to open wider still, telling Cord that he remembered. "Good," Cord said, and raised the pistol he had just taken from the dying man. Very deliberately, he pressed the muzzle against Creed's forehead and pulled the trigger. Then he stepped back and placed his foot against the dead man's chest and shoved the corpse over on the floor.

With a sudden need for air, Cord turned and walked out the door into the street. Behind him, he left a barroom rendered totally silent for a few moments until it then erupted with excited voices as Flo and Betty Lou hurried to Stony's side, and Clyde came from behind the bar to look at Levi Creed's corpse. He stood for a long moment, looking at the wide pattern of evil brain matter left upon his floor, unaware of the story it told.

Chapter 16

He suddenly felt exhausted. His neck and shoulders were stiff and sore, a result of the tense moments just past, and he decided he'd better sit down somewhere before his legs refused to support him. *Levi Creed is dead and on his way to hell right now,* he told himself, still finding it difficult to believe. And suddenly he was without direction as to what he was going to do for the rest of his life. He thought about Stony, now under Flo's and Betty Lou's care. He thought about Lem and Blackie and the others. And he thought about Eileen. Unless he was completely loco, she had dangled the possibility of marriage before him. Maybe she was just having him on, taking advantage of his naïveté to amuse herself. Then, unexpectedly, Birdie came to mind, and the picture of her bravely firing her pistol from the narrow part of that gully near the river—and her eager willingness to help in any endeavor. Why that came to mind now was something he couldn't explain. *What in hell have I got to offer a woman in exchange for her hand in marriage?* he asked, and immediately answered, *Nothing.* "I ain't ready to get married, anyway," he thought aloud.

He was still debating his future plans with himself when Betty Lou came out of the saloon looking for him. "Flo dug the bullet outta Stony's leg," she said when she found him sitting on the edge of the short boardwalk. "He's gonna be all right, but we think maybe it would be best if he stayed here for a day or two to make sure he doesn't come down with lead poisoning or something." When Cord made no reply in response, she said, "He wants to see you."

"All right," Cord said, and got to his feet. He followed Betty Lou back inside, where he found Stony sitting in a chair with his wounded leg propped on the table. He didn't appear to be suffering overly from his injury.

"I need you to help me get him upstairs to my room," Flo said. "He'll need to take it easy for a couple of days."

Stony did his best to affect a pitiable smile, but Cord wasn't convinced that his wound was that serious. "Sorry, Cord," he said. "I ain't doin' so good right now. I reckon they're right. I better take it easy with this wound. I reckon you're gonna have to drive them supplies back to the Triple-T. You know I would try to make it if I thought I could."

Cord smiled, just short of a smirk. "I know you would, Stony. You must be sufferin' somethin' awful."

"I hate to put the job off on you," Stony said, "but I knew you'd understand, the shape I'm in." He paused to affect a painful expression. "With this wound and all," he added.

"Oh, I understand," Cord assured him. "Don't worry. You can count on me to get the supplies back to Slop. I'll leave that sorrel I rode in on at the stable, and you can ride him home when you're ready. The previous owner ain't got no use for him anymore." He looked over at Flo, who seemed genuinely concerned. "Let's get him upstairs and put him to bed." He glanced at Clyde, who was still standing beside Creed's body, gawking at the size of it. "Let me help get Stony upstairs, and I'll help you drag that piece of shit outta here."

"I'd appreciate it," Clyde said, still fascinated by the portion of Levi's brain that lay scattered across his floor. "Big as he is, we might need to hitch up a mule to do the job."

Thinking the time might be right to make a little visit to the Roman-3, Cord drove the wagon back following the same route he and Stony had driven into town. When he reached the foot of the low ridge where the confrontation with Mace had taken place, he stopped and loaded the body in the wagon. Then he continued on to the Triple-T.

When he pulled up to the barn, Birdie came to the door of the hayloft where she had been working with a pitchfork, throwing hay in the stalls. "Oh my Lord!" she exclaimed in alarm upon seeing the corpse in the back of the wagon and thinking it was Stony. "Is he dead?" Not waiting for an answer, she ran back to the ladder and hurried down to help.

Cord waited to answer until she appeared in the barn door. "Yeah, he's dead, but that ain't Stony." He was about to explain when Lem and Blackie came running from inside, so he waited to tell them all what had happened.

"Well, I'll be!" Blackie exclaimed. "Stony shot, too. How bad is it?"

"Not bad enough to slow him down much. He's healin' up just fine in the lovin' arms of two whores," Cord said with a chuckle.

More concerned with another matter, Lem asked, "What did you bring that body here for?"

"Him?" Cord asked, and turned to glance at Mace's corpse. "I'm fixin' to return him to his owner."

"Now, damn it, Cord," Lem started to scold, but that's as far as he got before Cord held up his hand to silence him.

"No use wastin' your breath, Lem. I'm figurin' on endin' this damn range war with Roman-Three. That murderin' cattle rustler has gotten away with his killin' and changin' brands long enough, and I've had enough of it."

"It ain't up to you alone," Lem said. "All of us here have a part in it." He looked at Blackie for confirmation. "It appears that the war is over, anyway. There ain't been no trouble for a few days now."

"Whaddaya call that?" Cord asked, pointing to the corpse in the back of the wagon. Lem had no answer, and Cord continued. "As long as Striker is still on that piece of land, he's gonna be lookin' to hire on more men, and we're gonna go over the same ground again."

"So you're fixin' to ride over to Roman-Three and kill him?" Lem asked. "That don't seem like war to me. That sounds more like murder. Maybe you oughta think about this some more."

"Well, I'm thinkin' more about askin' him politely if he wouldn't mind packin' up and movin' someplace else," Cord replied. When he saw Lem shake his head, disappointed, he said, "This is somethin' I'll be doin' alone."

"It sounds like a dangerous thing to do," Birdie commented, a genuine look of concern on her face.

"Maybe," Cord replied, "if I get careless. We need to know what's goin' on over there just to be sure. We've all been sittin' around the last couple of days, pattin' each other on the back, sayin' we won us a range war." He motioned toward Mace's body again. "It doesn't look like they've given up after all, does it? I'm just fixin' to do something one of us has to do."

"Getting ready to ride off and do something that must be done again. Is that what I heard?" They all turned to see Eileen approaching from the house, her expression one of impatience. When no one answered her question, she leveled an accusing gaze at Cord. "Who is that?" She pointed to Mace's body.

"One of Striker's men," Birdie answered. "He tried to kill Cord and Stony. Stony's shot." She took a few steps away from Cord then in case Eileen thought she was too close.

"Oh," Eileen responded when she heard Birdie's answer, realizing that she had come on a little strong. "Where is Stony? Is he all right?"

"He's fine," Cord said. "I expect he'll be home in a day or two."

"Good," she replied. "Thank goodness for that." She looked directly at Cord then. "One of the other men can go over to the Roman-Three to see what's going on. I think you've done more than your share."

Cord shrugged. "I expect I'd better go, since it was my idea."

She fixed him with a hard stare. "But I want you to stay here," she said.

"I'll be careful," he replied.

She gave him a long, searching look before softly speaking, her voice barely above a whisper. "You don't understand. If you ride off again after I've asked you to stay, then there may not be any reason for you to come back at all."

It was the wrong thing to say. Birdie cringed while Lem and Blackie stared wide-eyed at the impetuous young woman. Astonished by what could only be an ultimatum, Cord could only gape in disbelief for a moment before speaking. "Well, I'd best be gettin' my horse saddled if I'm gonna make it to Roman-Three before hard dark. Blackie, gimme a hand throwin' that body on the back of a horse and tyin' it down, will you?"

"Sure thing," Blackie responded, pretending not to notice when Eileen stalked off toward the house in anger.

It took a little longer than he planned before he was ready to ride. The primary cause of the delay was due to the stiffness of Mace's body and the difficulty of securing it to the horse's back. After hours lying in the snow, the progress of rigor mortis was well advanced and helped along by the cold. When he was finally satisfied that the body was secure, he headed out the gate, leading his grim cargo behind him.

He had not ridden but a couple of miles when he was alerted to a rider coming up fast behind him. One of the hands from Triple-T, or another one of Striker's bushwhackers? He couldn't say, but the rider was definitely following his trail, so he figured it wise to prepare for the latter. Nudging the bay to pick up its pace, he headed toward a narrow ravine that led to a gentle rise in the prairie and followed it until it took a sharp bend. As soon as he rode around the turn, he hauled back on the reins, pulling the bay around so that he was facing the way he had just come. He pulled his rifle from the saddle scabbard and waited.

In a few minutes' time, he heard the beat of hooves on the snowy floor of the ravine. A few seconds later, the rider swung around the bend and pulled back hard on the reins to avoid colliding with him. Astonished, Cord blurted, "Birdie! Where the hell are you goin'?"

"I'm going with you," she replied, once she recovered from the shock of almost running into him. She pulled the chestnut mare up beside his horse, gazing frankly into his face, waiting for his response. When he was too astounded to reply, she continued. "I figured you might need some help, even though you said you didn't."

Finally finding words, he said, "Birdie, this doesn't make sense. You shouldn't be goin' with me. I don't know for sure, but I expect there's gonna be some real trouble before I'm through tonight. And I can't have you mixed up in it."

She patted the six-gun holstered on her side. "You'll have an extra gun now."

"Well, I appreciate it, but if I thought I needed another gun, I'da most likely asked Blackie or Lem to come with me. I can't take a chance on somethin' happenin' to you." He shook his head and told her, "Tell you the truth, I was thinkin' I might decide not to even go back to the Triple-T."

"That crossed my mind, too," Birdie said. "That's the main reason I came after you."

"To make sure I came back?"

"To make sure you didn't leave me, if you didn't come back," she confessed.

Dumbfounded, and not sure she was really telling him what it sounded like, he asked, "Are you sayin' you wanna go with me to, you know, be with me?"

"I don't know," she answered honestly. "I know that I don't want to be without you. I decided that much is true."

There was a long awkward moment of silence following her statement, with both parties surprised by the sudden turn of events. He gazed deeply into her eyes and suddenly she looked different to him as she returned his gaze. For the first time, he was aware of her intense blue eyes, the fine delicate nose and mouth, framed by her short dark hair that tended to curl over the top of her ears. "Your hair is growin' pretty fast," he finally blurted, aware immediately after that it was a dumb thing to say at this moment.

"Yeah, I guess it is," she replied. "I may really look like a girl before long."

Still finding it hard to believe, he had to ask again, "Why do you wanna go with me? I'm not sure where I'm goin' from here. I might even go back to the Triple-T."

"I just feel safe with you," she said. "I'm not saying take me as a woman, if you're not interested in that. I'll just go with you as your partner, just like Dooley, or someone else. And if things work out for us to be more than that, then I'm all right with that, too. But if you don't want me to go with you, just tell me, and I'll go back."

He realized at that moment, when she had given him a choice, that it was difficult to tell her to go back. After a moment's hesitation, he said, "Go on back to the house. I promise that when I'm through here, I'll come back and we'll talk it over."

"You'll come back?" she asked. "You swear?"

"I swear," he said, "if I have to walk."

She gave him one emphatic nod to seal their agreement, then turned her horse around and headed back to the Triple-T. He watched her until she was out of sight, then turned the bay to the north again.

Finding it hard to clear his mind of his startling conversation with Birdie, Cord rode up the slope of the same twin buttes he had watched the Roman-3 from before. Darkness was setting in quickly now as he tied the horses to a clump of sage. It was his intention to lead the packhorse in after hard dark and dump the body on Striker's front porch, so he settled down to wait for the proper time. After approximately thirty minutes had passed, it occurred to him that he had seen no sign of activity around the house or barn. It caused him to sharpen his focus on the buildings. Still after another long wait, there was no one evident, no lantern light in the bunkhouse or the main house. The ranch seemed deserted, but where were they? His first thought was the Triple-T. But if Striker and his men were off to raid the Triple-T, he would probably have met them on the trail beside Blue Creek. Maybe the seemingly deserted ranch was in reality an ambush, a trap waiting to close on him when he rode in. He quickly discarded that notion. There was nothing that would lead them to think they were going to be raided, and there was no way they could know that he had planned a visit. Thinking of his promise to Birdie, he decided to play it safe and do nothing more than watch the place.

After a couple of hours had passed with still no sign of any living souls about the ranch, he withdrew from his perch and went back down near the creek to find a place to build a fire and wait until morning to decide what to do.

When the sun broke through the deck of low clouds that had formed during the night, he made his way up the creek, approaching the ranch from a direction opposite the two buttes. When he came close enough to see the barn and house clearly, he stopped to watch for some activity of a ranch waking up. There was none. No one came from the bunkhouse. No one visited the outhouse. Certain now that the place was deserted, he walked out of the trees, leading the two horses, making his way boldly across the barnyard. When he reached the barn, he walked in to confirm that there was no one there. There were no horses, either. Back outside, he looked at the stiffened corpse on the pack-horse and decided to cut it loose. When it fell heavily to the ground, he turned to see if there was any response from the ranch house. There was none.

With his rifle ready, he walked up the steps of the house and opened the door, certain now that there was no one else on the place but him. There were no signs that anyone had prepared breakfast. The stove was cold. He walked down the short hall to the bedrooms.

In the larger bedroom was where he found Harlan
Striker, still in bed, a large kitchen knife buried to the
handle in his chest, his eyes screaming out with the
shock of his final moments. Cord studied the corpse of
the man who had caused so much grief for the folks at
the Triple-T, lying on the blood-soaked quilt, looking
so insignificant in death. "Well, I reckon that ends the
range war," Cord announced softly.

Before leaving the house, he checked the other bedroom, where he found the bed neatly made, but no sign
of any clothing left behind. He could only guess who
had killed Striker. Seeing nothing left for him to do, he
climbed up in the saddle and turned toward the Triple-T.
It was time now to think about the future, and what
part Birdie might have in it. He had a pretty good idea
what his decision was going to be.

Some twenty or more miles from the Roman-3, on a
trail toward Wyoming, the Crow half-breed woman
named Rena sat beside a narrow stream, eating smoked
meat she had prepared for her trip while her horses
rested. A thin smile parted her lips when she thought
about the last time Harlan Striker had threatened her
life. It had been just before he yelled for her to come to
his bed.

Read on for a look at
another exciting historical
novel from Charles G. West

SILVER CITY MASSACRE

Available from Signet in January 2014.

It had taken him a long time to make up his mind. Too long, he figured, but at last he deemed it time to put this senseless war behind him and get on with the rest of his life. Joel McAllister could look himself in the eye, knowing that he had given all that he had originally pledged to the Missouri Volunteers and General Joseph Shelby's Confederate cavalry. He had fought under Shelby's command for over two years, distinguishing himself in countless raids and skirmishes, enough so that he was awarded a battlefield promotion to the rank of lieutenant.

It had been more than two months since Lee surrendered at the little Virginia town of Appomattox, but Joe Shelby had defied orders to surrender his cavalry, saying he would never live under Yankee rule. Like several hundred of Shelby's volunteers, Joel had followed the fire-eating general when he left Shreveport and marched into Texas, determined to take his troops to Mexico. A sense of loyalty to his general had been the reason Joel had made that decision.

After some troublesome nights of serious thought, however, he found himself on the bank of the Brazos River near the little town of Waco, questioning the choice he had made. It was a hard decision to make, for he had felt it his duty to follow his superiors and not ask whether or not their orders were right or wrong. Over the last two days, he had labored over the question, and he realized that he was ready to say good-bye to war. Choosing to leave with some honor, he had informed his company commander, Captain Grace, that he was departing in the morning, having decided that his future did not lie in Mexico. The captain was disappointed, but assured him that the general would understand and wish him luck, just as he had with the majority of his command who had departed for home when the unit was in Shreveport.

"Where are you heading?" Captain Grace asked.

"About as far from this war as I can get," Joel answered. "I've been thinkin' it over, and I've decided to light out for Idaho Territory."

"Idaho?" Grace responded, obviously surprised. "What in hell is in Idaho? That's halfway across the world. You might as well go to California or Oregon."

"That's a fact, I reckon," Joel replied. "But maybe it's far enough away so there's no North or South, and this damn war ain't the only thing on everybody's minds. That ain't my only reason, though. I've got a brother out that way, and I reckon he'd be glad to have a partner to help him work his place. I've been thinkin' it over, and I ain't cut out for a career in soldierin'. I've got nothing to go back to in Missouri. The only family I've got left is my brother."

"Well, I wish you luck, McAllister. You're a fine soldier and a damn good man. I wish I could let you take your horse with you, but the general said any man who quits after we cross into Texas will leave on foot. I'm sorry. I surely am."

"I understand the general's feelin's on the matter," Joel assured him. "Our horse stock is needin' some help right now, so I didn't expect it any other way. I've got no problem with that. I'll turn my horse out with the others tonight."

"That's mighty understanding of you," Grace said. "I know the general will appreciate your attitude. You say you're planning on leaving in the morning?"

"Yes, sir. Right after breakfast."

"Good," Grace said. "I'm sure the general will want to have a word with you before you go. Maybe he'll make an exception of his order and let you take your horse."

Joel smiled and nodded. They shook hands then, and the captain turned and walked back toward his tent. Joel watched him walk away, remaining there on the bank until Grace entered the tent. He then returned to his own tent and the chestnut gelding tied beside it. The horse had been with him since his first day assigned to the regiment. It had more or less picked him to partner with. On the day they met, the gentle gelding left the herd of extra horses and walked right up to him when he approached them, bridle in hand. At the time, Joel had had no particular preference, so he accepted the chestnut's easy invitation, and there had been no reason to regret the decision ever since. Concerned about the horse's performance in battle, Joel had been pleased to find the chestnut willing and able during a cavalry charge and fleet of foot whenever a quick retreat was ordered. That characteristic of will- ingness inspired Joel to name him Willing, which he soon shortened to Will.

The captain had been right when he said the Idaho Territory was half a world away from Waco, Texas. But being the practical man that he was, Joel had no inten- tion of walking that distance and certainly no thought of leaving Will behind. He figured the regiment owed him a horse at the least, and a packhorse, to boot, which he planned to liberate from the herd of extra horses grazing in the narrow valley as soon as darkness set in a little more. There was a strong possibility that Grace was right in thinking Shelby would let him take the horse. But Joel preferred to bank on a sure thing, so he planned to leave that night, in spite of what he had told the captain.

He was about to enter his tent to finish packing up his saddlebags and bedroll when the familiar figure of Sergeant Riley Tarver suddenly appeared in the dimin- ishing light of evening. Even in the poor light, there was no mistaking the squat, solidly built Tarver as he approached on short legs, appropriately bowed for a cavalry trooper. Joel paused to await him. The sergeant was always found close to his lieutenant whenever the regiment was in battle. Joel was not oblivious to the fact that Tarver seemed to have taken a responsibility upon himself to ensure his safety. He had to chuckle when he stopped to think about it—Riley Tarver had selected him to watch over much the same as Will had.

And while he had never voiced it, he sincerely appreciated the sergeant's apparent devotion to him.

"Evenin', Sergeant," Joel greeted him. "You lookin' for me?"

"Evenin', Lieutenant," Riley returned. "Yes, sir. I was thinkin' on havin' a word with you, if you don't mind."

"All right," Joel replied, thinking he caught a sense of concern in the sergeant's manner. "What's on your mind?"

Tarver hesitated while he sought to organize his words. "Sir, can I talk kinda frankly?"

"Why, sure you can, Riley. Nothing ever stopped you before. Is something botherin' you?" It occurred to Joel that he was going to miss the burly sergeant.

Riley pushed his campaign hat back far enough to enable him to scratch his curly white hair, still hesitant to come out with what he had come to say. Finally, he spit it out.

"Lieutenant, you know, we've been in some pretty tight places over the past two years, and I hope you won't think it disrespectful if I say I've come to know you pretty well."

Joel stifled a chuckle. He was well aware of the sergeant's admiration. "Not at all," he answered. "I reckon we both know each other pretty well."

"Well, sir," Riley went on, "it looks to me like you've been thinkin' pretty heavy on somethin' for the last week and a half—like maybe that somethin's botherin' you. And if I was to take a guess, I'd say you ain't too damn keen about goin' down to Mexico." He paused when he saw that his comment had caused Joel's eyebrows to rise, but Joel made no reply, so he continued.

"It ain't none of my business, but I just wanted to tell you that I ain't lost nothin' in Mexico. If you're thinkin' about musterin' out of this army anytime soon—and you could tolerate a partner—why, hell, I'm your man. I'm ready to be done with this war, and the farther I can get away from it, the better."

Joel was stunned. Had he been that transparent? Or was Riley so devoted to him that he had learned to read his mind. He had given absolutely no thought toward having a partner on his long journey up the face of the country. It made for an interesting suggestion, however, one that called for his consideration. After thinking about it for a few long moments, it suddenly struck him as an amusing proposition, considering the timing. And he had to admit that if he were to pick one man with whom to partner, it would have been Riley Tarver.

Joel's lengthy pause caused Riley to worry. "If I've spoke out of line," Riley quickly offered, "I wanna say right here and now that I didn't intend no disrespect."

Joel needed no more than another moment to reply. "How soon can you be ready to go? 'Cause I'm leavin' tonight."

Riley's jaw dropped in surprise. "You mean I can go with you?"

"If you can get your gear together to leave tonight," Joel answered, "'cause I ain't figurin' on ridin' another day closer to Mexico."

"Glory be!" the sergeant exclaimed, scarcely able to believe it. "I knew there was somethin' workin' on your mind. I was wonderin' why you pitched your tent kinda off here by itself. Yes, sir, I'm ready to go right

ow." His grin was so wide that his face could scarcely
ontain it. "Where you figurin' on headin'? Not that I
are one way or the other."

"Idaho Territory," Joel answered.

"Idaho?" Riley responded, as surprised as Captain
Grace had been, but unlike the captain, he thought it
was a grand idea. "Well, now, there's a piece of luck I'd
say, 'cause I've spent some time up that way, back before
his war. I followed the rest of them fools out to Cali-
ornia lookin' for gold." He paused for a little chuckle
when he recalled. "I didn't find enough to buy tobacco
or my pipe."

"Maybe you'll have better luck this time," Joel said.
"My brother's sittin' on a claim out there near a little
own called Silver City. At least that's what his letter
said, but I didn't get the letter until six months after he
sent it. I reckon he's still in the same spot. That's what
'm countin' on, anyway. I can't say for sure what we'll
find when we get out there. My brother mighta moved
on somewhere else."

"I didn't know you had a brother," Riley said.

"Yep. Boone's two years older than I am. He went in
the army about six months before I did, got his leg torn
half off by a load of grapeshot at Vicksburg—crippled
him up pretty bad, so his soldierin' days were over.
Boone ain't the type to let anything stand in his way,
though. So when there was news that folks had found
gold in Idaho Territory, he decided he'd go, too. Accordin' to his letter, he thinks he's sittin' on a mountain of
it. He said there were a lot of folks who went to California that came back to prospect in Idaho. There may not
be any gold left to find when we get there, but I figured

I might as well go out there and see the country for myself. So if you're sure it'll suit you, then welcome aboard."

"It suits me just fine," Riley assured him. "I'm ready to go. We've done lost this war."

"There are a few things we have to take care of tonight if we're gonna get outta here before anybody knows we're gone," Joel told him. "How do you feel about horse stealin'?" He went on to remind Riley about General Shelby's policy regarding the horses. "I told Captain Grace that I wasn't leavin' till after breakfast tomorrow, 'cause I'm plannin' to borrow another horse to use as a packhorse tonight. I kinda gave him the idea that I was gonna turn my horse in with the others tonight and leave on foot after breakfast. Looks like we'll need two more now, and I wanna be long gone from here before reveille."

"Yes, sir!" Riley exclaimed, excited now with the prospect. "Horse stealin' runs in my blood on my mother's side. I'll go see if I can get us a little extra bacon and beans from the mess sergeant while he ain't lookin', and I can rig us up a couple of pack saddles for them horses we're gonna need." He paused to give his new partner a grin. "It'll most likely be a little easier to steal a couple of horses from that herd if there's one of us to distract the guard."

"I reckon," Joel replied with a matching grin. He reached out to accept Riley's extended hand, and the two parties sealed the partnership. "We'll need a couple of stout packhorses, 'cause I'm plannin' on loadin' 'em down with weapons and ammunition."

One thing the regiment had was plenty of both. After the surrender of the Confederacy, there were any number of arms stored at various magazines across Texas, and General Shelby had taken advantage of the opportunity to proceed to Mexico well supplied. Riley understood the lieutenant's thinking. The arms would be useful as trade goods to exchange for whatever supplies they might need along the way, plus there were a lot of Indians between here and where they were going.

Joel wanted to make sure that Riley had considered all the risks involved, so he paused to ask a question. "Are you sure you wanna make a long ride across this territory when it's just the two of us? You know there have been reports of Cheyenne and Arapaho raids all over parts of Colorado since that massacre at Sand Creek about a year ago, and the Comanches ain't ever been peaceful."

"Yes, sir, I'm aware of that, but I figure we'd be watchin' our asses pretty careful, and we'll have plenty of fire power to make it costly for any Injuns that light into us. Besides, I got me a strong hankerin' to see those Rocky Mountains again."

"All right, then. Get your stuff together," Joel directed, "and bring it to my tent after the camp settles down for the night. Then we'll see about gettin' ourselves a couple of horses."

"I'll see you in about an hour," Riley said. He paused just before lifting the tent flap. "I reckon you've figured on how long it'll take us to get to Idaho Territory. It's almost September now, and we ain't likely gonna be able to do much travelin' when the snow starts."

"Yeah, I know," Joel replied. "But I reckon I've got the rest of my life to get there, so I ain't worried about whether or not I make it before spring."

"Me too," Riley said.

ALSO AVAILABLE FROM

Charles G. West

**"THE WEST AS IT REALLY WAS."
—RALPH COMPTON**

Long Road to Cheyenne

Cam Sutton's quest for gold is delayed after he
rescues Mary Bishop and her daughters from a
stagecoach hold-up and decides to help search for
the missing Mr. Bishop. Turns out, he was
murdered—but not before finding enough gold to
make Mary a very rich woman. Cam offers to escort
the ladies on the long journey back to Cheyenne, but
with a greedy, cold-blooded killer on their trail, the
road is more treacherous than Cam anticipated...

National bestselling author

RALPH COMPTON

SHADOW OF THE GUN
DEATH OF A BAD MAN
RIDE THE HARD TRAIL
BLOOD ON THE GALLOWS
THE CONVICT TRAIL
RAWHIDE FLAT
THE BORDER EMPIRE
THE MAN FROM NOWHERE
SIXGUNS AND DOUBLE EAGLES
BOUNTY HUNTER
FATAL JUSTICE
STRYKER'S REVENGE
DEATH OF A HANGMAN
NORTH TO THE SALT FORK
DEATH RIDES A CHESTNUT MARE
RUSTED TIN
THE BURNING RANGE
WHISKEY RIVER
THE LAST MANHUNT
THE AMARILLO TRAIL
SKELETON LODE
STRANGER FROM ABILENE
THE SHADOW OF A NOOSE
THE GHOST OF APACHE CREEK
RIDERS OF JUDGMENT
SLAUGHTER CANYON
DEAD MAN'S RANCH
ONE MAN'S FIRE
THE OMAHA TRAIL
DOWN ON GILA RIVER
BRIMSTONE TRAIL
STRAIGHT SHOOTER
THE HUNTED

"A writer in the tradition of Louis L'Amour and Zane Grey!" —*Huntsville Times*

Available wherever books are sold or at
penguin.com

5543

THE LAST OUTLAWS
The Lives and Legends of Butch Cassidy and the Sundance Kid

by Thom Hatch

Butch Cassidy and the Sundance Kid are two of the most celebrated figures of American lore. As leaders of the Wild Bunch, also known as the Hole-in-the-Wall Gang, they planned and executed the most daring bank and train robberies of the day, with an uprecedented professionalism.

The Last Outlaws brilliantly brings to life these thrilling, larger-than-life personalities like never before, placing the legend of Butch and Sundance in the context of a changing—and shrinking—American West, as the rise of 20th century technology brought an end to a remarkable era. Drawing on a wealth of fresh research, Thom Hatch pushes aside the myth and offers up a compelling, fresh look at these icons of the Wild West.

Available wherever books are sold or at
penguin.com

S0464